Intently Dante stared at her, and he could feel the powerful beat of his heart. "Is there something you need to tell me?"

Justina nodded as a wave of emotion threatened to overwhelm her, but she held it back. *Don't act coy or ashamed or intimidated,* she urged herself. *Just deal with the facts.* "Is that a roundabout way of asking whether you're the father?"

"Am I?"

For a moment she hesitated, tempted to tell him that no, he wasn't. But then she thought of the child she carried. The baby who was currently kicking beneath her fluttering heart as if it was trying out for a fetal football team. Could she willfully deny her child the knowledge of its father, just because that father didn't love *her?*

"Yes," she breathed—and then she said it again, so that there could be no going back.

"Yes, you are the father, Dante."

D0683893

Dear Reader,

We know how much you love Harlequin® Presents®, so this month we wanted to treat you to something extra special—a second classic story by the same author for free!

Once you have finished reading *A Scandal, a Secret, a Baby,* just turn the page for another scandalous tale of celebrity from Sharon Kendrick.

This month, indulge yourself with double the reading pleasure!

With love,

The Presents Editors

Sharon Kendrick

A SCANDAL, A SECRET, A BABY

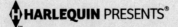

ISBN-13: 978-0-373-13128-0

A SCANDAL, A SECRET, A BABY

Copyright © 2013 by Harlequin Books S.A.

Recycling programs for this product may not exist in your area.

The publisher acknowledges the copyright holder of the individual works as follows:

A SCANDAL, A SECRET, A BABY
Copyright © 2013 by Sharon Kendrick

MARRIAGE SCANDAL, SHOWBIZ BABY!
Copyright © 2005 by Sharon Kendrick

Printed in U.S.A.

www.Harlequin.com

CONTENTS

All about the author...
Sharon Kendrick

SHARON KENDRICK started storytelling at the age of eleven and has never really stopped. She likes to write fast-paced, feel-good romances with heroes who are so sexy they'll make your toes curl!

Born in west London, she now lives in the beautiful city of Winchester—where she can see the cathedral from her window (but only if she stands on tip-toe). She has two children, Celia and Patrick, and her passions include music, books, cooking and eating—and drifting off into wonderful daydreams while she works out new plots!

Visit Sharon at www.sharonkendrick.com.

Other titles by Sharon Kendrick available in ebook:

Harlequin Presents®

A SCANDAL, A SECRET, A BABY

To Ruth Nehrebecka, who is a great inspiration (as well as being enviably blonde and effortlessly stylish!)

CHAPTER ONE

Dante D'Arezzo knew the exact moment his ex-fiancée walked into the cathedral. He heard the silence which fell and the whisper which followed.

'Look, there's Justina Perry.'

And the murmured response. 'Oh, *wow*!'

Dante could feel the punch of his heart as people turned their heads to look at her, to see if she'd changed. They wanted to know if she had any new lines on her face—or whether those lines had been ironed out by surgery. They wanted to know if she was heavier. Or lighter. They wanted to know every damned thing about her, because once she had been famous and fame made people think they owned you.

Dante knew that. He knew that only too damned

well. Hadn't he watched from the sidelines long enough to learn about the darker aspects of fame? The way it corrupted and corroded and spread into normal life like some sort of toxic acid?

His powerful body tight with tension, he watched her sinuous progress down the wide aisle of Norwich Cathedral, where the wedding of her ex-bandmate was shortly to take place. Her dark hair had been coiled into an elaborate confection at the back of her head and she was wearing an oriental-looking gown of pale satin, lavishly embroidered with dragons and flowers. At first glance the dress seemed disappointingly demure—until she moved forward on a pair of towering heels and a thigh-high split revealed the tantalising flash of one long, bare leg.

An unwanted wave of desire swept over him, quickly followed by a powerful surge of anger. So she still liked to show herself off like some kind of cheap *puttana*, did she? Did she still enjoy the sensation of other men watching her and wanting her—fantasising about that sinner's body coupled with the soulful face of a dark angel?

But his anger was not enough to diminish the exquisite ache in his body, and he watched as she took her place in one of the front rows, turning to smile at the person next to her as she sank down onto the pew. The embroidered satin stretched over her delicious bottom and all Dante could think about was how long it had been. Five long years since he'd seen her. More than enough time for him to have become immune to her feline appeal. So why was his heart thundering as he watched her staring up at the altar? Why was the hardening at his groin so pronounced that he was having to cover it up with his hymn sheet?

He tried to think about something else as the marriage service began—but it wasn't easy. Not when this wedding seemed even longer than weddings usually were—probably because the groom just happened to be a duke. Dante always played the part expected of him, and usually he would have been an exemplary and attentive guest. But today, his attention was focussed elsewhere and all the way through the service his thoughts kept straying back to Justina.

Justina writhing beneath him on a snow-white bed.

Justina with her ebony hair and magnolia skin and those amazing amber eyes.

He remembered the sweet tightness of her body. Those tiny little nipples which had been made to fit so perfectly inside a man's mouth.

Briefly he shook his head, for those thoughts disturbed him. He wanted to forget that for the first and only time in his life he'd made a mistake. His broken engagement was the only failure in a life which had been charted with resounding success. He was a proud man of noble Tuscan heritage. His ancestors had been scholars, soldiers and diplomats—an aristocratic line which had always been land-rich but cash-poor. But then Dante had become head of the family's business interests and had taken them soaring into the stratosphere.

These days the D'Arezzo family owned property over most of the globe, in addition to their vast vineyards in the beautiful countryside outside Florence. Dante had everything a man could possibly want, and yet inside his heart was empty.

There were bells ringing now—a triumphant peal of them heralding the end of the ceremony. And then came the somewhat unbelievable sight of Roxy Carmichael—all misty in white silk and pearls—clinging on to the arm of her new husband, the Duke. Dante shook his head in slight disbelief. Who would ever have thought it? The last time he'd seen Roxy she had been dancing around on a giant stage wearing little more than a sequinned pelmet which had been masquerading as a skirt.

That was what they'd all used to wear when she, Justina and Lexi had made up the Lollipops—the biggest girl-band on the planet. When for a while he had been little more than a member of their extensive posse.

The congregation had begun to file out behind the bride and groom and Dante found himself watching. Wanting to see Justina's reaction when she saw him sitting there. Did she ever regret the choices she'd made? The ones which had led to his rejection of her? Did she ever lie in bed thinking and fretting about what could have been hers?

Last night he had given in to a temptation he'd long resisted, and a quick search on his computer had told him that Justina remained unmarried, with no children—something which had given him pause for thought. She must be nearly thirty now, he realised. Wasn't she worried that these days women were advised to have children sooner, rather than later? A cruel smile curved the edges of his lips. No, of course she wasn't. What appeal would a child have to someone like her? Her career was everything to her. *Everything.*

His gaze flicked over her pale skin as she came towards him and for one suspended moment he saw her footsteps falter when their gazes met and locked. He looked into her amber eyes, which looked golden against the sudden snowy pallor of her skin. Saw them widen in disbelief and then saw a flash of something in their depths which he couldn't have defined even if he could be bothered to try. What Justina Perry thought or felt was of no interest to him. Not any more. But he wouldn't have been human if he hadn't enjoyed the sudden swallowing movement he observed rippling down over that swanlike neck of hers.

She was right beside him now. Close enough for him to catch a drift of her perfume, which made him think of jasmine and honey. And then she was gone, and he was aware of a pretty blonde in the row in front of him, who was turning round to give him a very bright smile indeed.

But the smile Dante returned was perfunctory. He hadn't come here today to find a woman. Though he hadn't really stopped to ask himself why he'd accepted an invitation he'd never been expecting to receive. Was it to lay a ghost to rest? To convince himself that he now felt nothing for the only woman who had ever managed to penetrate the stony exterior of his hard Tuscan heart?

He walked out into the crisp brightness of the day, where he could smell the powerful scent of the flowers which were arching around the vast doors of the cathedral. He looked across the courtyard to where Justina stood, surrounded by people clamouring for her attention—but she wasn't listening to them. Her attention was fixed on the door, as if she'd been waiting for him to appear, and as her eyes found their target in him he felt the thrill of something he could never have described—not even in his native tongue.

He began to walk towards her, only vaguely aware of the women who turned to watch his progress—women watching him was something which had happened throughout his charmed life. He saw Justina's teeth dig into the pink cushion of her bottom lip, and as he remembered just what those beautiful lips were capable of a stab of lust threatened to overwhelm him.

He had reached her now, and the people surrounding her grew quiet as faces were turned towards him in open curiosity. He guessed that the novelty of his dark Italian looks was enough to arouse interest in this most English of settings. And maybe his face looked as forbidding as he intended it to look, because they quickly moved away, so that the two of them were left alone.

'Well, well, well,' he said. 'Look who's here.'

Justina stared up at him, her heart pounding in a way it hadn't done in a long, long time. She could feel her senses firing into life as if someone had just set light to them. She could feel the prickle of her breasts and the instant pooling of liquid heat and she was praying that the cheating bastard wouldn't guess. She didn't *want* to desire him. She wanted to present a cool and unruffled exterior. But it wasn't easy. Not when his face was just inches away from hers—a face more beautiful and yet more elementally savage than any other she'd ever seen. His dark eyes were boring into her and his powerful body was imprinting itself into her consciousness. She felt weak. As if someone had just drained away all her blood and replaced it with water.

Well, you're stronger than that, she told herself. *You aren't going to show any sign of weakness. Because this is Dante D'Arezzo. The man who confuses love with control. Who dumped you because you wouldn't behave like his own personal puppet. Who cold-bloodedly took another woman to his bed and…and….*

She saw a bed with rumpled sheets. A mass of

ruffled blond hair and a high, pert bottom. And Dante, his eyes closed, a smile of ecstasy on his cheating lips as the naked woman administered to his every need.

The vivid images of his betrayal were like jagged pieces of glass at the edges of her mind and Justina only just managed to blunt them—just as she'd spent the last five years blunting them. She mustn't think of that. She couldn't afford to. She had to focus on what was important—and the only thing she could think of right then was making him go away and leave her alone.

She kept her expression unwelcoming, her voice a cool drawl. 'Thanks for ruining what could have been a perfectly good day,' she said. 'Who invited you?'

Dante hadn't been expecting such *open* hostility, and for some reason that he wasn't quite able to work out this pleased him. Was it because the prospect of a fight with her was almost as tantalising as the thought of spreading her over the bonnet of that nearby car and riding her until he came?

He took a stealthy step closer. 'Who do you think invited me? The bride, of course. Or did you imagine that I gatecrashed?'

Justina couldn't suppress a faint shiver as his

powerful form cast a shadow over her like a dark omen. As if Dante had ever had to gatecrash anything in his life!

'Really?' she questioned, wishing that she could stop reacting to him like this.

She felt as if her body had suddenly started thawing after spending years in some arctic waste. As if she would die if she didn't touch him again, or feel those hard lips pressing down on hers. She found herself remembering the way he'd used to put his head between her legs and lick her there, and she shivered with shameful longing. How did he *do* that? How could he still make her want him when she hated him so much?

'I didn't even think you were still in touch with Roxy.'

'I wasn't. We lost contact a long while ago—about the time when you and I split.' His dark eyes mocked her. 'But presumably she was feeling generously disposed towards the world when she found herself a duke to marry, and so she decided to track me down.'

Justina knew exactly why Roxy had done it. A man like Dante would be a luminary on any guest list; his grandness and stature would be a boost to any hostess's street-cred. And, of course, his outstanding good looks would guarantee that all the single female guests would be purring with contentment. But why the hell hadn't Roxy bothered to warn her about it beforehand? Had her ex-bandmate guessed that she wouldn't have come within a hundred miles of the church if she'd known *he* was going to be here?

Yet surely she should be immune to him by now? She hadn't seen him for nearly five years. She was older and supposedly a whole lot wiser—wise enough for his undeniable sex appeal to leave her cold. *So why wasn't that happening?* Why were her breasts tingling as his arrogant gaze skated over her, that molten aching at her thighs making her feel embarrassingly self-conscious?

With a feigned composure she stared at him—praying for an objectivity she'd never been able to apply to this Tuscan aristocrat. He was wearing a suit, like every other man there—apart from the few guests in uniform —but something about the *way* he wore it instantly marked him out as someone special. The exquisite cut of the charcoal cloth hugged his powerful frame, emphasising the narrow jut of his hips and the definition of his long legs. Yet despite his highly sophisticated exterior, with Dante D'Arezzo all you were aware of was the primitive man beneath. He was the sort of man who saw what he wanted and went out and took it. Who made women cry with pleasure. And with pain, she reminded herself. With terrible and lasting pain.

'Maybe Roxy was short on numbers and that was the reason for your out-of-the-blue invitation,' she said as she glanced up at the cathedral with a flippant shrug. 'It's a pretty big church to fill. And I expect a token Tuscan aristocrat is on every bride's wish list.'

He smiled, as if her insult meant nothing to him—as if he guessed that it was all for show. 'It's been a long time, Justina,' he said softly.

'Five years.' Her smile was fixed. 'Time flies when you're having fun—something which was certainly in short supply when I was engaged to you.'

But he didn't appear to be listening. His gaze was drifting slowly over her body as if he still had the right to look at her that way. As if she was his possession and he owned her.

'You've lost weight,' he said.

She felt her heart miss a beat, unsure if it was caused by disappointment or anger—because wasn't that just typical of Dante? For him to take something she felt proud of and make it sound like something bad. She'd worked very hard for this body. Dragged herself out of bed on the most inhospitable of mornings to pound the pavements, come rain or shine. When she was travelling, she was a frequent visitor to hotel gyms—padding the anonymous carpeted corridors at unsociable hours while she listened to music from her earphones. And hadn't her strict regime rescued her from the essential loneliness of those solitary hotel stays?

She never ate carbs after 5:00 p.m., and she rarely drank alcohol. She was disciplined about her lifestyle because it was harder to stay fit the older you got. And physical fitness helped her to cope. It kept her fresh and alert in an industry where youth was everything—an industry which she'd seen claim the lives of those who couldn't cope with its impossibly high demands. And she had sacrificed too much for her to career to do anything to ever jeopardise it.

'Well, isn't that fortunate? Since losing weight was what I was aiming for,' she responded, her gaze flicking over his charcoal-grey suit, which was doing nothing to disguise the hard musculature beneath. 'You might try working out a little yourself some time, Dante. Try for the leaner look—it's very fashionable, you know.'

'I don't think so. I get all the exercise I need without the narcissistic need to spend hours down at the gym.' He leaned forward by a fraction, noting the automatic dilatation of her eyes as he did so, and suddenly he wanted her. Wanted her so badly that he could have pulled her into his arms and crushed those cushioned lips beneath the hungry clamour of his own. His eyes glinted. 'My body is hard in all the places it needs to be hard.'

Justina felt her face grow hot, as unsettled by his sudden closeness as by the unashamedly sexual boast, and she took a step back. 'You're disgusting.'

'You think so? You used to like my particular brand of disgusting, as I recall.'

'That was a long time ago. Fortunately I've grown up since then. My tastes have matured and I'm no longer attracted to the Neanderthal type.'

'Then you really *must* have changed. I've never known a woman who was so turned on by a man being masterful in bed.'

His silky taunt whispered towards her and brought back memories Justina thought she'd buried for ever. Memories of Dante kissing her. Dante pushing his hardness deep into her warm, wet heat. *Dante doing that to another woman.* She wanted to scream. To lash out at him and ask why he'd done it—*why?* But she would not give in to the pointlessness of resurrecting the past. The past was over. Her life was now and her future didn't involve him.

And she needed to get away from him.

Directing her gaze to an imaginary spot behind his head, she forced her mouth into a smile of recognition, as if she'd just seen someone she knew, so that by the time she allowed herself to look into those dark eyes again she had composed herself enough to adopt a convincing air of indifference.

'You really mustn't let me monopolise you any longer, Dante. I'm sure there are lots of people who are longing to speak to you. In fact there's a young lady over there who seems eager to catch your eye. I'm sure you'll still be quick enough off the mark to have her in your bed before the day is out.'

And then she began to walk away, half afraid that he might try to stop her. But he did no such thing. She saw the brief narrowing of his eyes as she turned on her towering heels and walked across the cathedral square, and she was aware of the burn of his gaze as she allowed herself to be swallowed up in a group of guests. Her hands were trembling and her heart was racing and for a moment she contemplated leaving the wedding right then. Nothing was stopping her. She could hurry back to the hotel she'd booked into, pack up her stuff and head back to London. She could run away from her ex-fiancé and all the painful memories that seeing him again evoked.

But Justina knew she couldn't do that. She and Roxy had only recently been reunited, and she couldn't let her old friend down on such an important day. Averting her face from a paparazzi camera which seemed to have sprung from out of nowhere, she gave a ragged sigh. She was just going to have to behave like a grown-up and deal with it. She would go to the wedding reception and avoid Dante. How hard could it be? She was good at avoiding people—and she doubted that he'd be on his own for long.

She made her way towards the line of red double-decker buses which had been hired to take all the guests to the reception and found a seat, smiling politely at the man who immediately slid in next to her and started to introduce himself. But it was difficult to concentrate on what he was saying, even though he was doing his level best to flirt and was wearing a whole row of bright medals on his military uniform. He was probably some kind of dashing war hero, she thought gloomily, as well as being handsome in that blond and square-jawed sort of way.

So why could she never be attracted to someone like him—the sort of man she knew she *should* be attracted to? The dependable type who might easily adore her if only she'd give them half a chance. Wasn't it a mark of her own emotional failure that nobody had ever come close to making her feel the way that Dante had done? And wasn't that the main reason why she was still single as thirty loomed on the horizon—with no stable relationship and the chances of having a baby receding with every year that passed?

She remembered the magazine interview she'd given only last week, when the persistent journalist had managed to make her confront that uncomfortable fact. That if she waited too long she might never have a baby of her own. Feeling cornered, Justina had said that of *course* she wanted a baby. And then had added jokily that first she would need to find someone to be her baby's father!

The double-decker bus lumbered through the narrow Norfolk lanes before turning in to the grand gates which led to the Duke's estate. A long, gravelled drive swept up to the groom's ancestral home and as the bus halted outside, Justina felt the breath catch in her throat as she glanced up at the perfectly proportioned golden building which Roxy had told her so much about.

Surrounded by green parkland, Valeo Hall was guarded by two snarling bronze lions which stood on top of two plinths. The pillars lining the steps up to the massive oak door were garlanded with the same fragrant white flowers which had decorated the cathedral, and Justina breathed in their sweet scent as she stepped down onto the forecourt. Lucky Roxy, she found herself thinking. A new husband and a new life. A whole new future just sitting waiting for them. Surely she wouldn't have been human if she hadn't felt a moment of wistful envy at that moment?

Standing in line, waiting to congratulate the newlyweds, she gave the handsome Duke a quick hug and seconds later was enveloped in a cloud of tulle and white lace as his bride stepped forward to embrace her tightly.

'Oh, Jus.' Roxy beamed. 'I'm so glad you could come! Did you enjoy the service?'

'It was gorgeous. *You* look gorgeous—the loveliest bride I've ever seen. But you didn't tell me that Dante was going to be here,' Justina whispered.

'Should I have done?' Roxy smiled in a conspiratorial way which made her look about nineteen again. 'I know you aren't together now, but I thought I'd invite him anyway—because for a while, Dante was a big part of my life. You don't mind, do you?'

Justina gave a wry smile. What could she say? That seeing him again had been like revisiting an unbearably dark and painful place? She looked at Roxy's luminous face and reminded herself that this was about more than her own hurt pride and wounded heart. This was *Roxy's* day—and surely she could suffer seeing Dante one more time for her sake?

'Of course I don't mind,' she said cheerfully. 'Always good to get a blast from the past.'

Touching her fingertips to her diamond tiara as if checking it was still there, Roxy frowned. 'So there's nothing going on between you any more?'

'You're kidding?' Justina's denial was vehement and heartfelt. 'Dante and I are history.'

She moved aside to make way for the next

guest and took a glass of champagne from a passing waitress. Raising the glass to her lips, she drank more quickly than normal—but the quick hit of fizzy wine made rebellion begin to simmer inside her as she walked towards the reception. Why *should* she allow herself to be intimidated by Dante D'Arezzo when she was strong enough to stand up to him? She was an independent woman, wasn't she? Not some little mouse. If she ran into him at the reception—and that was a big *if*, since she intended to stay as far away from him as possible—then she would stonewall him, just as she'd managed to do outside the church today.

She looked around. Guests were beginning to file into the vast banqueting hall which had been laid with individual tables. The golden and white room was hung with chandeliers, blazing splintering light over the heirloom crystal and silver. Here there were more pillars, all woven with ivy and spring flowers, and Justina had the sense of having walked into an enchanted glade where anything could happen.

She found her name on the seating plan, pleased to discover that she was sandwiched between a brigadier-general—which meant that he would probably be about eighty—and a Lord

Aston, who she'd never heard of. But her main source of pleasure came from the fact that she was nowhere near Dante. At least Roxy had been diplomatic enough to seat them on opposite sides of the room.

She made her way across the shiny floor of the banqueting hall towards her table, but her extra-high heels and her cheongsam dress meant that all her attention was focussed on making the journey without mishap. She wasn't really paying attention to the other guests who were taking their places, and it wasn't until an olive hand reached over to pull out her chair that some internal warning system began to sound.

Justina froze with a terrible sense of inevitability as she looked down into the brilliant dark gaze of the man she had once thought would be her husband.

CHAPTER TWO

HER HEART RACING with fury and an unwanted kind of excitement, Justina stared into Dante's dark face—wishing she could wipe that supercilious smile from his lips. 'What the hell are *you* doing here?' she said viciously, and an emerald-decked redhead sitting opposite jerked up her head in surprise.

'Do keep your voice down, Justina,' he said. 'This is an aristocratic wedding where name-calling will almost certainly not be tolerated.'

Justina could have shaken him. Or punched against that solid wall of a chest. Or...*something*. Something which involved stamping her foot like a child and demanding that he be removed from her proximity as quickly as possible. As it was, she could do little except sit down in the chair which he was now pulling out for her. Because he was right. This was the wedding of one of her oldest friends and she could hardly cause a scene by demanding that she be moved to a different seat, could she?

He had risen to his feet and was helping her into her chair, his fingers briefly brushing over her shoulders before he slid into the vacant chair beside her.

She turned to look at him, careful to keep her voice low even though she could feel her nerve ends screaming in response to that unexpected touch of his hands. 'I'm surprised you even know the meaning of the word "tolerate",' she said. 'How did you manage to get here before me when I was on the first bus?'

'I drove.'

Justina nodded. He'd driven. Of course he had. Could she really imagine him obediently trooping onto the transport provided like everybody else? He was the ultimate control freak, and whatever happened it always had to be on *his* terms.

She sucked in a deep breath. 'What I don't understand is why you happen to be sitting *here*?'

'For exactly the same reason as you, I imagine. Waiting for the wedding breakfast to begin, and with it the opportunity to toast the bride and groom and wish them many happy years of wedded bliss.'

'Please don't wilfully misunderstand me, Dante. That's not what I meant and you know it.' Reluctantly Justina's eyes focussed on the hard planes of his face, which were softened only by the sensual curves of his lips. She saw the faint shadow at his jaw which always appeared, no matter how often he shaved.

Why did he have to be so damned *sexy*? she thought. And why was her traitorous body reacting so hungrily to him as she breathed in his warm and earthy scent?

'I looked at the table plan and your name was nowhere near mine. I was just celebrating my good fortune at such a sympathetic placement and now I find you next to me. So how did that happen, Dante?'

'Simple. I changed the names,' he said unrepentantly.

Justina glared at him. How could she have forgotten his high-handedness? That way he had of just blazing in and taking whatever it was he wanted as if the world was just one giant boardroom? 'You can't turn up at a posh society wedding and start rearranging the seating!'

'I just did.' He sat back in his seat and glittered her a lazy smile. 'And since no one else has a problem with it I suggest you go with the flow and enjoy yourself.'

'Enjoy myself? With you beside me? That's a joke, right?' She bent to put her bag on the floor, mainly in an attempt to disguise the sudden tremble of her fingers. 'If I wanted to spend the afternoon in the company of a snake I'd head for the nearest pit.'

Dante saw the mutinous look on her face as she lifted her head again and for a moment he almost smiled. How could he have forgotten her outrageous defiance—the only woman in the world who had not deferred to his wishes? Who had been determined to get her voice heard and insisted that her career was just as important as his.

For a while he had enjoyed their delicious battle of wills, with the subsequent make-up sessions which had been all about red-hot passion. Until he'd been forced to realise that she meant what she said. That her objections had not been some sustained sexual tease and that she had no intention of compromising her lifestyle after their marriage. She was a singer and a performer, she'd told him, and she'd been given opportunities which came along all too rarely. She'd told him she couldn't—no—she *wouldn't* turn them down. She'd also smilingly had the nerve to tell him to stop being such a dinosaur and to respect how important her career was. But behind her smile had been the definite glint of steel, and that had unsettled him. He remembered being furious and then—surprisingly—hurt. Until he'd forced himself to be grateful for his lucky escape. Because her attitude did not bode well for a long-term relationship with someone like him.

His thoughts cleared and he found himself looking into clear amber eyes which were framed so exquisitely by her dark lashes. He waited until their wine had been poured and then let his gaze linger on her bare left hand.

'So. No wedding band. I note that you have not been as fortunate as your bandmate in the matrimonial stakes,' he observed.

Pausing midmouthful of wine, Justina almost choked with indignation. 'The matrimonial *stakes*! It's not some kind of horse race!'

'No?' He shrugged. 'But it *is* a race, all the same. Most women like to be in a permanent relationship by the time they're your age because they are thinking about the inevitable ticking of their biological clock. What are you now, Justina? Thirty-one? Thirty-two?'

'I'm not even thirty!' she gritted out, and it wasn't until she saw the answering gleam in his eyes that she realised she had fallen into some horrible sort of trap.

She'd ended up sounding defensive about her age, just because she was about to leave her twenties behind without a wedding ring on her finger. Dante had managed to do what Dante always did so well—he'd made her feel bad about herself.

So don't let him! She slanted him an adversarial look. 'I think these days you'll find an emerging breed of women who don't need the mark of a man's possession to define themselves.'

'I see your rather aggressively feminist stance hasn't softened with time.'

'Feeling threatened, are you?'

'Believe me, Justina—I'm feeling something a lot more basic than threatened.'

His mocking gaze had flickered to his groin and Justina felt her cheeks grow hot with a mixture of anger and desire. Viciously, she jabbed her fork into an unsuspecting spear of asparagus, though she couldn't quite bring herself to eat it. What was the *matter* with her? He was insulting her, and even if he *did* underpin the insults with a deliberate sensuality why the hell was she responding like this?

She put her fork back down. Perhaps that was what absence did? It hadn't made her heart grow any fonder, but it had certainly awoken a sexual appetite which she had thought gone for ever. And Dante was the last person she wanted to make her feel this way. As if she'd been wandering around, starved of all comfort and pleasure, until he had suddenly reappeared, symbolising everything she'd been missing in one dark and very dangerous package.

'Did you go to all the trouble of rearranging your seat just so that you could spend the entire meal being objectionable?' she questioned.

'Oh, come on, Justina. You know exactly why I did it. Surely you can appreciate that I am a little *curious* about you—especially considering that we were once planning to be man and wife?'

'You mean until you decided that you'd have sex with that…that…' She wanted to spit out the word *tart* or *whore*—but that might give him the erroneous impression that she still cared. Picking up her wine glass, she knocked back a large mouthful. '*Woman*,' she finished acidly.

'Will you stop rewriting history?' he demanded. 'You know damned well that we'd already broken up by then.'

She opened her mouth to object, and then shut it again—because what was the point? He arrogantly refused to see that he'd done anything wrong and nothing she said was going to change his mind. *So let it go. Stop reacting to him, because that's what he wants you to do.*

Yet it felt like hell to be this close to him. Trying like mad to pretend that she felt nothing when inside her heart was beating so loudly she was surprised that someone hadn't told her to turn the volume down.

She played around with the food some more, before forcing herself to look into his face. 'Okay. Let's do it your way and get the niceties over with. What are you doing these days? Still living in Rome, I suppose?'

'Not any more. These days I have an apartment in New York.'

'Oh?'

'You sound surprised.'

'Not really. Surprise would imply a degree of interest, which I simply don't have.' She pushed her plate away and—forgetting her no-carbs rule—started nibbling on a piece of bread instead. 'It's just that you used to act as though paradise was a place in Italy, sandwiched in between Umbria and Emilia Romagna.'

'My love of my homeland has not diminished, Justina,' he said silkily. 'And I go home whenever I can—though that is becoming increasingly less these days.'

'Business is doing well?' She made the question sound as if it was a bore to have to ask it.

He attempted a modest shrug, but she reflected with a growing feeling of frustration that modesty was one of the few things he didn't do well.

'Business is doing excellently. We've expanded our interests in North America and I love the vibrancy of New York. Okay, it isn't Tuscany—but you can't have everything.'

Justina ate some more bread—as if that could help fill the emotional hole which Dante had exposed with his words. She didn't want to think about Tuscany—or the *palazzo* where the D'Arezzo family had lived for centuries. She had been blown away by the dramatic beauty of the region and the country itself, but her visit there hadn't been a success. Actually, that was a complete understatement. Dante's aristocratic family had disapproved of his English pop-star fiancée—especially as her visit had coincided with the release of a promotional video. The one where she'd been dancing energetically while not wearing a bra. Even she had been appalled by how *raunchy* the finished product had appeared to be—but it wouldn't have seemed very credible for her to come out and say so at the time.

She had been deemed an unsuitable girlfriend for one of the D'Arezzo men, as well as being a potentially bad influence on his younger sister, and their trip had been cut abruptly short. At the time Justina had accepted what had seemed a rather harsh verdict because she'd had no choice other than to accept it. But it had been yet another nail in the coffin of their relationship.

'Can't have everything?' she echoed sarcastically. 'But I thought you were the man who always believed he could. Who made "having it all" into an art form!'

'Oh, how *brittle* you sound, Justina,' he murmured. 'I do hope that your attitude isn't motivated by envy or avarice. Career taken a nose-dive, has it?'

She was tempted to tell him to go to hell, but some remnant of pride stopped her. *Let him know that you've carved a respectable life for yourself,* she thought. That the sacrifices she'd made had been worth it. She was independent and *proud* of it. *And she was never going to be like her mother.*

'On the contrary, I'm living in London and still writing songs,' she said. 'But for other people now.'

'And you're successful?'

'Oh, I do okay.' Justina kept her smile tight. She could have told him about her recent chart-topping song, or the invitation to write the score for an upcoming musical, but he wouldn't be impressed. Dante didn't approve of ambition unless it came from a man. 'It keeps me in shoes.'

'Very expensive shoes, by the look of them.' He lowered his gaze to study her skyscraper heels before lifting his head to let his eyes drift lazily over her face. And it was still the most beautiful face he had ever seen. Her pink lips were pressed together as if she was trying to decide what to do with them and Dante felt a rush of pure and potent lust. It hit his skin like the buffeting of a powerful wave. It turned the blood in his veins into a heated flow as he imagined kissing her again.

And in that moment he knew that he was going to have her one last time. That this fever wouldn't go away unless he did. He realised then that his desire for her was like a disease which had lain dormant all these years and the sight of her had suddenly reactivated it all over again.

He felt the heavy aching at his groin as he leaned forward a little. 'And what about men?' he questioned softly.

'Men?'

His gaze was steady; his voice was not quite. 'Nobody in your life you like enough to bring him along today as your "plus one"?'

Justina met the blaze of his eyes, determined he wouldn't discover the truth. Because wouldn't he laugh—or, even worse, act *smug*—if he knew that her time with him had ruined her for other men? That she'd been unable to trust another man enough to get close to—even if she'd found anyone else attractive enough to want to try.

So why not play games with him? Why not pretend that she loved men just as they loved her? Surely pride demanded something along those lines? For Dante was traditional and old-fashioned enough to see her still-single status as some kind of failure.

She took another sip of wine. 'Oh, I do all right with men,' she said, and the sudden darkening of his face gave her a brief thrill of pleasure. Because if that was *jealousy* then it was only a fraction of what she'd felt when she'd walked into his hotel suite that day and seen that naked woman writhing all over him. Fighting back a sudden feeling of nausea, she raised her eyebrows, as if daring him to continue his interrogation.

'But nobody permanent?' he persisted.

'Nope.' She made it sound like a conscious choice instead of an unwanted situation into which she had been cast. She hadn't realised that love would be so difficult to find second time around. She hadn't realised that she would look at other men, compare them to the arrogant Tuscan—and be left completely cold. 'I don't do permanence. And now, if you don't mind, Dante, I think we've exhausted pretty much everything we need to say to each other.'

Very deliberately, she turned her back on him and started talking to the Brigadier, who was sitting on her other side—although it took her a moment before she had composed herself enough to concentrate. But the old soldier was a lucky choice of companion. He knew lots about the groom's ancestral home, and once he got going there was no stopping him. Acting like balm on her ruffled senses, he made for unexpectedly engaging company—especially to someone like Justina, who'd had such an erratic education.

Her mother's louche and nomadic lifestyle had meant that Justina had changed schools as often as most people changed their wardrobes. By the age of seventeen she'd had a wealth of experience, but not much in the way of formal teaching—unless you counted her mother's weekly master classes in gold-digging. But from an early age she'd learnt the art of asking the right questions, and the Brigadier was able to answer them all to her satisfaction. He told her all about the battles which had been fought around the beautiful Norfolk estate, and described in detail all the house's treasures—including the rare Titian painting in the picture gallery.

If only she could have blocked out the occasional drift of Dante's accent as she heard him entertaining his side of the table throughout the meal. The redhead wearing emeralds had a particularly piercing laugh, and Justina had to stop herself from wincing every time she heard it. If only she could have blotted out her aching awareness of his presence, too. She could almost feel the heat from his body and detect the raw, masculine scent which was so uniquely his.

Someone began banging a spoon against the

side of a glass, and as the bride's father stood up to make his speech Dante leaned over to speak in her ear.

'You turned your back on me, Justina—and nobody ever does that.'

'Shh. I know you love talking about yourself but you really must be quiet. The speeches are about to begin.' She caught the brief look of frustration on his face, before sitting back in her seat and fixing her eyes on the top table.

The bride's father began to speak, his crumpled linen suit and long hair making him stand out from the rest of the guests. He told a few inappropriate anecdotes which should have had the aristocratic relatives groaning—but it was such a happy occasion that people just started giggling in response. Justina looked around at all the laughing faces and a terrible emptiness started to gnaw away at her. Suddenly it felt as if everyone was sitting within the warm circle of a fire while she was alone on the outskirts, in the dark and cold. The outsider who had no real sense of belonging. And hadn't it always been that way?

She sat through the rest of the speeches and laughed in all the right places, but after the ceremonial cutting of the cake she picked up her satin clutch-bag and looked around. Dante was busy talking to the redhead and she doubted whether the Brigadier would miss her too much. She'd make as if she was going to the washroom and leave without anybody noticing. She'd have the early night she needed and sleep away her jet-lag—and tomorrow she would wake up and start forgetting about Dante all over again.

She managed to slip from the room without comment, but had got no further than the pillared entrance hall when her search to locate her cell phone was halted by the deep caress of a familiar accent.

'Going somewhere?'

She turned to find Dante effectively blocking her path, and she hated the shiver which whispered its way down over her spine. Hated even more the way she seemed mesmerised by the sardonic curve of his lips. 'Trying to,' she said pointedly. 'If you'd be so good as to get out of my way?'

'But there's dancing.'

'I know there is. But I've had enough.' *Of you.* She didn't say the words out loud; she didn't need to.

He frowned. 'So you're travelling back to London?'

'Not tonight, no. I've booked into a hotel in Burnham Market.' She gave a little sigh as she met his raised eyebrows. 'It's a town not far from here.'

He nodded as he delved into the pocket of his suit trousers for his car keys. 'I'll drive you there.'

'Thanks, but I'd prefer to get a cab.'

'Don't be melodramatic, Justina. A cab will take ages and my car is parked by the stables.'

In the cool shadows she could see the bright gleam of his eyes.

'What are you so afraid of?'

She wondered how he would react if she told him the truth. She was afraid of wanting him. Of wanting him to kiss her, despite knowing that it was wrong. Because what did it say about *her* that she should still desire him after everything that had happened?

'I'd hate to drag you away from the party.'

'I'm happy to be dragged. As it happens, I'd intended driving back to London tonight anyway—I have a flight to the States tomorrow.'

Put like that, it made her continued resistance sound unreasonable—or maybe she just didn't have the strength to oppose him any more.

Justina accompanied him outside as he handed

his keys to a valet. While they were waiting for his car to be brought round he turned to her.

'Whatever happened to Lexi?' he asked suddenly.

Justina met his curious gaze. It was a long time since anyone had mentioned Alexi Gibson, the third member of the Lollipops—or 'Sexy Lexi' as the press used to dub her.

'You know she went solo?' she questioned. 'That it was her desire to go it alone which led to the break-up of the band?'

'No, I didn't know that.' Up until the day he'd received the wedding invitation he'd deliberately excised all references to the Lollipops from his life, as carefully as a surgeon might remove an area of diseased tissue. 'Is she here?'

'Nope. Nobody ever sees her since she married one of Hollywood's biggest players.' Briefly, Justina found herself wondering if Lexi was happy—and for the first time in a long time, she turned the question on herself. Am *I* happy? she wondered. The answer hit her with a jolt. She wasn't. Successful and fairly contented, yes— and certainly fulfilled in her choice of career. But happy? No way. Not compared to the happiness she'd known in the past, with Dante.

The valet had arrived with Dante's sports

car—a low and gleaming machine which made wriggling into the passenger seat something of a challenge, despite the accommodating side-split in her cheongsam dress.

'Name of hotel?' he questioned steadily, as if the sight of her bare thigh hadn't just sent his blood pressure shooting through the ceiling.

'The Smithsonian.'

She watched as he keyed the details into his sat-nav and then sat back as the powerful car pulled away from the big house with a small spurt of gravel. The silence which descended hung heavily on the air—with what they *weren't* talking about filling the space around them and making the atmosphere feel claustrophobic. The elephant in the room was alive and well, thought Justina wryly, and currently crammed into a powerful car in Norfolk.

They drew up outside the lighted hotel which stood in a pretty Georgian Square and her fingers were unsteady as she tried to unclip her seat belt. Despite her relief that the awkward journey was over, she felt strangely reluctant to get out and just walk away. It was funny, but the older you got, the more you realised the significance of goodbyes. At twenty-five she hadn't really thought about whether or not she'd see

Dante again because at that age she hadn't been thinking beyond her heartbreak. This time she was aware that their paths were unlikely to cross again, that this was probably the last time she would ever see him—and she was unprepared for the sudden twist of pain in her heart.

'Justina?'

The soft dip in his voice was distracting, and so was the false intimacy created by the limited space inside the vehicle. In the dim light she could see the gleam of his eyes and she became aware of just how close he was. 'What?'

There was a pause. 'You know that I still want you.'

She thought how *blatant* he was. How only Dante D'Arezzo would have the nerve to come out and say something like that. 'Well, tough. The feeling isn't mutual.'

'Oh, come on. You've been undressing me with your eyes since you walked down the aisle and saw me at the cathedral.'

'I think you must be mistaken. I'm not interested in a man who spreads his favours so thinly.'

There was a heartbeat of a pause, and when he spoke his voice was harsh. 'You know damned well that it was over when I went with her! How many times do I have to tell you that?'

Justina looked down at her lap. Yes, it had been over between them—certainly as far as he'd been concerned. Her determination to go on tour with the Lollipops had led to Dante abruptly ending their engagement. But she had missed him. She had missed him more than she'd thought it possible to miss anyone. The reality of life without him had hit her hard, and his absence had felt like falling down a bottomless black hole. So she had flown back to England unexpectedly, planning to go to his hotel and ask him if they could try again, to give it one more go—because deep down she'd thought that they loved one another enough to overcome their fundamental differences. But she had been cruelly mistaken.

Her last memory of Dante was bursting into his hotel suite and seeing him in bed. But he hadn't been alone. His eyes had been closed and something had been moving at his groin beneath the sheet. Justina's horrified gasp had made the movement stop and a head had emerged. It had been a tousled blond head, and somehow that had only driven the knife in deeper. As if he was piling on cliché after cliché. Not just taking another lover—taking a *blonde* lover.

Justina had managed to turn on her heel and make it all the way to the lift. She'd even managed to hold it together enough to hail a taxi outside the hotel. But her heart had felt as if he'd stamped on it with a metal-studded boot.

She had cut all communication with him from that moment and done everything she could to try to forget him. No one could have been more assiduous than Justina in cutting all references to Dante from her life. She had destroyed every photo of him and had sold all the jewellery he had showered on her and then donated the proceeds to charity.

She was aware that his dark eyes were still fixed on her questioningly, and she vowed that he would never know the true depths of her heartbreak. 'I wasn't expecting you to move on with quite such insulting speed!'

'You think I should have waited?' he questioned heatedly. 'When already you had kept me waiting for so long? Waiting while you did your world tour. Waiting while you did more of your television interviews and your damned newspaper spreads. You knew the kind of man I was, Justina. I was young and I was hungry and I ex-

pected the woman I loved to be by my side, sup-
porting me. I had certain *appetites* which needed
to be fed—and I could not tolerate the life you
were forcing me to lead. Our very separate lives.'

'It's done,' she said flatly, her heart contracting painfully as she heard him say it. *The woman
I loved*. Past tense. The love was gone—for both
of them. 'It's in the past, Dante—and it was best
for everyone in the long run. It certainly made
for a clean break.'

His eyes searched her face and in that moment
he felt a pang of regret washing over him. Guilt,
too. And he was unprepared for the way it made
his heart clench, as if someone was squeezing
it with icy fingers. 'You know, you were never
meant to find me with her,' he said. 'I'm sorry
if I hurt you.'

Justina nodded. Once she would have given
anything to have him acknowledge the pain he'd
caused. But now it sounded like a patronising afterthought. Almost as if he suspected that she'd
never really been able to move on from him
without this final sense of closure.

And yet was that so far from the truth? Despite all her best intentions she'd never really
got over him, had she? Part of her was still stuck
inside her old self, still remembering the lover

he'd been—against whom all subsequent men had been measured only to fail.

Maybe she had continued to idealise him. Maybe his undeniable qualities as a lover had made her place him on an impossibly high pedestal which had subsequently distorted her views on men. Was that what had caused her to erect these high barriers around herself, which nobody else had ever been able to scale?

Pride helped her form careless words, and a career on the stage meant that she was able to utter them with a degree of conviction. 'The hurt I felt was just a part of growing up,' she said. 'You were simply a necessary part of my sexual education, Dante.'

For a moment there was a stunned silence, and when he spoke his voice was underpinned with a dark note of anger. 'I must say that I've heard myself described in many ways—but never quite like that before.' The tip of his tongue slowly traced the outline of his upper lip. 'And did I provide you with good grades during this sexual *education* I gave you?'

Justina's heart skipped a beat as her body began to ache with half-forgotten hunger. She told herself she ought to get out of the car while she still had a chance, but it was as if someone had turned her limbs to stone. 'I don't…I don't remember.'

'You don't? That's such a pity. Then maybe I ought to refresh your memory for you.'

She met the challenge in his shadowed eyes and saw the way his lips had parted. Did she murmur something—or indicate with her expression that she wasn't averse to the idea? Was that what made him move closer?

And suddenly they were kissing. Kissing as she'd forgotten how to. His hands were at her waist and she was reaching for his shoulders. In no time at all he was running his fingers over her satin-covered breasts and she was moaning like a woman in pain.

He snapped his seat belt free, swiftly followed by hers, but the space inside the car was cramped and already the windows were starting to get steamed up. It was hard to move, because there was nowhere *to* move, and her cheongsam made it even harder. The realisation that they were sitting right outside her hotel didn't even enter the equation until she heard Dante mutter something urgent in Italian. He dragged his mouth away from hers and she could see the look of frustration burning in his eyes.

'Not here,' he bit out, shaking his dark head.

'Not like this. Take me inside, Justina.' He bent his head to drift his lips over hers. 'Take me into your body before I explode.'

CHAPTER THREE

HER HOTEL ROOM was pristinely tidy. It was one of the things which Dante remembered as being uniquely Justina. While the rest of the band had existed in a rubble of half-eaten room service food and discarded wine bottles she had lived in her own neat little bubble, sitting writing her songs in the middle of all the chaos. He remembered her telling him that it was her particular antidote to a messy and erratic upbringing.

But his thoughts about her orderliness lasted for about as long as it took for the door to close behind them, for him to take her into his arms again and for his mouth to crush down on hers in another hungry kiss. He could feel the restless movement of her body as she writhed against him, but he got the sense that her mind was screaming out all kinds of objections.

Very deliberately, he grazed his mouth over hers with a slow and erotic brush. 'I want you,' he said, his words coming out unsteadily. 'I have never wanted a woman as much as I want you in this moment.'

Justina closed her eyes as his lips moved to her neck, her fingers tangling themselves luxuriously in the thick darkness of his hair. 'Dante...' she whispered, knowing that the rest of the sentence went something like, *You know we shouldn't be doing this.* But the words remained unspoken—and how could they be spoken when he had started touching her breasts like that?

'What the hell kind of dress is this?' he questioned as he felt around for a zip.

'It's called a...a cheongsam. I...I bought it in Singapore and I—'

'I'm not interested in its history!' Roughly, he cut through her stumbling explanation. 'The only thing I'm interested in is how to get the damned thing off.'

'There are buttons down the side,' she gasped.

'*Sono mille!*' His fingers were trembling as he began to fumble them open. 'How many?'

She felt cool air rushing onto her skin and told herself to call a halt to this madness. But she couldn't. She just *couldn't.* Her body was too hungry, her desire too strong to be able to resist what he was doing to her. Hadn't she spent the past five years wondering if she'd ever feel like this again? Wondering if her body would ever feel this incomparable rush of desire? And suddenly Justina knew that she didn't want to be passive. That if this was to be their swansong then they would come together as the equals they'd never really been. She was no longer the virgin lover he had needed to teach. She had graduated with honours, and maybe it was time to remember just how much she'd loved having sex with this man.

She kicked off her high heels and sent them flying across the room before beginning to tug at his tie.

'Impatient?' he queried, thinking that in the past she would have slid the shoes tidily from her feet.

'Aren't you?' she whispered back as she turned her attention to his shirt. She slid open the buttons and greedily peeled it away to reveal the honed torso beneath, bending her head to graze her teeth against his skin, her tongue licking luxuriously against its silken surface.

'*Dio.*' He shuddered, and tore at another button of her dress. He pulled the garment away from her with hands which were shaking, and if such a reaction was unheard of for someone of his experience he didn't care. He unclipped her bra in one deft movement. Her panties he disposed of by ripping apart the delicate lace with his fingers, and he heard her little gasp of pleasure as they brushed over her honeyed heat.

'You always liked me to play a little rough, didn't you, *tesoro*?' he demanded as he tugged off the last of his own clothing—and was taken off guard by her fervent passion as she pushed him down onto the bed.

She moved over him, her face filled with an expression he could never remember seeing before as she straddled him. Her eyes were slitted so he couldn't read them, and she was biting her lips as if she was trying to stop them from trembling.

'Do it,' he commanded.

But Justina shook her head. Tonight *she* was going to call the shots. This was going to be her therapy, the recovery she needed. She would feast on his body until she'd had her fill. She would let the harsh light of reality shine down on this demi-god of her imagination and by morning she would see him for the mortal he really was. This was *sex*, she told herself fiercely—and she wasn't going to make the mistake of confusing it with love.

'I'll *do it* when I'm good and ready.'

Dante moaned as she circled her hips to brush her feminine core over his steely erection so that he could almost feel her—but not quite. She was close enough for him to be able to plunge inside her, and yet she kept her moist treasure almost tantalisingly out of reach. His head fell back against the pillow and for a moment he felt almost helpless. This was not how he liked it to happen—at least not with Justina. He liked to be in control, to play the dominant role, and yet she was writhing around on top of him like some teasing whore. And, God help him, he *liked* it.

'*Per favore*,' he groaned. '*Please.*'

His heartfelt plea made something inside her snap, and despite revelling in her fleeting moment of power Justina knew she couldn't wait any longer. Positioning herself, she slid down and slowly took his hard, silken length deep into her body. She heard him groan as he filled her and for a moment she couldn't move. She wanted to fall against him. To collapse against his chest and hug him, clinging tightly as if she would never let him go. To tell him that nothing had ever felt as good as this and nothing ever would.

But she wasn't going to be passive, was she? Or weak. She was going to enjoy her body and make the most out of a situation she had never thought would happen.

Nor should it be happening, taunted a mocking voice in her head, but she shut the door on it as she began to move. Their warm bodies met and reacquainted themselves as she eased his throbbing shaft in and out of her eager flesh. She groaned as he played with her breasts, and when his thumb began to rub against her clitoris she flung her head back and gave a low and shuddering cry. It felt so amazing that she never wanted it to stop, but it didn't last as long as she wanted it to. How could it, when they were both so close to the edge? She tried to prolong the erotic dance for as long as possible, but the hot waves were too powerful to hold back. Dark impulses danced over her skin as she gripped his shoulders and pushed her hips forward, driving him in right up to the hilt.

'Justina!' he gasped.

'Dante!' she moaned in response as she felt the first shimmering tugs hovering at the edge of her consciousness—and then, as she began to go under, he flipped her onto her back, his powerful body dark and tense as he drove into her with increasing speed. Her body felt as if it was exploding with pleasure as the first of the spasms hit her, and then she heard him give his own ragged cry as his head sank down against her neck.

Justina kept her eyes tightly shut as their bodies gradually grew still and felt a brief pang of melancholy wash over her. But she was damned if she was going to let it show. She wasn't going to start dwelling on how amazing it had been because that was nothing new. And she wasn't going to start wishing that they could go back to what they'd had before. Because they couldn't, could they? You could never go back.

Even if you could she wouldn't want to—not with Dante. *Especially* not with Dante. Because he was bad news. Or had she forgotten that? Had the urgent greed of her body made her conveniently push away the bitter truth? He'd hurt her more than she'd thought it was possible to hurt and he had the power to do it still. And he would. She knew that. She knew all about the complex factors which motivated him. She knew that he'd seen some of her behaviour as humiliation to his macho pride, and perhaps this was his way of getting even. Taking her body with careless disregard for her feelings.

She wriggled a little, aware that they were still locked intimately together. He was sleeping—or at least he seemed to be doing a good impression of sleeping, with the dark arcs of his long lashes feathering his sculpted cheeks. Once there would have been love as she looked at him, but that emotion had been replaced by a mixture of anger and regret. How could she have done that? How *could* she? She'd brought him up here to her hotel room and just had sex with him—without any of the usual preliminaries. And why, of all the men in all the world, did it have to be *him* and only him who could make her feel like this? The only man she'd ever been intimate with was the man who had hurt her. Who had destroyed her trust completely.

She felt him stir inside her. She felt his burgeoning erection and remembered how deliciously *insatiable* he'd used to be. Once he would have lowered his head to kiss her and started to make love to her all over again. But she wasn't going to let that happen. *Please give me the strength to push him away,* she prayed— but Dante got there first.

His silent withdrawal from her sticky body seemed fraught with symbolism—all of it dark. He hadn't said a single word, and the silence in the room seemed to be growing bigger by the second. He was levering himself up onto one elbow and appeared to be viewing her as dispassionately as a scientist might look into a petrie dish, to see what rogue organisms had sprung up overnight.

'That was some sex,' he said, and Justina met the cold expression in his eyes.

She kept her own response deliberately light. *Don't let him know how you feel. Hide your hurt, your anger and your shame and be the kind of woman he usually ends up in bed with. Casual. No-strings.* She even managed to curve her lips into the faintest of smiles. 'You liked it?'

Dante's face darkened. 'I'm sure you don't need me to tell you how good you are.' He paused and his voice took on an empty, hollow quality. 'I'd forgotten quite how good.'

But he had never known her quite like that before, he realised. And, despite his own very comprehensive love life since they'd parted, he felt sick at the thought of her doing the same. He tried to tell himself that it was a *good* thing to realise that she'd changed. That she was no longer the sweet innocent he'd initiated into sex. He hadn't expected her to be, had he? *Had* he?

'I expect you've learnt a lot from all the other men you've known in the interim,' he said.

Justina gave her naked shoulders a little wriggle. 'I always make it a rule not to discuss other lovers when I'm in bed with a man. It strikes me as particularly bad manners.'

Her words made his mouth harden and he pushed back the rumpled bedclothes before getting out of bed. She watched as he headed for the bathroom, just as she'd watched him do so many times before. His naked olive body was magnificent, the perfect globes of his paler buttocks contrasting with the dark musculature of his powerful thighs.

He emerged minutes later and without another word reached for his clothes and began getting dressed.

'Going?' she questioned, still in that same studiedly casual voice.

He paused in the act of pulling on his shirt, his dark eyes flicking over her with a look which was half lust, half disgust. 'I have a flight to the States in the morning. I told you that.'

'Of course.' She didn't want him to think that she minded him leaving so she got out of bed herself, reaching for the silk robe which was lying neatly folded on the chair by the bed.

'Would you like a drink before you go?' she questioned. 'I can ring down for coffee if you like. It's a long drive back to London.'

A dark spear of jealousy lanced through him. Dante wondered if she knew how *seasoned* she sounded. As if she asked men that kind of question most days of the week. He saw her slide the slippery robe over her luscious nakedness and quickly averted his eyes. Maybe she did.

'No, thanks.'

Justina began pulling the pins from her mussed-up hair and shaking it free. 'Is there something particular in New York?' she questioned. 'Something which can't wait?'

He curled his tie into a gleaming coil and slid it into his jacket pocket. 'There's a big party I don't want to miss.'

'Oh?' He might as well have been talking about the stock market for all the emotion she put into her next question. 'Something special?'

Dante looked at her. Her hair was now free of all the pins and had tumbled down around her shoulders and she was brushing it. It wasn't as long as he remembered, but it was still thick and raven-dark. It made her look like some beautiful dark angel, he thought, and for a moment he wanted to kiss her again, to ravage her. To tumble her back down on the bed and thrust right into her all over again until he had emptied himself inside her. But he couldn't. Or rather, he wouldn't. Because while once had been a mistake, twice would be insanity. They were too different. They always had been.

He shrugged. 'Just a party.'

'Oh?' Justina fought against the instinct which was telling her to leave it alone and instead let her finger hover over the self-destruct button. 'Whose?'

'A girl's.'

Beneath her silk robe Justina felt her skin ice to goose bumps. Had he…had he done it again? Taken her to bed when he was in a relationship with someone else? Her heart felt as cold as her skin, but somehow she managed another of those light smiles—as if they'd just done nothing more daring than enjoy a cup of tea together, instead of romping wildly on the bed. Because she was *not* going to fall to pieces.

'Well, drive carefully,' she said. 'And I hope you have a safe journey back to America.'

Dante's mouth twisted. How dismissive she sounded. As if what they'd done had meant nothing. Because it *had* meant nothing, he reminded himself bitterly. They both knew that.

His mind began to play back an erotic tape of what had just happened. Justina straddling him. Justina riding him. The way he'd ridden her back until that sweet release had claimed them both. The forbidden ache of sex throbbed thickly through his veins and in that moment of renewed desire he despised himself almost as much as he despised her for what they had done.

But not enough to stop him from pulling her into his arms and lowering his lips to a mouth which was now closed and resisting. A couple of seconds was all it took for that resistance to vanish, for her lips to part again and allow his tongue to slip inside. A couple of seconds more and she was kissing him right back, her fingers tangling in his hair the way they always did when she was turned on. If he'd given it any longer he suspected that he could have taken her again—right there on the floor on which they stood. He suspected that if he slid one finger between her legs he could make her come in seconds, the way he'd always been able to do. And wasn't he tempted to do just that? *Wasn't* he?

But Justina was pushing at his chest with two balled-up fists and tearing her mouth from his. Her eyes were dark with anger as she took a few unsteady steps away from him, and her breathing was ragged as she struggled to control it.

'You've got what you came for—now get out of here,' she snapped, because never in her life had she felt so *used*. 'Go back to New York and get the hell out of my life.'

For a moment they stared at one another as rage and desire simmered in the air around them, and then Dante picked up his jacket and slung it over his shoulder.

'Goodbye, Justina,' he said, and the smile which curved his lips was bitter. 'Thanks for the memory.'

CHAPTER FOUR

THE NIGHTMARE COULDN'T possibly get any worse.

It just couldn't.

As warm, fat raindrops teemed from the sky Justina hurried into a shop on the busy Singaporean street as fast as her bulky frame would allow—but it wasn't easy. The huge swell of her baby made movement difficult, especially in the sultry heat which characterised this vibrant city. A minute was all it had taken for her to get soaked right through, and now she stood shivering as the icy blast of the shop's air-conditioning blasted over her damp skin.

Trying to conceal her shape behind a rack of designer clothes, she peered out through the blur of rain. People were hastily putting up their umbrellas. Others were standing huddled beneath bus shelters as they sought to avoid the daily spectacle of the tropical storm. Nobody seemed to be looking in her direction. Nobody at all.

Justina swallowed down the sudden dryness in her throat. Was she simply going crazy— imagining that someone was following her? That another photographer planned to leap out to take a picture? She couldn't understand why the press were so interested in the fact that she was having a baby when loads of women had babies out of wedlock these days without stigma.

Yet she couldn't deny the media interest—especially since the Lollipops *Sweetest Hits* had been re-released just before Roxy's wedding and had stormed up the charts all over the world. She still had a public profile, which had become higher as a result of those renewed sales. On days where there wasn't a lot of news around she could still sometimes find one of those rather depressing pieces about 'unlucky in love' Justina Perry hidden in the back pages of the newspapers—the ones which wondered why she was still single.

Only now she had given them an even bigger story—*STILL SINGLE AND NOW EXPECTING! WHO'S THE MYSTERY FATHER, JUSTINA?*

After she'd gone through the first stages of

dismay and denial, she had tried to conceal her pregnancy for as long as possible—and when that had become out of the question she had stayed out of the limelight as much as she could. But the press were like hungry dogs. One sniff of a juicy story and they came looking. Lately there'd been a whole spate of articles speculating about the identity of her baby's father—she was just praying that nobody had seen her disappearing from Roxy's wedding with Dante D'Arezzo. That was the kind of snippet which would find its way into a gossip column, forever linking her name to the Italian billionaire.

'Can I get you a chair, ma'am?'

Justina turned round to find a shop assistant regarding her with concern. Perhaps she was worried that the tired-looking Englishwoman was about to give birth in the middle of her shop and it wasn't really Justina's role to reassure her that she wasn't due for another five weeks.

'No, thanks. I'm fine. I'll take a cab back to my hotel. The rain looks as if it's stopping now.'

'You're sure, ma'am?'

'Yes, thank you.' From somewhere, she summoned up a smile. 'Quite sure.'

But during her shivering journey back to Raffles Hotel, where she always stayed when she was in the city, Justina couldn't seem to halt the thoughts which seemed determined to keep any peace of mind at bay. Round and round in her head went the indisputable truth. She was pregnant with Dante's baby and terrified he would find out.

Distractedly, she rubbed at her temples. He was bad news. He was a player. He was everything that was dangerous in a man—especially where she was concerned. He had taken her to bed and soared with her to the stars before they crashed back down to earth again. And she couldn't just blame Dante for what had happened, because she had been culpable, too. She'd practically ripped his clothes off and ravished him, despite all the terrible history between them.

She felt the sudden clench of her heart, but it was more with anger than with pain. She had been headstrong and stupid. She had given in to desire without thinking about the consequences and that's why she found herself in this position. But there was *no way* she was going to go running to him. Not when he'd made it clear that what had happened had been a regrettable one-off.

She kept telling herself that interest would

die down if she kept her counsel. She lived the kind of international life where it was perfectly acceptable to be vague about the identity of her baby's father. The people she wrote songs for wouldn't have cared if the devil himself had claimed paternity. The only person who was really interested was the London doctor whose care she was under—and he wasn't making any moral judgements. That was the sum total of people it really affected. She certainly wasn't relying on any help from her mother, whose re-action to the news had been entirely predict-able—if a little sad.

'I'm not ready to be a grandmother!' Elaine Perry had snapped, not seeming to notice Jus-tina's white-faced response.

Justina had stared at the woman with whom she had such a complicated relationship. Her once-beautiful mother, who was unable to ac-cept that her looks were now fading and who tried to compensate for that by slapping on far too much make-up. 'But, Mum—'

'Don't "Mum" me! If you think I'm spend-ing my time knitting bootees or acting as an un-paid babysitter, then you're mistaken, Justina.' A coy smile had followed as the older woman had fiddled with hair which was growing thinner by the year. 'I *do* still have a busy social life of my own, you know.'

And Justina, feeling sick for all kinds of reasons, had not responded. What compassion could she expect from a woman whose life had been spent as mistress to a series of wealthy men she'd milked for every penny she could? Who was now reduced to living with some creepy and aging *roué* in the centre of Paris?

Justina still felt shaky as her cab drew up outside the hotel and she went inside to collect her key from the desk in the spacious lobby. The atmosphere of the iconic hotel usually had a soothing effect on her. The faded brocade chairs and tall potted palms always made her think of a more elegant time, and whenever she stayed there she felt part of it. Only today the magic of Raffles wasn't working. She felt as if she was on a tiny raft, bobbing around in an unforgiving sea, with no real place to go and drop anchor.

Maybe she needed the restorative power of a deep bath and a strong cup of tea, and then she would—

'Justina.'

Someone was saying her name in a way which only one person ever could. Disbelief made her skin turn to ice as she heard the voice which had haunted her waking thoughts and troubled dreams for the past seven and a half months. She shook her head in hopeful denial. She was imagining it. She *had* to be imagining it.

Slowly she turned to see the dark and forbidding figure of Dante D'Arezzo, and her heart began to flutter wildly in her chest. No. She wasn't imagining it. Nobody else spoke like that. And nobody else looked like that either. Dante was here in the flesh—vibrant with life and looking immaculate in cool, pale linen, his face an intimidating study of dark fury as his gaze seared into her.

The angled slant of his cheekbones cast shadows over his features and his mouth was grim and unsmiling. She had never seen his powerful body look quite so tense. The only thing about him which moved was a little muscle which was flickering at his temple. For a moment she swayed with the sheer shock of seeing him, but maybe he'd anticipated that kind of reaction for his hand reached out towards her. Strong fingers clamped around her forearm to steady her, and she could feel the burning warmth of his flesh digging into her icy skin. And God forgive her but her body instantly thrilled to that touch, even though it was more the touch of a captor than a lover. She could feel her shivering response to him, and she wondered if he could feel it, too.

'What…what are you doing here?' she demanded shakily as his brilliant gaze scorched through her.

Dante's heart began to accelerate with anger as he looked into her white face. What did she *think* he was doing here? Doing a leisurely tour of the Far East and bumping into her quite by chance? Did she imagine he was going to ask her to the bar to join him for one of the hotel's famous Singapore Slings?

'You and I need to talk,' he said grimly.

Justina bit her lip as distracted, crazy thoughts began to rush into her head. What if she called out and told the staff that she was being harassed? Wouldn't that sound bad, coming from a heavily pregnant woman? Wouldn't he instantly be ejected from the hotel, and probably from the country itself?

She wasn't so sure that he would. Dante could smooth-talk his way through most things. She could imagine him turning the full force of his charm on hotel security and managing to convince them that it was her *hormones* at work. And when it all boiled down to it her hormones *were* the only reason he was here. He wasn't here because he missed her or because he wanted her back in his bed. He wanted to speak to her about something which was glaringly obvious to both of them and she must accede to his wishes. She owed him that much, at least.

'Not here,' she said, her throat so dry that her words sounded strangled. 'We can go and have coffee in the Writers' Bar and—'

'No,' he snapped, imperiously cutting through her suggestion. 'I don't intend to have this conversation while you play to the crowd, Justina. Take me to your room.' He saw the brief look which hovered in her eyes and his mouth twisted with derision as he lowered his voice to a deadly hiss. 'Oh, please don't worry that I'm about to seduce you. Because let me assure you that's the last thing on my mind right now. In fact, let me put it even more plainly, just so that we can be very clear about where we stand. If you and I were alone on a desert island I think I'd gladly embrace celibacy rather than risk coming within two feet of you, you manipulative little bitch.'

The vitriol in his voice made Justina's hand fly to her lips in horror as she looked at him. Did he really hate her that much? But even if he did he had no right to talk to her that way. She was carrying a baby beneath her heart, and even if he wished it wasn't *his* baby it was certainly *her* baby, and she would defend it with every ounce of strength in her body.

So stop letting him intimidate you. Have the talk he wants—the talk you know you owe him.

Because wasn't this what she had been expecting—and dreading—for months? Wasn't this very meeting the reason why she'd taken on so many travelling commitments since discovering she was pregnant? Not daring to be in one place too long in case he found her, she had become a kind of bulky fugitive. A woman who was running away from the inevitable— only now the inevitable had caught up with her.

She shrugged. 'Okay. We'll talk. But it might be a good start if you stopped manhandling me like that.' Pointedly, she glanced down at the olive fingers which were still gripping her forearm, and then up into the hard gleam of his dark eyes. But the terrible thing was that she *liked* him touching her. For all his cruel words, and her fear of what he wanted, she liked the way he made her feel. And, shamefully, it was deprivation rather than relief which washed over her when he let her go, and her footsteps were a little unsteady as she turned and headed for the staircase.

Justina was aware of people watching them as they made their way from the public area of the hotel towards the residential part and guessed they must make a bizarre couple. She was all damp and bedraggled after being caught in the tropical storm, and Dante looked so indomitable as he shadowed her, his savagely beautiful face and powerful body making every female guest in the building glance at him twice.

In silence they walked towards her suite, and the dark gleam of the wooden verandas, the raffia furniture and the scent of flowers drifting up from the courtyard garden failed to calm Justina's mounting sense of anxiety. By the time she pushed open her door she felt like a piece of elastic which had been stretched so tightly that the faintest movement would violently snap it.

But she couldn't carry on feeling frayed and vulnerable like this. She had to stay in control and remember that she was dealing with a man for whom control was key. Some primitive part of her wanted to leave the door open—but she knew that the sound of their voices would carry and she couldn't risk that. With a heavy sigh of resignation, she closed it behind them.

'I need to use the bathroom,' she said.

It seemed almost too intimate a thing to

say—which was a bizarre thought in the circumstances—but Justina needed to do more than relieve her pregnancy-weak bladder. Pride made her tug a brush through hair which was hanging down her back like rats' tails, and to slick on some pink lipstick which seemed to be the only colour in her white face.

She still needed to suck in a deep breath as she prepared to walk back in and face him. She felt sick with nerves—the way she'd used to feel just before she went out on stage—only this was much worse. On stage, her crippling fears had used to vanish the moment she heard the first chord of music and professionalism began to kick in. Today she had no idea how she was going to react to what lay ahead of her. These were new and uncharted waters—and she'd never seen anything more forbidding than the expression on Dante's dark face as she pushed open the door and walked into the lavish sitting room.

He was standing in front of the massive floor to ceiling windows which overlooked the veranda and yet somehow he made them look insignificant. His face was hard—like granite—and his eyes were cold as they flicked over the massive swell of her belly, as if he couldn't quite believe what he was seeing.

'You'd better sit down,' he said heavily.

She shook her head. *Damn* him for trying to act concerned. If he was so concerned then he wouldn't have leapt out at her like that, downstairs in the foyer. 'I'd prefer to stand,' she said.

For a moment Dante felt immense frustration shimmer over his skin. Wasn't that typical of Justina? So damned independent that she'd refuse to do the sensible thing. Even though her face looked as pale as flour, she was stubbornly refusing to sit down simply because *he* had been the one to suggest it.

'Have it your own way.'

'I intend to. How did you find me, Dante?'

'It wasn't difficult. You don't exactly blend into a crowd at the moment. I saw the erratic press reports about your…*condition*, and I worked out that the baby could be mine. I kept thinking that if that *were* the case you would contact me.' There was a pause and his eyes burned into her. 'I kept waiting for you to get in touch, and when you didn't I thought…'

His words tailed off. He'd thought that maybe he'd been mistaken, that it wasn't his baby at all. And hadn't the thought of *that* eaten him up with jealousy? The idea that he might have been just one in a line of men who had graced her bed? But the feeling hadn't left him, and neither had the strange *certainty* which had flooded through him. It had been certainty which had made him track her down. Which had made him board his private jet to Singapore, where he had been informed that she was staying alone in Raffles Hotel.

Intently, he stared at her, and he could feel the powerful beat of his heart thundering in his chest. The crazy thing was that he wanted to go over there and place the palm of his hand on her belly, as if to convince himself that this was real. And if he did that could he guarantee that the same dark hunger wouldn't flicker into life, the way it always did? Why was it that, no matter how much he tried to convince himself otherwise, he could never seem to stop wanting her?

'Is there something you need to tell me?'

Justina nodded as a wave of emotion threatened to overwhelm her, but somehow she held it back. *Don't act ashamed or intimidated,* she told herself. *Just deal with the facts.* But it was far from easy, because as she faced the accusation in his eyes a terrible yearning threatened to flare up inside her. She found herself wishing this could all have been different. That they were the same two people they'd once been—a couple in love who were planning to be together for the rest of their lives.

But it was not like that. It was nothing like that. Pointless to waste her time wishing that it was. *Pretend you're doing a television interview,* she told herself. *Act calmly. Take the emotion out of the subject and try not to turn this into a confrontation.*

Her voice was almost gentle. 'Is that a round-about way of asking whether you're the father, Dante?'

CHAPTER FIVE

'AM I?' DANTE STARED at her, and his eyes had never looked colder than they did right then. 'Am I the father of your baby, Justina?'

For a moment she hesitated, tempted to tell him no. Because wouldn't that be easier all round? He could go back to New York and the life he'd made there. She would never have to see him again. *Never*. Financially—and hopefully emotionally—she could manage to be a good, single mother. Lots of women were.

But then she thought of the child she carried. The baby who was currently kicking beneath her fluttering heart as if it was trying out for a foetal football team. Could she wilfully deny her child the knowledge of its father just because that father didn't love *her*? Wouldn't that be the most selfish thing she could ever do—especially since she knew the pain and deprivation of growing up without a father? She knew how that could leave an empty hole which nothing could ever fill. She felt fiercely protective of this new life within her—and if she was being protective then that ruled out being selfish, didn't it? It might be better for *her* if Dante was out of her life, but it wouldn't be better for the baby.

'Yes,' she breathed—and then she said it again, so that there could be no going back. 'Yes, you are.'

For a moment he said nothing. He could hear the loud ticking of a clock as a surge of adrenalin flooded through him—his body automatically gearing itself up for fight or flight. He stared down at the elegant table beside him, on which stood a bowl of fruit so perfect that it might have been made from wax. For a split second he wanted to smash his fist through it. To see the apples disintegrating into pulp and the squashed oranges spurting out their juice. The desire was so strong that his big hands clenched into tight fists and he almost raised one. Until he forced himself to face facts as well as to re-exert the habitual control which had momentarily threatened to desert him.

Don't forget that this is a very single-minded woman, he told himself, as he stared into her wide amber eyes. *Who will do anything to get what she wants out of life.* He had witnessed her steely ambition first-hand. He had seen how she'd always put her career before him—it had been the main reason why he'd called off their wedding. So he needed to find out *all* the facts—not just the ones she had chosen to tell him.

'How can you be sure it's mine?'

Justina heard the rough challenge which distorted his voice. The question hurt—mainly because it sounded genuine and not asked simply as an attempt to insult her. Did he really think she behaved that way? Picked up men at weddings before taking them back to her room to have sex with them? She wondered how he would react if she told him that he was the only man she'd ever been intimate with, and that was how she knew he was the father. Would he laugh at her or simply pity her for spending the past five years without being able to move on?

'I just am,' she said flatly.

He shook his head. 'You'll have to do better than that.'

'What are you talking about?'

His mouth twisted. 'If you recall, you told me

that you did "all right" with men.' He remembered the casual way she'd said it, and his own corresponding stab of jealousy. The overpowering sense of *darkness* which had shadowed his soul at the thought of other men making love to her the way he'd done. 'I got the distinct feeling that I wasn't the only one who shared your favours—not least from the enthusiastic way you climbed on top of me and ground those hips of yours so expertly against mine. I certainly didn't think that what happened between us on the night of the wedding was in any way unique.'

It was the cruellest thing he could have said, and Justina prayed that her face didn't register the hurt which was curling up inside her. He thought she was a tramp. He'd just come out and said so. 'Then why are you here if you believe that?' she questioned. 'Why this dramatic appearance—ambushing me in the lobby of my hotel as if you were in some kind of movie?'

'I'm here because I want the truth.'

'Why not just phone me up and ask me? Surely that would have been simpler for a man as busy as you?'

His gaze was steady. 'Would you have taken my call?'

Beneath his intense scrutiny, Justina shrugged. She wanted to save face. She wanted to hurt him back, as he had just hurt her. And instinctively she wanted to do the one thing she suspected would appal him so much that he might even contemplate going away and leaving her alone. She wanted to deny him. To let him know that she didn't need him. She wanted to offer him the freedom to walk away and leave her to face this on her own. 'Probably not,' she said eventually.

He nodded his head and turned to stare out of the window. Somehow it was easier to contemplate the courtyard gardens than continue to confront the fecund swell of her belly—though the white frangipani blossoms on the trees might as well have been lumps of snow for all the notice he took of them. But the brief respite was all he needed to regain his composure, and when he turned back he nodded.

'So it is true,' he said, his voice filled with silken venom. 'I have often been accused of cynicism, but even I couldn't believe that a woman could be quite so manipulative as you have been. It seems I was wrong.' There was a pause as his gaze raked over her, and even as the words formed on his lips he could feel the betraying leap of desire. 'You just wanted a stud, didn't you, Justina?'

'A stud?' Justina stared into eyes which resembled flat, dark metal. 'What...what are you talking about?'

His mouth twisted. 'I'm talking about the interview you gave just before Roxy's wedding. The one where you said how much you regretted not having had a baby and how much you'd like one.'

She heard the condemnatory tone which distorted his voice and for a moment felt vulnerable. Yes, she'd said that—but sometimes you said things which were only half-truths for all kinds of reasons. Especially when a journalist got you on the back foot. He *knew* that—and surely there was enough history between them for her to explain why she'd done it?

'Because that's what I felt I was *supposed* to say,' she defended. 'Because women who don't want babies are seen as monsters.'

'But I thought you *didn't* want babies.' His dark brows shot up. 'How could you possibly want them when your damned career was always so important to you and took precedence over everything else? You told me that there wasn't enough *time* in your life for children—and I can't see that having changed.'

Frustratedly, she shook her head. Hadn't he realised that at the time she'd said that it had been fear which had motivated her—as well as ambition? Her career had mattered to her because it had been a symbol of her own survival, as well as her success. She'd still been on the way up, and it had meant too much to her to simply let it slide just because that was what he wanted. But Dante had also wanted her pregnant as soon as they were married, and that had scared the hell out of her—and not just because she'd been so young. She had tried to explain that it was partly down to the awful experience she'd had with her own mother, which made her want to wait, but he had been immovable. Women married and then they became pregnant—it was as primitive as that to Dante.

'You don't understand, Dante.'

He shook his dark head and gave a cynical laugh. 'Oh, but I do, Justina. I understand only too well. You had sex with me—what? Five years after we'd last seen one another? Most women would have slapped my face for even trying it on. But not you. Oh, no. You wanted me from the moment that you saw me in the cathedral—I could read it in your eyes as clearly as if you'd come straight out and propositioned me.'

'I'm sorry if I don't match up to the saintlike status of your other lovers!'

'We didn't even use any protection!'

'I didn't realise that was solely the woman's responsibility.'

'I assumed you were still on the pill,' he snapped, knowing that he should have stopped to find out. But he hadn't. He hadn't cared about anything other than finding himself in the tight, molten slickness of her body again after so long. And hadn't it felt good? Hadn't it felt like *heaven*? He swallowed as he tried to force the erotic memory to the back of his mind—but he couldn't. It had been haunting him ever since— so how could he expect it to disappear when the woman who had so lured him was standing right in front of him? 'Why would you take such a risk with a man you were never likely to see again after that night?'

Justina stared into the cold condemnation on his face. Because she hadn't been thinking straight, that was why. So blinded by passion that common sense hadn't got a look-in. Oh, *why* did it have to be him who'd made her feel all these things? Why did he *still* make her feel them even now? If he walked across the room and started to kiss her, she honestly didn't know how she'd respond.

'You tell me,' she said tonelessly.

'Okay. I will.' His eyes grew hard and his voice was calculating—like a detective who was poised on the brink of a breakthrough. 'I'll tell you exactly how I think it was. Maybe you wanted a baby. You'd reached a time in your life where you realised you'd better get a move on if you wanted to be a mother. Only maybe you wanted a baby without all the added trouble of an accompanying man. Isn't that what every successful career woman craves these days, Justina? The designer baby to go with her designer life?'

Justina flinched. Did he really believe her capable of doing such a cold-blooded thing? 'That's the most absurd thing I've ever heard.'

'And what better candidate for her baby's father than me?' he continued, as if she hadn't spoken.

'You?'

'Yes, me.' Automatically he pulled his powerful shoulders back as his proud words hissed into the air. 'Strong and virile. The alpha of the pack. Women are programmed to want a man like me to father their child. That's why they thrust themselves on me at every opportunity.'

For a moment she was tempted to point out that he had been the one doing the thrusting, but she recognised that this was no time to attempt humour. Not when he was essentially accusing her of having used him as some sort of unknowing *sperm donor*.

'I'm not continuing with this ridiculous discussion any longer,' she said. 'Go and mull over your crazy conspiracy theories somewhere else. I'm tired and I need to pack. I have a plane to catch.'

He watched as she rubbed two fingers tiredly across her forehead. 'You're going home?'

'Yes, Dante—I'm going home. I'm only just within the legal requirement for flying, if you must know.'

'Why the hell *are* you flying? Why aren't you doing what most women would do in your position—lying on a sofa with your feet up instead of trekking halfway across the globe?'

'I've been working.'

'Of course. I should have guessed.'

'I know that for you it's a dirty word when it comes from a woman's lips—but that's just the way it is. I was working—and now I need to pack. So if you wouldn't mind leaving me to get on with it, I'd appreciate it.'

'As it happens, I would. I'd mind very much.' For the first time he saw the faint shadows which darkened her eyes. 'I presume you're booked on to a scheduled flight?'

'I wasn't planning on flapping my arms and flying to England, if that's what you mean.'

He let out a low breath of irritation. 'That is a completely unsatisfactory state of affairs. You will travel with me instead. On the D'Arezzo jet.'

For a moment she hesitated. 'You've got your own plane now?'

'Yes, I've got my own plane,' he snapped. 'I told you at the wedding that the company was doing well—you didn't bother to ask *how* well. But I don't know why that should come as a surprise, when *my* career never made you sit up and take notice. It was always about *you*—wasn't it, Justina?'

He said it in a way which filled Justina with rebellion. Already he was trying to take over. To use his power and his wealth to control her movements. Earlier in the day she'd been feeling lonely—but now she could see that there were worse things than having to deal with an unplanned pregnancy on her own. Like having

Dante call the shots and expect her to fall in with his wishes.

'I will not travel on your plane,' she said quietly. 'I already have my ticket and I'm intending to use it. Before you ask, I will be travelling in first class and I will be perfectly comfortable. I don't need your money and what it can buy. That's why I've always made my own. Why I've always been so protective of my career and my independence. Don't you realise that I'm not impressed by your wealth, Dante? I never was.'

There was a pause while their eyes clashed in a silent battle of wills. Yes, he thought bitterly, she had always made it perfectly clear that she didn't need *him*.

'But I'm not trying to impress you,' he said quietly. 'On the contrary, I am merely trying to make you see sense. Because this is no longer just about you and what makes *you* happy—although God knows that's been your main consideration for so long that it's difficult to see how you could ever change your behaviour. You seem to forget that you carry my child within you, and I have a responsibility towards that unborn life.'

She felt her heart contract. 'But you don't—'

'Now, we can do this one of two ways.' His

unequivocal words cut through her protest. 'You can force me to carry you kicking and screaming through the foyer of this beautiful hotel—with all the attendant embarrassment and publicity that will cause. Publicity which will be abhorrent to me and to the D'Arezzo corporation. But if I have to do it, then I will. Be under no illusion about that.' There was a pause as his dark gaze scorched through her. 'Or we can do this the easy way. You can go and do your packing and let me fly you back to England and all you have to do is sit back and let it happen. Which is far better for you—and for the baby. Surely even you can see that?'

Justina pursed her lips together, afraid that she was going to do something stupid—like bursting into noisy tears of frustration. He still thought he could march right in and take over her life. Even worse, he didn't just think it—he was actually going ahead and *doing* it, in that powerful and pig-headed way of his. He had her backed into a corner and she knew it—just as she knew that his forceful words were underpinned with truth. It *was* better for the baby, and this *was* no longer just about her.

And if she was being brutally honest hadn't his words produced a flicker of comfort somewhere deep inside her? A feeling which was distracting, because comfort had been absent from her life for so long. For months now she'd carried on travelling and working as she'd done all her life while her belly had got bigger and bigger. She'd tried to convince herself that she was a perfect example of an independent woman who could do this on her own. But lately it had felt lonely, and sometimes in the middle of the night it had even felt scary.

At this precise moment she felt tired—and Dante was standing in front of her like a symbol of everything which was strong and vital. But it was *dangerous* to buy into that. Everything that he did came with some sort of clause. He never offered something without demanding a whole lot back in return. She should remember that.

'It seems that you've got your own way as usual,' she said.

Dante gave a bitter laugh as she spoke the sulky little phrase without any apparent sense of irony. Didn't she realise that she was the one person who had *stopped* him getting his own way and thus had marred his personal track record of success? That she was the one and only person who had ever defied him?

'Maybe you should hold on to that thought, Justina,' he said. 'It might save you from useless rebellion in the future.'

CHAPTER SIX

'THIS IS WHERE you live?'

Justina fought against an inescapable feeling of weariness as Dante stood like a dark avenger in the centre of her apartment and bit out his critical question. Despite the undeniable luxury of his private jet she was exhausted after the long flight, and the traffic from the airport to her East London home had been horrendous. And now she was being forced to stomach the sight of Dante dominating her private space, which was making her feel edgier still. She wished he would just go away and leave her alone—and yet she knew him well enough to realise that he wasn't going anywhere.

Because nothing between them had been settled.

No decisions had been made about the baby

during that flight from Singapore. He had settled down to tackle a huge pile of work and largely ignored her. At the time she had been grateful for the respite—relieved not to have to tackle a difficult subject beneath the eyes of the gorgeous stewardesses who worked on his plane. She'd even pulled her notebook from her bag in a retaliatory gesture, but she'd been far too het-up to be able to concentrate on her latest song.

She had tried to buffer herself against the curious volatility of her emotions during that long journey, and yet it had proved almost impossible to remain calm and immune to him. She despaired of the ever-present desire she experienced whenever he was near—as if her body had been hard-wired to make her want him even when she was this pregnant. She didn't know how to make it go away. And now she was beginning to realise that they couldn't keep putting off the inevitable talk about the future.

'Yes, it's where I live,' she said, putting a pile of unopened mail down on the table. 'What's the matter with it?'

Dante glanced around, not bothering to hide his disapproval. It was a vast open-plan apartment which was perfect for a career woman, but not for a baby. There were too many sharp corners, too many glass surfaces—and the furniture was coloured an impractical shade of oatmeal. He'd been to many sophisticated apartments like this but they always left him cold. In Tuscany he had a *palazzo* which was centuries old, and in New York his home was a faded brownstone filled with antiques. He didn't *do* modern—and wasn't that yet another great difference between him and this woman? She had no great love for the past. She'd once told him that was because her own history was so full of gaps—and yet *his* history was what defined him.

Walking over to the window, he stared out at the stately dome of St Paul's Cathedral and the glittering skyscrapers beyond, before turning round to face her.

'This is no place for a baby,' he said.

There had been several times recently when Justina might have been inclined to agree with him, but hearing Dante say it was different from thinking it herself. 'Don't tell me—a baby can't be happy unless it's living in some cute little house with roses growing around the door?' she said sarcastically. 'Or, as in your case, some whacking great *palazzo* nestling in the Tuscan hills?'

'Don't be naïve, Justina. How many other women in this block have babies?'

She frowned. 'What's that got to do with it?'

'So already we're talking social isolation.'

'For a *newborn*?'

'For you, too!' he snapped. 'New mothers need people around them for all kinds of reasons. And what about that tiny elevator?'

'What about it?'

'How the hell are you planning to get a buggy in there?' He looked around again, only this time he appeared to be seeking out something in particular. His dark gaze finally settled on her. 'Where *is* the buggy?'

'Buggy?'

His voice was dangerously quiet, and he appeared to be choosing his words with care. 'Please tell me you've bought our child something in which to transport it. Just like you've bought a cot and clothes and all the other things he or she will require. Do you have all those very necessary things, Justina—and, if so, would you mind telling me where they are?'

Still reeling from that wholly possessive 'our child', which had flowed so fluidly from his lips, she met his eyes, unprepared for the wave of guilt which washed over her. 'No,' she said, and her voice was little more than a whisper. 'I haven't bought a thing. Not yet.'

For a long moment there was silence, before Dante slowly took in her words. 'Not yet' she had said, while looking so ripe with child that he wouldn't have been shocked if she'd suddenly gone into labour right there on the oatmeal sofa. No, that wasn't quite true—he *would* be pretty shocked if that happened.

'Why not?' he demanded. 'What are you waiting for?'

His words were like bullets, and Justina felt as if she'd just removed the vest which might have bounced them back at him. All the fight went out of her—because how could she possibly explain that her life had been non-stop activity for the past thirty-five weeks? That she'd been afraid to turn down any work since she'd first stared aghast at the telltale blue line which had confirmed her pregnancy? That she hadn't wanted people to think she was going to retire or start taking things easy because she still needed to work—baby or no baby? She was going to have to work for all kinds of reasons—the main one being her own sense of crippling insecurity, which always lurked just below the surface of her life.

Hadn't it been easier to cram her life full of jobs? Much easier to have things which kept her busy rather than to have to think about a future she'd never envisaged and which she still couldn't quite imagine. But as she met Dante's gaze she could see that her actions might easily be interpreted as selfishness. And hadn't that always been one of his number one accusations against her? That she was one of a terrible breed of women who refused to put other people first—or rather put their man first?

'I kept putting it off,' she said. 'Maybe it was an extended form of denial that it's actually happening. I've been to all the childbirth classes....' Her voice tailed off as she remembered the ignominy of *that*. Everyone else had been part of a gleeful couple—each man proudly patting his partner's bump at every opportunity and religiously doing all the breathing exercises. One man had even given up soft cheese and alcohol in order to 'share his wife's experience'. Justina had just felt such an *oddity* in their midst. Maybe they'd found it slightly embarrassing that she didn't have a partner—that she'd clammed up whenever they had tried to quiz her about her baby's father. And hadn't she felt so unbelievably *lonely* as she'd tried to stem her envy of their seemingly uncomplicated and ordinary lives?

'It just seemed so unreal,' she continued slowly. 'Like it wasn't really happening to me. As if I'd wake up one morning and find that it had all been a mistake.'

His gaze was still fixed on her and she waited for some control freak tirade to follow because she'd dared to neglect the material requirements of the D'Arezzo heir. But to her surprise there was no outburst. Just that same faintly despairing expression in his dark eyes, which was infinitely worse. She thought that he'd never seemed more distant as he stood there, his powerful body seeming to absorb all the light in her usually airy apartment. But there was something compelling about him which drew the eye so that it became impossible to look anywhere else other than at him.

'What do you do to relax?' he asked suddenly.

The question was so unexpected that she didn't have time to concoct a convincing answer. Instead, she shrugged. 'I'm not very good at relaxing.'

'I can tell. You look worn out,' he said softly. 'So why don't you think about the baby for once—instead of your unquenchable desire to be number one in the music business? Go and take a bath, or something. Isn't that what women usually do to relax?'

'You would know about that better than I do, Dante.' She was about to add that she would have a bath when *she* wanted one—and preferably after he'd gone—but his phone had started ringing and he'd clicked to answer it. And unbelievably, he was holding up a forefinger to silence her while he listened.

She contemplated telling him to go and take his calls somewhere else—but she was damned if she was going to stand there like some sort of simpering secretary, waiting patiently for him to finish his conversation. Instead, she stomped into the bathroom and locked the door behind her, turning the taps full on and recklessly dolloping in far too much lime and mandarin bath foam, before she hit the music button and then lowered herself into the foamy water.

When she'd first moved into this apartment she'd had a sophisticated sound system installed which played music in all the rooms. Usually she pressed the 'shuffle' button, so that she never knew which track was coming next. But today she selected *Metamorphosis*—which had been one of the Lollipops' most successful albums. A success which had come at a cost.

It was the album she'd been writing when her relationship with Dante was breaking up. She hadn't been able to listen to it for years but her reasons for needing to hear it now were important. No, they were vital. She needed to revisit that dark place she'd been in. She needed to remember the heartbreak and the desperation she'd felt as it had all slipped away from her. To remind herself that the occasional twinge of isolation was nothing to the pain she'd suffered in the past.

She lay back in the warm water, the shiny mound of her belly emerging from the white suds as the sound of the music filled the bathroom.

It hurt. It hurt more than she had expected it to. The lyrics of one song in particular felt like having a bucket of salt poured over an open wound, and she flinched as the memories all came flooding back. It was a song which had soared up the charts. Women had bought it in droves. She'd even been approached about having it used in the film score of a romantic comedy, but she had said no—even though her agent had hit the roof when she'd told him. She hadn't been able to bear the thought of having it associated with comedy when it symbolised the bleakest time of her life. In fact, she'd always regretted releasing it as a single. It had been played on the radio so much that for a while she'd stopped listening in order to preserve her sanity.

She'd written it when she'd got back from finding Dante in bed with that blonde, pouring all her feelings out into a song because she hadn't been able to bear the shame of telling anyone else what had happened. She'd entitled the track 'Her' and the words were still unbearably painful to hear.

Does she know the things you said
When you were lying in my bed?
Your words of love became a slur
When you whispered them to her.

Justina wanted to scream. To turn the music off and with it the images it brought back—but she couldn't move. She was marooned in a great tub of bath water, feeling and looking like a beached whale, her usual agility long gone. So she closed her eyes and waited for the track to finish.

The water was almost cold by the time she

carefully got out, hoping that Dante would have taken the hint and gone.

But he hadn't gone. He was still talking on the phone, looking out of the window as he conversed in his native tongue. He must have heard her enter the room—even though she was moving soundlessly on bare feet—for he turned round, his eyes narrowing when he saw her.

Maybe she should have put on some jeans and a sweater, not the full-length silken robe which she'd wrapped tightly over her baby bump. But why *should* she start turning her whole life around to fit in with him? She was dressed for bed and she intended to go to bed—perhaps he might take the hint and leave her to it.

His voice slowed as he watched her push a lock of damp hair back behind her ear, and he said something in Italian before cutting the connection and sliding the phone back into his jacket pocket.

'I thought you'd have gone by now,' she said ungraciously as she slumped down onto the sofa.

'I was listening to the music. Unsurprisingly, the acoustics in your apartment are the best I've ever heard.' His smile was brief, but damning. 'Tell me, do you always listen to your own songs when you're lying in the bath?'

If she said *'never'*, wouldn't that indicate that he could still unsettle her enough to make her behave in an uncharacteristic way? *And she didn't have to justify herself to him.*

'That's none of your business. I can listen to what I like. Frankly, I'm surprised you're still here—not least because that last song must have made you feel intensely uncomfortable. Or maybe not.' Her eyes challenged him with a bravado she was far from feeling. 'Maybe it feeds your massive ego to hear yourself written about in a song.'

'Not that particular song, no,' he reflected. 'It was unforgivable for you to take our private disagreement and throw it into the public arena.'

'Perhaps if you hadn't behaved like a total sleaze then I might have found something good to write about you.'

'"A total sleaze"?'

His eyes narrowed, but she could tell by the way that he was tapping his forefinger against his lips that he was furious.

'Is that what you think I am, Justina?'

He was walking towards her now, with a look on his face which was making her shiver. Actually, it was making her do much more than shiver. It was making the soft, curling excitement at the pit of her belly slowly begin to unfurl. She knew she ought to move, to run away—but her slumped position on the sofa meant that she wasn't able to run anywhere. *And deep down she knew she didn't want to.*

'It doesn't matter what I think you are,' she said.

'No?'

'No. You're nothing to me any more, Dante.'

For a moment their gazes locked, and Justina held her breath as he walked round the back of the sofa to stand behind her, so that she couldn't see him. She could feel a strange kind of tension begin to shimmer in the air around them.

'I think it does matter.' There was a pause as he brushed a fingertip over the back of her neck. 'You don't like me very much, do you?'

She shook her head. 'No.'

'Brutal, but honest,' he mused, his fingertip retracing the path it had just taken, as if he was fascinated by the innocuous column of flesh he found there.

She tried to fight against the sudden whisper of pleasure that touch had given her. 'What are you doing?'

He began to massage her shoulders, briefly expelling a breath as he felt her soft flesh beneath his fingers again. 'I'm trying to make you relax, but it isn't easy because you are very tense, *tesoro*,' he observed softly. 'Very, very tense.'

Justina swallowed. She ought to assert herself. She ought to tell him to stop. But how could she bear to do that when it felt this good? His fingers were kneading at the tightness in her shoulders and she could feel the tight knots dissolving as if by magic. His thumbs began to circle rhythmically at the base of her neck and it was impossible not to just go with it. She told herself that the caress of his fingers on her skin was dangerous. She knew that. But it had been so long since she had been touched. Not since that night back in Norfolk, when their baby had been conceived.

She closed her eyes. 'Dante—'

'Shh.' His fingers continued with their steady movement. 'Don't talk.'

'You shouldn't be doing that.'

'All I'm doing is making you relax.'

But that wasn't all he was doing. He must know that. Because the tension which had melted away had now been replaced by a very different kind. She could feel it building in the air around them—like the heavy electricity you got before a violent thunderstorm. She could feel the melting ache of heat between her thighs and the insistent tingling of her breasts as she yearned for him to touch them. And wasn't it appalling that the woman who was due to give birth in a few short weeks should be feeling this rising tide of need?

So stop him!

Her throat felt dry, her mouth so parched that she could barely get the words out. 'I don't think—'

'Good. Don't think. Just feel.'

And—oh, God—it was all too easy to do that. Sinfully easy. His hands were working deeper into the flesh around her shoulders and he had drifted two thumbs down over her ribcage. Her heart was fluttering wildly in response. Surely she was mistaken but had he…had he just brushed his hands over her breasts? Yes. There it was again. Definitely. The whisper of his fingertips was butterfly-light but achingly accurate.

'Dante—'

'For once in your life, will you just shut up?' he questioned, splaying his hand over one peaking nipple and letting his thumb circle over the tight bud.

She began to squirm with excitement. She couldn't help it. She wanted to call his name out loud. She wanted him to walk round to the front of the sofa, to pull her into his arms and start kissing her and make love to her properly. But he wasn't doing that. He was… He was…

She gasped as he leaned over her, so that his lips were on the top of her head. She could hear the heavy sound of his own breathing and it was echoing the sound of her own. She could smell the sandalwood scent of his aftershave and feel the warmth of his flesh as he touched her. His hand had skated down over the swollen mound of her belly and he was pushing aside the folds of her silken robe. She could feel her thighs parting—as if she was a puppet and someone was pulling her strings. Well, *he* was. That was exactly what he was doing. He was skating little circles over the cool skin of her inner thighs until she was gasping helplessly with pleasure. And then his finger flicked over her moist and eager flesh until it alighted on the tight little nub and she opened her thighs wider. She gave another gasp as he began to make that achingly familiar movement, her hunger briefly tempered by the fear that he might stop.

But he didn't stop. He carried on with what he was doing. Stroking his finger against her aroused flesh until she was past caring about anything—victim to her own urgent needs as she called out his name like a betrayal.

It happened in a rush. One minute she was climbing towards the blissful summit, still shadowed by the fear that the peak might elude her, or that it might not happen at all. But Dante always delivered. Every time. Only never like this. Never quite like this. She found herself making little cries that sounded like pleas as she spasmed helplessly around his finger.

Time shifted and slowed as she drifted back down from a dazed state of bliss, unsure what to do next even if her weighted limbs had been capable of any kind of movement. All she knew was that he was tugging her robe back into place before dropping a light kiss on top of her head almost as an afterthought.

He walked around the sofa and stood facing her with an expression on his face which she couldn't fathom, even if she'd had the energy to try. She could feel the colour still flooding her cheeks, and the intense dryness in her mouth which made the thought of speaking seem like a chore. Her head felt as heavy as lead but she forced herself to keep her chin lifted, because she wasn't going to cower away and pretend that nothing had happened.

'What...what did you do that for?'

He gave a short laugh. 'You're now going to

tell me you loathed every minute of it, I suppose?'

She wished that the telltale heat in her cheeks would magically disappear. 'That's…' And why was her voice sounding so infuriatingly *husky*? 'That's not the point.'

'I thought it was exactly the point.' He shrugged his shoulders in a particularly Italian way and his lips curved into a smile of undeniable satisfaction. 'You were uptight, so I started to massage your shoulders. And then you seemed a little…*turned on*…so I did exactly what you wanted me to do.'

For a moment she looked at him in disbelief, but the unrepentant expression on his face was nearly as damning as his words. 'You hateful… *bastard*!'

'Guilty as charged.' His eyes narrowed. 'But while you might hate me, Justina, I hope you won't be hypocritical enough to deny that you still want me. You made that pretty clear.'

Just as he wanted her. Her face was flushed and belligerent and she was glaring at him, and he was tempted—oh, how he was tempted. Would it be the end of the world if he joined her on that great big sofa and started to kiss her? He could feel the throb of desire at his groin and imagined the sweetness of her fingers stroking him there. Imagined her guiding him into her sticky warmth. He found himself wondering what position he would have to take to make it more comfortable for her, because he had never made love to a pregnant woman before.

He shifted his weight as desire fought a fierce battle with reason. She was *pregnant*, he reminded himself, and she was pregnant with *his child*. Maybe he shouldn't have touched her like that—but hadn't the restless wriggle of her curiously sensual body made it impossible to do otherwise?

Averting his gaze from the anger which was still sparking from her eyes, he glanced at his watch. 'And, much as I hate to miss out on today's dose of character assassination, I really must go. My plane will have been refuelled and I'm flying back to the States.'

Justina hugged the lapels of her robe closer. 'That's the best bit of news I've had all day.'

'I'm sure it is. But don't worry, because I'll be back in time for the birth.'

'You don't have to.'

'Oh, but I do. You may not need me, Justina— but my baby does.' He pulled a business card from his wallet and put it down on the table next to her handbag. 'You'll find all my details there, including my private number.'

'Gosh, I *am* privileged. Or maybe not. How many women are in possession of one of these, I wonder?'

'You'll also find the number of my assistant, who has been instructed to help you,' he continued smoothly, as if her interruption had been nothing but a minor irritation. 'Anything you want, you ring Tiffany—she's very efficient. If you can't face furnishing the nursery yourself—as seems to be the case—then she can do it all from New York.'

Justina's post-orgasmic lethargy was replaced by a growing feeling of rage. Tiffany? Who the hell was Tiffany? He wanted his *assistant* to go out and buy stuff for *her* baby, did he? While managing to make *her* sound useless and helpless in the process?

With an effort she stopped slumping against the cushions and sat up to glare at him. 'And what else does *Tiffany* do?' she questioned. 'Is it part of her job description to provide extras for the boss?'

'I try never to mix business with pleasure,' he answered coolly. 'And you really shouldn't be getting yourself worked up like that. You've already had enough excitement for one afternoon, so why don't you go and get some rest?'

'Oh, just go,' she said, shutting her eyes to block out the sight of his undeniably gorgeous face. She kept them closed until she'd heard the front door click behind him, and when she opened them again he was gone.

She sighed. If only it was as easy to get rid of the memory of what she'd just let him do to her.

CHAPTER SEVEN

'DANTE WANTS TO KNOW whether you've received the brochure, Miss Perry?'

Justina's fingers tightened around the telephone receiver as she listened to the transatlantic accent of Tiffany Jones and wondered why the hell she hadn't just let this call go through to her answering service. She was feeling lumpy and lethargic enough without having to endure yet another of these polite and all-too-frequent queries which had been coming from Dante's personal assistant in his New York office.

But it would be demeaning to give in to what she really wanted to say, which was: *Are you sleeping with the father of my baby?* Surely a situation like this demanded that she act with an unflappability equal to that of the cool-sounding Tiffany.

'Yes, thank you. I've received it,' said Justina, recalling the ritzy attachment which had pinged through on to her computer last week, offering a cornucopia of luxurious items for the more privileged baby.

'And did you like it?' Tiffany's voice was eager. 'Would you like us to go ahead and order the crib for you—and the stroller?'

Us? *Us?* Justina's hand wrapped itself around the receiver as if it was Dante's neck she was squeezing. Resisting the urge to tell the woman that in England they were called a cot and a buggy, she walked into the smaller of her two bedrooms to see one of each standing there, all new and shiny-bright. The primrose-yellow walls of the nursery been adorned with a giant jungle scene, and a mobile of tigers and lions swirled down from the ceiling, adding to the storybook feel of the room. A smile of satisfaction curved her lips. From all the fuss that Tiffany had been making from New York you'd have thought that decorating and furnishing a nursery was right up there with brain surgery.

'Can you please tell Dante that none of that will be necessary?' she said crisply.

'I can tell him,' said Tiffany doubtfully. 'But

I think he'd prefer to speak to you himself, Miss Perry.'

Well, why didn't he pick up the phone himself, instead of asking his wretched assistant to make the call? 'I'm afraid that I don't really have the time—'

'Justina?'

Dante's velvet-edged drawl came on to the line and Justina could have screamed. Why weren't any of them listening to what she was saying?

'What do you want?' she questioned ungraciously.

'I want to know how you're feeling today.'

'Honestly? I'm tired, and I'm feeling like a whale, and I'm fed up with these regular interrogations of yours—'

'And have you given any more thought to my question?' he interrupted smoothly.

'I've given it a good deal of thought and my feelings haven't changed.' She sucked in a deep and determined breath. 'I don't want anyone there with me at the birth—especially you. It isn't mandatory to have a birthing partner, you know.'

She could hear what sounded like Dante tapping his finger against the phone. 'I know it isn't

mandatory,' he said. 'But it's certainly prefer-
able. You can't do it all on your own, Justina.'

'On the contrary, I can—and what's more, I
intend to.' She paused for a moment as her abdomen tensed with a sharp and disturbing kind of
twinge. 'I don't need anyone while I go through
what is a perfectly natural procedure. And it
isn't as if we're in some kind of *relationship*,
is it?' Her mind took her back to the last time
she'd seen him, when a seemingly innocent massage of her shoulders had turned into a sensual
act which still made her cheeks burn with embarrassment whenever she thought about it. No
wonder he thought she was some kind of puppet when she'd behaved like that. *So show him
you're not some kind of puppet.* 'I'm an independent woman, Dante. Just in case you'd forgotten.'

'How could I possibly forget,' he questioned
acidly, 'when you never fail to remind me?'

'Then why don't you try listening to me for
a change instead of forcing your will on me? I
could—' But the rest of the sentence froze in her
throat as an iron-hot band of pain clamped itself
around her belly.

'Justina? Are you still there?'

The intensity of the pain was so unexpected
and so powerful that she clapped her hand over

the phone so that he wouldn't be able to hear her panting her way through it. It wasn't until it had passed that she spoke again, in a voice which was unnaturally bright. 'Sorry about that—I thought I heard someone at the door.'

She could hear the frown in his voice. 'Are you okay?'

'I'm *fine*.'

'When you did you last see the doctor?'

'When I was supposed to see him—last week. I have all my appointments written down neatly in my diary and I have been following them to the letter. Now, will you stop fussing?' she said. 'I'm perfectly capable of having a baby without having you checking up on me every five minutes like some kind of demented midwife. And I really have to go—I'm in the middle of writing a song and I must get the words down before they go out of my head. Don't worry, Dante. I'll let you know the minute something happens.'

She cut him off without another word and walked over to the window, trying to shake off her strange feeling of restlessness and the power he always had to unsettle her. She didn't need to feel any more unsettled than she currently did and it couldn't be good for her *or* the baby. She felt as if the air was pressing down on her, and the rain which had been falling for seven days straight showed no sign of stopping. She'd been stuck inside all day, and yet the last thing she wanted was to go outside and brave the elements.

She should watch a film—or read that book she'd bought, which everyone was raving on about—the one whose hero seemed to have modelled himself on the Marquis de Sade. She knew that relaxation was vital during these late stages of her pregnancy, but her strong work ethic meant that she always felt guilty if she did nothing.

She flicked through the TV channels and found a woman yelling at a weaselly man who really needed to do something about his skin. The woman's inarticulate insults were at first amusing—and then a touch disturbing. Because Justina realised that what motivated them was frustration that the man wouldn't do what the woman wanted him to do—which was to love her.

I'm never going to be that woman, Justina vowed fiercely as another sharp band of pain tightened across her abdomen. *I'm never going to have hopeless expectations of a man who can never meet them, because that's a sure-fire rec-*

ipe for unhappiness. Much better to be independent and free of emotional pain.

But then another very physical pain caught her by surprise. It was so strong that she had to stand perfectly still and cling to the back of the sofa. It wasn't until they started coming regularly that she realised she was in labour.

She tried to stay calm and remember what to do. *Stay at home for as long as possible. Time the contractions and call the hospital.* Another wave clamped like a burning iron around her middle, and she was gasping a little as she picked up the phone and spoke to a midwife.

'Come in now,' said the midwife. 'Have you got someone with you?'

'I'm on my way,' said Justina, neatly avoiding the question.

But they asked her again when she'd been checked in to the birthing suite as she lay on the bed, having her blood pressure monitored.

'Is the father on his way, Miss Perry?'

'No.' Justina shook her head. 'He's in New York.'

'Does he know that you're in labour?'

She thought about Dante seeing her like this. She thought about how nothing but a capricious fate had brought them together. Hadn't she told him that she was independent and that she didn't actually *need* him? Well, that hadn't just been bluster—she'd *meant* it.

She shook her head. 'No, he doesn't know.'

'Someone here could easily—'

'I don't want him here,' declared Justina.

Did she imagine the look of disapproval which passed between the midwife and her student? But then another pain came, and it was so powerful that it obliterated everything, and she stopped wondering if she was being judged for her morals or her cold-heartedness.

Time slowed and she felt disorientated— only the relentless contractions brought reality into sharp and clear focus. Hours passed by in a blur of pain as Justina tried to remember all the things she'd learned at her antenatal classes and put them into practice. She paced the floor. She crouched down on her hands and knees as sweat poured from her brow. She tried not to gasp, but not gasping became impossible when the midwife examined her and announced that she'd gone into 'second stage'.

'I don't care what stage I'm in! I just want this bloody baby out!' shouted Justina recklessly.

She heard the sound of some commotion at the door, where the student midwife stood talking to someone. She heard an unmistakable Italian accent speaking low words edged with fierce intent.

'Just ask her. Please.'

The student came over to the bed, her cheeks looking flushed. 'There's a man outside who says he's the father of your baby and he wants to come in. He says his name is Dante D'Arezzo and please could I ask you.'

In a brief respite between contractions it occurred to Justina that this was possibly the first time in Dante's life that he'd had to ask for anything without being guaranteed the desired response. But her reasons for wanting to exclude him seemed *petty* in the light of what was happening. Justina looked towards the door and there he stood—six feet plus of dark and brooding determination. And *strength*, she realized as she registered the tension in his powerful shoulders. Couldn't she use a little of that strength right now?

'Let him in,' she croaked, and he must have heard her because in an instant he was at her bedside, his expression impenetrable as he looked down at her. But the words of recrimination she'd expected were absent as he brushed aside a lock of matted hair with a hand which was remarkably gentle.

'I'm here now,' he said simply.

'Is that supposed to make me feel better?'

'I'm rather hoping it might.'

For some reason his words made her feel bad. 'Dante, I didn't want to—'

'Shh. I doesn't matter. I'm here,' he repeated. 'And that's all that matters.'

She swallowed. 'It...*hurts.*'

'Then hold on to me. Go on, hold on—as tight as you like. Hurt *me* instead, if it makes you feel better.'

She told herself that it was stupid to want to cling to him. To hold him so tightly so that he would never let her go. But all her inhibitions seemed to be melting away as the demands of her body took over and she clutched him like a drowning woman snatching at a floating branch.

'I'm hot,' she added.

'Then lose the gown.' The corners of his lips curved. 'It's not the best thing I've ever seen you in.'

She almost smiled back as he helped her tug the sweat-soaked hospital issue garment from her body and the coolness of the air washed over her naked skin. But then came another of those contractions, and when she had breath enough to speak she shuddered out the fear which was threatening to overwhelm her.

'I'm so scared that something's going to go wrong.'

His black gaze caught hold of her and enveloped her. He lifted up the hand which wasn't digging into his and briefly touched it to his lips. 'The chances of that happening are infinitesimally small. You're in the best possible hands. You know that, Jus. You've told me often enough. How did you put it? A perfectly natural procedure that women have been going through since the beginning of time.'

Had she really said that? Had she really sounded so stupidly confident when now she felt as nervous as a child on the first day of school?

Her fingernails dug even farther into his hand. *'I want to push!'*

Dante flicked a glance at the midwife, who nodded. 'Then push, *tesoro,*' he urged softly. 'Go ahead and push all you like.'

'Arrgh!'

Her anguished cry made him feel helpless— Dante felt more powerless than he'd ever felt in his life. Frustration washed over him as he watched her writhe, but he did what little he

could to help her. He smoothed away her hair
when she thrashed her head wildly against the
pillow, and dabbed cool water at her temples
which briefly made her moan with gratitude.
But only briefly.

All too soon the tension in the room increased,
along with the rising sound of her cries. Dante
watched as the movements of the midwives became brisker, though one of them paused long
enough to raise her head and ask, 'Do you want
to come and see your baby being born, Signor
D'Arezzo?'

Dante met Justina's eyes and wordlessly she
nodded. For one minute he thought she might be
about to make some smart comment, and perhaps if she hadn't been in the middle of giving
birth she might have done, but she closed her
eyes again and screwed up her face with a fierce
concentration.

And then it all became very urgent. The air
pulsed with taut words and fractured cries as
Justina gave an almighty push. His breath caught
in his throat as he saw a dark slick of hair appear, followed by the seemingly impossible appearance of a bruised and bloodied baby as she
pushed again. And his heart clenched as the in-

fant opened its mouth and howled and somebody said, "It's a boy!"

They put the slippery infant into the cradle of his hands as they cut the cord, and Dante's throat was so tight he could barely breathe. His baby. His son. So tiny and so helpless. He could feel the tears pricking at his eyes as the midwife took the baby from him. She cleaned him, before placing him onto Justina's breast, where he began to suckle, his eyes fixed on his mother's as if they'd known each other for a very long time. Silently, Dante watched as Justina touched a finger to the newborn's smooth cheek and gave a secretive kind of smile.

And in that moment he had never wanted her quite so much.

CHAPTER EIGHT

JUSTINA WATCHED AS Dante's fingers moved with remarkable dexterity over the tiny baby, his dark head bent as he focussed intently on the task at hand. He was so *careful*, she thought, as if Nico was made of porcelain rather than of flesh and blood. But every so often the intense concentration on his features would soften a little, and he would smile and murmur something in Italian. With an unwanted rush of emotion she acknowledged how tender he could be—and how gentle—and something dangerously close to nostalgia flickered over her.

Forcing her thoughts away from the wistful and back to the purely practical, she looked at the ebony gleam of Dante's head. 'I never thought I'd see you change a nappy,' she observed.

Dante gave Nico a final kiss on his little belly, before raising his head to look at Justina, who sat with an expression of serene interest on her face as she watched him. It was hard to get his head around the fact that she'd given birth less than a month ago, for although she was definitely curvier than she'd used to be she was still as slim as a reed. She looked more casual than he'd ever seen her, with her hair caught into a single plait which fell over one shoulder and a face completely free of make-up. Yet he didn't think he'd ever seen a woman looking as delectable as she did right now. Her skin was soft and clear and her eyes were bright. He found himself wondering whether this was another of wily Mother Nature's safety mechanisms—that a man should feel such overwhelming lust towards the woman who had just borne his child.

'Changing a nappy isn't difficult,' he said as he lifted the drowsy Nico from the changing mat and placed him carefully in his cot.

'Obviously not,' answered Justina, wishing that he'd stop being quite so...*reasonable*. Because this was Dante, she reminded herself. Powerful Dante, who didn't say or do anything without an ulterior motive. She raised her eyebrows in ironic query. 'But I thought that a macho man like you...'

Her words tailed off and he gave a wry smile. 'You make me sound like someone who bares his chest and wears a medallion. There's nothing in the rule book to say that the most masculine of men can't be hands-on with his own baby.' He gave a shrug. 'Although obviously things were very different in my father's day. I'm sure he never changed a nappy in his life.'

Justina started to fold one of Nico's tiny vests as Dante's words forced her to confront something which up until now they'd managed to avoid. 'You haven't really mentioned how your family have reacted to the news. I assume you've told them?'

'Of course. I rang them the night he was born.' She saw his ebony eyes soften with memory. 'My mother is over the moon. This is her first grandchild and she's eager to meet him. All my family are.'

Justina nodded. Of course they were—and she knew they had every right to be. Just as she knew that she couldn't keep putting off the inevitable meeting. She felt as if she'd been living in a bubble since Nico's birth—a feeling which had only been strengthened by Dante's unexpected help with the baby. Had he been worried that she'd be unable to cope or that she'd sink into a mire of postnatal depression? Was that why he'd seamlessly relocated from New York and booked in at the nearby Vinoly Hotel, so that it was easy for him to drop by and visit his son?

She had returned home from the hospital to a delivery of the most beautiful flowers. Gardenias and roses and stephanotis and lily of the valley had been massed into a bouquet so enormous that she'd hardly been able to get it through the front door. The fragrance had been intoxicating, and the brief accompanying note of thanks had made her want to cry. But crying was the last thing she could afford to do. The last thing she ever did. Crying made you weak, and never had she needed her strength as much as she needed it right now.

She remembered turning on Dante as if he'd sent her an explosive device, aware of the sudden tremble of her fingers as they had brushed against the white petals. 'Why did you send me flowers?'

'Isn't it normal for the father to send flowers to the new mother?'

Justina had shaken her head. Of course it was *normal*. But *they* weren't normal, were they?

None of this was. A baby had been born to two people who were no longer together. Who didn't even like each other. *And Dante was not a man she could trust.* She should remember that above all else. He might be ladling on sweet words and consideration, but he would be doing it for a reason. And it seemed that one of those reasons had now arrived.

She drew in a deep breath as met his eyes. 'Your mean your mother wants to come and visit?'

He shook his head. 'My mother hates to travel. I was thinking that you and I might take Nico to Tuscany instead. I think it's time he was introduced to his Italian roots.'

She wanted to protest that at four weeks old Nico would barely be conscious of which cot he was in, let alone which country. But Justina knew Dante well enough to realise that her words would fall on deaf ears. He had always been passionate about his homeland, and no amount of reason was ever going to alter that. In fact she was surprised that he had waited this long to bring it up. *That's why he has been so unusually reasonable,* she told herself. The flowers and the nappy-changing and the insistence that she relax in the bath while he looked after

Nico—they had all been velvet-coated weapons in his battle to get what he wanted.

But despite the sensation of being manipulated Justina had no intention of refusing his request, no matter how difficult she might find it to return to his family home. Because Nico *needed* family—and her own was never even going to make it past the starting line.

'Do they still hate me?' she questioned, in a voice which didn't actually sound like her voice.

'I think that's an unnecessarily emotive way of putting it, Justina.'

'I thought one of your complaints about me was that I wasn't emotional enough?' That was the main accusation he'd used to hurl at her, usually just before one of her tours, so that they'd always seemed to part with some sort of atmosphere simmering between them. 'I remember you telling me that no woman with a heart could leave her man while she went away on tour.'

Dante met the amber glitter of her eyes. It was true he'd found it unbelievable that she could bear to be away from him for any length of time. He'd thought that her career would pale in comparison to being with the man she professed to love. But apparently not. She had refused to temper her ambition and he had grown impatient with her frequent absences. In the end those absences had chipped away at their relationship, so that many of their snatched reunions had been spent getting to know one another again. Sometimes it had felt as if they were going backwards instead of forward. When it had finally come, his furious ultimatum had seemed inevitable.

'My family didn't hate you,' he said slowly.

There was a pause. 'They didn't make me feel very welcome when I met them.' She could hear that whisper of insecurity in her voice again.

'I think they tried their best.' He reached down into the cot and stroked Nico's head. 'But my mother is an old-fashioned woman who didn't approve of your choice of career—or all the things which came with it.'

'Like mother, like son!' observed Justina wryly, though she recognised that it hadn't just been his mother who had been opposed to her. Dante's brother Luigi had also disapproved—and all the male D'Arezzo cousins had clearly felt the same.

Her mind went back to the welcome party which had been thrown during her first and only visit to the D'Arezzo estate. If only Dante's sister hadn't insisted on playing the Lollipops' latest DVD! Justina remembered the entire family sitting and watching in horror as she'd cavorted across the screen wearing a tiny tutu and a minuscule vest-top. After that they'd treated her as if she was some kind of stripper instead of a legitimate songwriter and performer.

'They didn't think I was the right person for you,' she added. 'I was unsuitable. And of course being English didn't add to my general allure.'

'All Italian mothers want their sons to marry an Italian girl,' he said with a shrug.

'As opposed to an illegitimate nobody whose mother has a track record for breaking up other people's marriages?'

'I think she wondered how our relationship was going to work when you were travelling the world.' There was a pause as his black eyes glittered a question. 'And you must admit that she had a point.'

Justina glanced down at where Nico lay sleeping and tried to imagine Dante ever being this tiny or this helpless. Unsurprisingly, she failed. 'So how did your mother react when you told her who the mother of your baby was?'

Dante hesitated as he considered how best to convey his mother's words. He had expected anger. Rage. A tirade against the Englishwoman who had made those brazen promotional films and flaunted her half-naked body to the world at large. He had thought there would be a dramatic outburst about a woman like *her* returning to the scene and ensnaring her powerful son by becoming pregnant.

But he hadn't bargained for the softening effects of age, nor the primitive desire to see their powerful family line continued. His mother had been widowed for a long time and Dante was her eldest son. It was right that his offspring should be the firstborn, she'd said. The thought of a whole new generation of the D'Arezzo family was enough to sweeten the pill of the mother's identity—and the fact that he wasn't married to her.

'But you will have to marry her, of course, Dante. If this baby is a D'Arezzo, then he must be legitimised.'

Dante remembered his mother's immediate assumption. The way she had smiled the smile of a woman who knew that a hundred candidates would have married her son in an instant. But Dante knew it wasn't as easy as that. Not with Justina. Most women *would* fall over backwards to become a D'Arezzo bride—but not this woman who took such pride in her independence. Who would see no point in marrying for the sake of a baby—especially when their relationship had failed last time around. Yet despite all this, one irrefutable fact remained—*his own fierce familial pride would not countenance his son being illegitimate*.

'Dante?'

He looked up. 'What?'

'I asked how your mother reacted when you told her she was going to be a grandparent.'

'In the same way that any grandparent would react, I guess. With joy and with excitement. I expect your mother was exactly the same?'

Justina twisted the end of her plait with restless fingers. 'You *are* joking?' she said. 'She thinks she's way too young for that particular role.'

'That figures,' he said. But despite her flippant comment, Dante glimpsed the hurt which had briefly clouded Justina's eyes and felt a surge of anger on her behalf. Couldn't her mother have behaved *normally* for once? Couldn't she just have cooed a little and been there for her daughter? 'Did she send anything for Nico?'

Justina laughed. 'A silver napkin ring which he'll probably never use.'

'You know, we'll need to get him a passport as

soon as possible,' Dante said suddenly. 'If we're taking him to Tuscany.'

Justina realised that they'd slipped seamlessly from talking about a hypothetical trip to Tuscany to acquiring a passport for the journey—and wasn't that Dante all over? He would always try stealth before he tried coercion but the end result was always the same: he got exactly what he wanted.

Their journey plans were set in motion and Justina went shopping for new clothes, since none of her own seemed right. She wanted to wear something normal and flattering after months of being swaddled in loose clothes, but it was more than that. The last time she'd seen Signora D'Arezzo had been at the height of her fame, when she had very definitely been dressed like a pop star. She'd been into glitter and pizazz and making a statement—but nearly six years down the line her tastes had changed. She still bought trendy, but these days she gravitated towards the less garish.

She loaded up her shopping basket with silk and cashmere and splashed out on some new underwear, telling herself that she was only buying it because her shape had changed. But she felt a flare of colour in her cheeks as her fingers drifted over a lacy thong and she imagined Dante removing it.

Loaded down with baby equipment, they travelled to a private airfield north of London, where the D'Arezzo jet was ready and waiting. They left England on a drizzly day and touched down in Tuscany, where only a few faint clouds floated in an azure sky, and Justina tried to remember the last time she'd had anything approaching a holiday.

At Pisa airport they were whisked straight through the various border controls with the kind of adulation which Justina hadn't witnessed since she'd been on the road with the Lollipops. But then, Dante was on his own territory here, she reminded herself. People knew him. They revered and respected him. The D'Arezzo family had lived in the region for centuries, and his aristocratic air had never been more evident than when people stopped to compliment him on the baby.

Yet she felt wistful as she watched him carry Nico through, while officials beamed and touched the baby's raven curls. And she noticed the sideways looks which greeted her as she followed in his footsteps—the glances at the fingers of her left hand, noticeably bare of a wedding ring or any kind of show of commitment from Dante D'Arezzo.

Perhaps they think I'm the nanny, thought Justina as they walked out to a waiting car. She touched the heavy silk of the jacket she was wearing over black skinny jeans as if to remind herself of who she really was. This was a jacket she'd paid for herself—not gone crawling to a man for an allowance to finance it. She was self-supporting and she should be proud of that.

'You okay?' questioned Dante, looking up from where he'd just finished buckling Nico into a baby car-seat.

'I'm fine,' she said, trying to ignore the butterfly nerves which were building in her stomach.

'You look amazing,' he said softly as the car pulled away.

His statement caught her by surprise and Justina glanced up, slightly appalled to hear herself trotting out that most predictable of responses. 'Do I?'

'You certainly do. Nobody would ever guess you'd had a baby so recently.'

'Until they see the baby, of course,' she said pleasantly, trying to ignore the instinctive sizzle of her skin. She told herself that he was good at making a woman feel as if she was the centre of the universe—heaven only knew he'd had enough practice at it. *He's a player,* she reminded herself, *and all players do that. He went to bed with someone barely a week after your engagement had broken down. That is not the behaviour of a man who professed to love you and only you.*

She thought about all the things which remained unsaid between them. That strange *intimacy* which they'd shared during the birth, when Dante had been there for her in a way she'd never imagined he could. He'd been strong and protective and gentle, and in those highly emotional moments she'd felt close to him again. She had thought she wouldn't want him there, but now she didn't like to imagine what it might have been like if he hadn't been.

But there were other things which also remained unsaid—things she wasn't proud of. Neither of them had mentioned that erotic encounter on the sofa, after which he had just walked out of the door as if nothing very remarkable had happened. And he hadn't made any move on her since, had he? Even now that her body had pinged back into shape and she'd begun to forge her own routine around Nico, Dante still hadn't looked at her with anything approaching desire.

She kept telling herself that having no physical intimacy made sense on every level. It was too easy to build dreams when a man was making love to you... But that didn't stop her wanting him or being so *aware* of him. As if her body had been programmed to react with excitement whenever he was close.

Turning her head, she stared out the window as the car drove past high green mountains and tried to concentrate on the beauty of the Tuscan countryside. All she had to do was be a good mother to her baby—that was the most important thing.

Before long, the motorway gave way to more rural roads, and although it had been over five years since she'd last been here Justina was surprised by how familiar it all seemed. The D'Arezzo home wasn't immediately visible from the road—mainly because the gardens and estate had been planted so that it would blend into the land around it. A long drive led up to the house and behind it soared more green hills, studded with ancient olive trees and a variety of fruit orchards, and lower down were the prize-winning D'Arezzo vines themselves.

The *palazzo* grew closer, with its dark golden walls and its shuttered windows. Justina stared up at its clock tower and all the different wings which had been added over the years and couldn't fail to be impressed—just as she'd been the first time she'd set eyes on it. Here lay centuries of stability and continuity and a definite place in the local community. It was something she'd never had herself, and a lump rose in her throat as she realised that this was not just Dante's heritage but Nico's, too. That his blood made him part of this place and she had no right to deny him that heritage.

The big car came to a halt in the courtyard, and she was surprised to see Dante's mother waiting for them. In the past, the housekeeper had greeted them, and the meeting with Beatrix D'Arezzo had been postponed until the formal pre-dinner drinks.

Justina watched as Dante carried Nico towards his mother and hung back a little as she saw Beatrix lean eagerly towards the baby. Saw her touch his cheek with wondering fingers before exclaiming, *'Caspita, e uguale a suo padre!'*

Justina smiled as Beatrix came forward to greet her. Her crash course in Italian years earlier might have only left her with a rudimentary grasp of the language, but she understood the gist of *that*. Baby Nico *was* certainly the image of his father!

'Justina!' said Signora D'Arezzo with a smile. 'Welcome back. And congratulations on the birth of such a beautiful little boy.'

The words sounded genuine and Justina nodded, acutely aware that Dante was watching her.

'*Mille grazie,* Signora D'Arezzo,' she answered, and then she smiled back. 'He's gorgeous, isn't he?'

'Gorgeous, indeed, and the image of his father at the same age!' said Beatrix indulgently. 'But you look tired, Justina. Travelling is always tiring—especially for such a new mother. Would you like to see your rooms, so that you can all settle in?'

Justina gave a grateful smile. 'That sounds perfect. Thank you.'

'Dante?' Signora D'Arezzo turned to her son and said something in Italian before turning back to Justina. 'We haven't had a baby here for a long time, but we will do our best to make you feel at home.'

It was Beatrix's *kindness* which was affecting her more than anything, Justina realised as she nodded her thanks. Or maybe it was more complex than that—because Signora D'Arezzo was exhibiting a *motherliness* towards her which she wasn't used to. *Her* mother had never been big on hugging—unless it involved a man with a big wallet. She'd treated her daughter more like an adornment than a real person—and hadn't that been one of the things which had made Justina determined to be as hands-on as possible with her own son, determined that he should feel her love from the start?

She followed Dante as he carried the baby through the winding corridors of the ancient villa before stopping before an enormous set of wooden doors. Inside, the main room was tall and arched, lined with ancient books on one wall and with a huge fireplace big enough to roast a hog in. Windows on three sides overlooked the undulating Tuscan landscape, and Justina gave a sigh of pleasure.

'Like it?' asked Dante.

'Who could fail to like it?' She looked at the paintings and the dark furniture, the silken rugs on the cool floor. 'It's the kind of place people dream of visiting.'

He pointed to an open door through which she could see an antique cot on which sat a battered-looking teddy bear.

'Nico's going to go in there. Obviously.' He smiled. 'Would you like to see where we'll be sleeping?'

At first Justina pretended she had misheard him. But her heart started to race as he pushed open an adjoining door, where a large room was dominated by one enormous bed.

'We're sharing a room?' She gave a light laugh. 'Are you serious?'

'Totally serious.' The shrug of his shoulders was unapologetic. 'My mother is making an effort to be modern, and she has put us in together because she thinks we're a couple now.'

'And you haven't bothered to enlighten her that we're not?'

'I haven't told her that we find ourselves here as a result of a one-night stand, if that's what you mean.'

His assessment was brutal—was that deliberate?—and it *hurt*. 'How ironic that when we *were* here as a couple we were at opposite ends of the house,' she observed, swallowing down the sudden lump in her throat. 'Meaning that you had to come creeping into my room at the dead of night.'

'I don't remember you objecting too much at the time, *tesoro*. As I recall, the subterfuge rather turned you on.'

Justina bit back the objection which had sprung to her lips, because it hadn't been the subterfuge which had turned her on—it had been *him*. Dante had only used to look at her and she would be melting with desire. She met the mockery in his eyes and the sudden flip in her stomach made her realise that nothing very much had changed. He could still turn her on with just a look—and wasn't that *dangerous*, given this new proximity? On one level she was honest enough to admit to herself that she was desperate to have sex with him again, but on another she knew that it would be complete madness.

Nico stirred and she held out her arms for him, relieved to be able to press her burning cheek onto his downy little head. 'I'd better feed him,' she said.

Dante nodded. He had seen the look of confusion which had clouded her amber eyes and he wondered how hard she was going to fight him. And fight herself. 'Why not go over there?' he said, indicating an old rocking chair which sat in front of one of the windows. 'While I unpack.'

Justina carried Nico over to the window, crooning a little as she did so, before unbuttoning her silk shirt and latching him on to her breast. She'd never sat in a rocking chair before, and the creaking rhythm was oddly soothing. It made her feel timeless—and safe. Dreamily, she stroked the baby's head as he fed, and in the background she could hear the sounds of Dante pulling open drawers and shutting wardrobes.

By the time she was finishing he had returned and was standing watching her. His eyes were as soft and dark as molten jet and suddenly she felt almost shy. But how could she possibly feel *shy* in view of everything that had happened between them?

She tried for flippant instead. 'What do you think you're looking at?'

'At you. You look unbelievable. Like a Madonna. A Madonna in skinny jeans.'

'Will you stop it?' She could feel her cheeks getting hotter by the second. 'I'm busy feeding your son.'

'And you do it so well.'

'It's a biological function, Dante,' she said drily. 'Every woman does it.'

But every woman did *not* do it. Dante knew that. And once again Justina had surprised him. Hadn't he thought that she would be itching to wean Nico and leave him in the care of a nanny, so that she could concentrate on her songwriting? But she hadn't. She had embraced motherhood with an enthusiasm he could never have envisaged. And wasn't that what made this whole scenario seem almost *miraculous*? Justina sitting in a rocking chair at the D'Arezzo *palazzo*, feeding their baby. She looked light years away from the black-eyed temptress who had once strutted the stage to the appreciative roars of thousands of fans.

He continued to watch as she settled Nico down, but he sensed a certain restraint about her as she moved away from the cot—as if she'd also moved away from her comfort zone. And he didn't want her uptight. He wanted her soft and giving—the way he'd been fantasising about for too long now.

'The bathroom's through there,' he said. 'You might want to go and freshen up.'

Glad to escape from his unsettling scrutiny, Justina went into the bathroom, where she stripped off and stood beneath the warm torrents of water and tried to put Dante out of her mind— easier said than done when desire kept straying into her mind with dark and dangerous thoughts. And she couldn't hide in the shower all day.

She wandered back into the bedroom, clad only in a towel and found Dante standing there, his expression unfathomable as he watched her walk in. She supposed she should say something on the lines of *I didn't know you'd be here*— except that would have been a lie. Where else would he be when they were supposed to be sharing a bedroom?

'Is Nico okay?' she questioned awkwardly.

For a moment he didn't move, and when eventually he nodded Justina could see that his powerful body looked as tense as she felt.

'Fast asleep. Want to see?'

Nodding, she followed him into the adjoining bedroom, where their son lay sleeping in the antique cot, the wood very dark against the pristine whiteness of the bedclothes. For a moment she just stood and watched the steady rise and fall of his little chest, marvelling at the thought of the tiny heart which beat within it and the fact that she and Dante had created this living miracle between them. Out of one reckless act of passion this beautiful little child had been born.

And what of Nico's life? she wondered suddenly. Would he suffer as she had suffered because a man and a woman had come together as she and Dante had done? Not thinking about the consequences of their actions, thinking of nothing but the heat of the moment and the overwhelming lure of desire? Growing up, she had hated her own illegitimacy, and yet now she had bequeathed that same pain to her child.

With a strangled little sound she turned and walked back into the bedroom, scarcely aware that Dante was close behind her. At least not until his hand had reached out to her bare shoulder and was turning her round.

'Justina? What's wrong?'

She shook her head. How could she admit to the great cauldron of insecurity which was bubbling away inside her when all she could think about was the burn of his fingers on her bare flesh?

'*This* is wrong—this whole farce of us coming here with our baby and being put in this room together as if we're all some kind of happy family,' she said desperately, shaking his hand away. '*We're* wrong!'

'No!'

His voice was fierce as he pulled her into his arms, his voice unsteady as he pressed his face close to hers. So close that she could feel the heat of his breath fanning over her skin.

'We have never been wrong. How can it possibly be wrong when it feels like this whenever I touch you?'

'Dante—'

'Kiss me,' he growled. 'And then tell me again that we're wrong. Do that and I'll never lay another finger on you.'

She opened her mouth to say that was cheating. That she didn't want to kiss him. But that would have been a lie. Because hadn't she wanted this all along? Deep down hadn't she been yearning for this—the hard pressure of his kiss and her own urgent response to it? Hungrily, her lips sought his, and he tugged at the towel and let it slither to the floor, so that she was completely naked.

For a moment he pulled away so that he could look at her, sucking in a breath as his gaze burned over her, and she was so lost in the moment and the way he was making her feel that she did nothing. She could feel her nipples springing to life beneath his hungry scrutiny, and the melting desire which was pooling insistently at the fork of her thighs.

'Dante,' she breathed. 'This is...'

'Inevitable,' he bit out, as he began to tug at his belt. 'It's been inevitable for a long time now. Because you are beautiful. The most beautiful woman I have ever seen. And I am aching for you. I am crazy for you, *tesoro*.'

No, *this* was crazy, she thought. Dante was

talking with an emotion she hadn't heard in a long time and stripping off his clothes with ruthless efficiency, while she just stood there and watched him! She bit her lip as she saw his erection springing free, and a rush of desire flooded over her as he splayed his hands over her bare hips and pulled her down onto the bed.

'Dante,' she whispered, 'we can't do this.'

'Want to bet?'

'But your family,' she said desperately.

'Dinner isn't for hours.'

'But—'

'No more buts, Justina. Especially when we both know you don't really mean them. Don't you realise this is siesta time and you're in Italy now?'

His lips were trailing fire as they brushed over her neck and her eyes closed as her head fell back against the pillow. 'Oh,' she said indistinctly.

'I want to kiss every inch of you,' he breathed. 'I want to touch every part of your body. Do you know that?'

Now his finger was stroking its way over her breast, teasing over the aching mound until it alighted with teasing precision on the nipple. 'I… Oh…'

'Your breasts are bigger than they used to be.'

'And do you…do you approve?'

He smiled against her lips. 'Mmm. One hundred percent.'

His finger had moved down over her belly and quickly she sucked it in. 'Dante!'

'Relax. Why are you holding your breath like that?'

'Because my breasts aren't the only things which are bigger. My stomach is *huge!*'

He laid the flat of his hand over the slight cushioning of her flesh. 'Your stomach is perfect. Just as you are perfect.'

'No, I'm not.'

'Will you shut up and come here?'

He bent his head to kiss her and Justina could feel herself almost drowning in the sweetness of that kiss and the things he had just said to her. *He thought she was perfect!* She clung to him as his fingers drifted to her bare knee and then made an almost careless journey up her thigh. He skated teasing little circles there until she was gasping, and then his finger flicked against her sticky heat and she gasped some more. And suddenly his possession became more important than immediate pleasure. She wanted to *feel* him. She wanted him deep inside her again.

'Dante…' she whispered.

'What?' he whispered back.

'Please.'

'Can't wait any longer?'

'N-no.'

'Me neither, *tesoro*. Me neither.'

She held her breath as he moved over her, and the world seemed to stand still as he entered her with one deep and possessive thrust. She felt a great warmth suffuse her, and the breath she'd been holding escaped. She thought she felt him smile against her lips before starting to kiss her again. And Justina let go. Suddenly it was easy to let go. To forget about what had brought them here and concentrate instead on the way he was making her feel.

'Oh,' she breathed again.

Through the dark mists of his own pleasure he managed to get words out. 'Does that hurt?'

'God, no. It feels…incredible.'

'I know it does. For me, too.' He closed his eyes as he lost himself in the rhythm. He'd thought that the sex would be different, and it was—just not in the way he'd imagined. Justina was as tight and delectable as she'd ever been, but it felt… Dante groaned. It felt more than sex had ever felt before. Something which went deeper than physical pleasure. Was that because this body had given birth to his baby—because part of him had grown deep inside her?

He felt her thighs wrap themselves around his back and her fingers digging into his shoulders. He could feel her climax building, and even though he could have come in an instant he held back. He held back even though it nearly killed him—and only when she started to come did he let go and he thought his orgasm was never going to end.

For a while the room was silent, save for the shuddering sounds of air being gulped back into their starved lungs, like two people who had just been saved from drowning. And when their breathing was steady he kissed her for a long time—until the need to yawn became unbearable.

'Charming,' she said, stroking a fingertip over the rasp of growth at his jaw as he opened his eyes and looked at her.

'I do my best,' he murmured.

She could hear the sleepiness in his voice and for a moment Justina lay in the warm circle of his arms and let sensation ripple over her skin. His lips were pressed against her neck, and in that moment she felt utterly protected. She wanted to tell him that nobody else had ever made her feel this way. She wanted to blurt out the secrets she'd held hidden in her heart for so many years.

But Dante had hurt her. He had hurt her badly. Why would she risk that happening all over again? Why jeopardise everything with an emotional outburst when it was far better to play safe? She needed to protect herself against the threat of heartbreak—as much for Nico's sake as for her own. Because a heartbroken mother did not make a good mother. She of all people knew that.

So sleep, she told herself. *Take this opportunity to rest. You're tired, you're a new mother and you've got a family dinner to get through tonight.*

Dante heard the slowing of her breathing as she snuggled against him and he stared down at the ebony hair which spread like treacle over the pillow. He studied the dark curve of her eyelashes and the paper-pale skin against which they brushed. She was pressed so close that he could feel the beating of her heart, and something like certainty crept over him.

He thought about the baby who lay sleeping in the next room. He thought about the harsh and unequivocal words of his lawyer as he acknowledged one fundamental truth. That he wanted this...this family. Just like she'd said, he wanted it all. Nico. Her. All of them together.

And Justina was going to have to start seeing things his way.

CHAPTER NINE

JUSTINA WOKE ALONE from a restless sleep, where images of green mountains were interwoven with the intimate caress of a man's strong body and a silence where there should have been a baby's cry. Startled, she sat bolt upright in bed.

A baby's cry!

Momentarily disorientated, she looked around, trying to get her bearings, blinking back her faint feeling of disbelief. She was in Dante's family villa. More accurately, she was in Dante's bed. She stared down at the empty space beside her. Only he'd gone. Where…?

She jumped out of bed, grabbing at one of the rumpled sheets to wrap it around her naked body before stumbling into the adjoining room to find Nico's cot empty.

A whimper erupted from her throat as she fought to control a rising feeling of panic. Where was her baby? She rushed back into the bedroom and threw on jeans and a sweater, before slipping her feet into a pair of flip-flops as she ran from the room to look for him.

But the *palazzo* was vast, and although she called out Dante and Nico's names in an increasingly concerned voice her calls were met with a resounding silence.

She ran outside, her eyes skating over the horizon, over the distant mountains and the sunlight which was gilding the leaves of the olive trees. Only then did she see him, down among the neat rows of the vines. A tall, dark man pushing a buggy, silhouetted against the classic Tuscan backdrop. Her heart lurched with relief, but she felt the shimmering of something else as she began to run towards them. Something which felt uncomfortably like fear.

'Dante!'

She saw him stop. Saw him lean down as if he was saying something to the inhabitant of the buggy. And then he straightened up and stood, perfectly still, watching her run towards him until she finally reached them, her breath coming in ragged gasps.

'What are you *doing*?' she demanded, her eyes raking over the cot. Her anxiety was only allayed when she saw that Nico was lying there, sleeping peacefully.

Dante heard the breathless accusation in her voice and something inside him hardened. 'What does it look like?' he demanded. 'I brought Nico out for a walk in the fresh air.'

Her fears—which had seemed so real—now began to evaporate. 'I thought…'

'What did you think, Justina?' he questioned acidly. 'That I'd kidnapped our son?'

In the beauty of the Tuscan afternoon her response now seemed faintly ridiculous. 'I woke up alone.'

'I thought you could use the sleep.'

'I've…' She struggled to explain, wanting to wipe that cold, hard look from his face. 'It's all been a bit of an adjustment. Not just coming here, but getting used to having a baby around. This is the first time since he's been born that he hasn't been…' She sucked in a deep breath. 'That he hasn't been there when I've woken.'

Slowly Dante nodded as he acknowledged what lay behind her behaviour, but he also knew that her actions were motivated by something that went much deeper than maternal anxiety. He had never wanted nor asked for the judgement of a woman until now, but for the first time in his life he could see that he needed to give voice to the one question which had remained unspoken.

'Don't you trust me, Justina?' he asked quietly.

Justina looked at him. She knew what she should say. She should tell him that, yes, of course she trusted him—because wouldn't that smooth things over? He would smile, and then they would kiss, and then make a fuss of Nico. And to anyone watching from the house they would look like the perfect family. But this wasn't some sort of play, she reminded herself. This was real life—and being in bed with him this afternoon had made some of her defences come tumbling down. She couldn't keep hiding from the truth simply because it was painful. Dante had asked her an unexpectedly honest question which deserved nothing but an honest answer.

'Actually, no,' she said. 'Not really.'

He stilled, because somehow hadn't he expected—hoped for—a different response? 'So me being there for you during the birth and afterwards counts for nothing?'

Her gaze was steady. 'I didn't realise you were doing it to score Brownie points.'

'I *wasn't*,' he defended, indignation catching in his throat as he looked at her long dark hair which was blowing in the breeze. And suddenly he wanted to make it very clear to her exactly where he stood on the subject of other women. 'Don't you realise that I haven't looked at another woman since I met you again at Roxy's wedding?'

'How would I know that?' she asked quietly. 'I'm not a mind-reader.'

'Let me tell you what it was like when I saw you again after all those years,' he said slowly. 'You blew me away—just like you did before. I couldn't get you out of my mind. I kept telling myself to stay away from you. That we were bad for each other. I knew that. Only the temptation to come and find you was eating away at me.'

She didn't say anything, because his words didn't sound like affection or anything close to it. They sounded like *addiction*. Was Dante addicted to the emotional danger which had always existed between them? Was she?

'And then I discovered you were pregnant,' he said. 'And my desire very quickly became anger. Anger that you didn't bother to tell me. That you were prepared to keep me in the dark about the fact I was going to be a father.'

'Surely you can understand why I did that?'

'Not really, no. Was it power that made you keep it secret?' he questioned. 'Or control?'

Standing silhouetted against the dying apricot light of the Tuscan day, Justina thought that she had never seen him looking more indomitable, and yet his inherent arrogance almost took her breath away.

'I'm amazed you can say all that to me with a straight face,' she said. 'You told me that it was never meant to be anything more than a one-night stand—so why would I foist on you the repercussions of that meeting? You were going to have a baby with a woman you despised. No... please.' She lifted her hand as he opened his mouth to speak. 'Let me finish, because it's important. I thought that a baby would be the last thing you wanted and so I didn't tell you. I can see now that was wrong, but I was trying to be independent.'

'Of course you were.'

She ignored the sardonic note which had hardened his voice. 'I should have given you a choice about how much involvement you wanted instead of assuming that you wanted none.'

'Or was that what *you* wanted, Justina?' His voice was silky-soft now. 'For me not to have any contact with our child?'

She looked into his eyes. Weren't lies sometimes kinder than the truth? She knew it would be easier all round if she just denied it. Yet she also knew that they had passed the point of twisting the truth in order to spare each other's feelings. 'Of course it's what I wanted,' she said. 'I didn't want you back in my life in any way. You bring with you too many complications, Dante.'

Dante heard the cool determination in her voice and saw the candid gaze from her eyes. Her words hurt far more than he had expected them to, but her honesty was curiously refreshing. It told him exactly where he stood and it told him just what he needed to do. 'I guess that pretty much concludes all we need to say on the subject of paternity,' he said. 'Maybe we should now do something inherently civilised—like going inside to drink some coffee.'

She nodded, shaken by the frankness of the exchange but pleased at the unexpected turnaround which the conversation had taken. 'That sounds exactly what I need.'

As if on cue, Nico began to stir. Justina looked down at him, a fierce love swelling up in her heart as his long lashes fluttered open. 'Hello, you,' she said softly. 'Are you hungry?'

They walked back to the house, where Justina fed and changed Nico, and soon afterwards Dante's mother knocked on the door and asked if she might take the baby to show to the staff.

'And, no, I don't need you to help me!' she said very firmly to her son.

There was a moment of silence once Signora D'Arezzo had gone. The two of them stood listening to the echoing sound of her retreating footsteps, and then Dante turned to Justina and lifted her fingertips to his lips.

'Coffee?' he questioned.

She shivered, all their disharmony dissolved by that first touch. 'If you like.'

'Or bed?'

She told herself that coffee was the safer option—so why was she nodding with that schoolgirl-shy smile and letting him lead her through to the bed, where the sheets were still rumpled from before? She bent to straighten them, but the drift of his fingertips over her bottom halted her.

'Don't,' he said roughly. 'It's a waste of time.'

She turned to face him, and he pushed her down on the bed and began to kiss her.

Some of the tenderness of earlier had gone—

had been replaced with an unmistakable urgency. He tugged off her clothes with impatient fingers, and somehow she managed to accomplish the same with his. Their bare bodies met in a warm collision of skin, and Justina felt the instant shock of familiarity and lust. He seemed so powerfully dark and dominant as he moved over her, his carved features rigid with restraint as she touched the hard, silken length of him.

'Don't,' he groaned.

She drifted her fingertips upwards and downwards in a light and teasing motion. 'Sure?'

Eyes glinting, he removed the offending hand, circling it with his fingers and holding it above her head so that she was effectively imprisoned beneath him. He looked so dark and dominant and powerful, she thought. And she was discovering that she liked that. She liked the feeling that this was beyond her control, that she was submitting to Dante's will—because didn't that stop her thinking too deeply about whether or not she should be doing it at all?

Her orgasm came swiftly, and afterwards she drifted in and out of sleep until the clock chimed seven and she forced herself to go and take a shower. The room was very quiet when she returned. Dante was already dressed and fastening a pair of pale gold cufflinks. He glanced up to find her watching him, and he smiled as his gaze took in the white towel which was wrapped around her.

'I'm getting a distinct feeling of *déjà vu*,' he drawled. 'You do realise that you'll have me in a permanent state of arousal if you insist on walking around looking like that?'

She could still feel his heated gaze on her as she went over to the dressing table and sat down. She took a wand of mascara and held it to her eye, but Dante had followed her. He was standing behind her and lifting the dark curtain of damp hair before leaning down to press his lips against the back of her exposed neck.

'You smell delicious.'

'It's only soap.'

'Then it is a very delicious soap.'

She closed her eyes. 'Dante...'

'Mmm?'

'We...we don't have a lot of time before dinner.'

'I know we don't, *tesoro*—but I want you to know that I'm crazy about you. That I want you very much and that we have a lot of making up to do.' His hand splayed over her breast and she opened her eyes to see the erotic image of his dark fingers star-fished over the white towelling reflected back at her in the mirror.

'Just go,' she whispered.

'I'm going—but all through dinner I shall be thinking about how much I am going to enjoy touching you later, just like this.'

She felt a wrench of longing as he moved away, leaving her to apply her make up with fingers which were now trembling and to slip into the new underwear she'd bought. All the time she was aware of him watching her. And somehow he could make her feel more self-conscious than she'd ever been on a stage in front of thousands of people. He made her feel...*exposed*. As if the tough skin she'd formed to protect herself could be stripped away by a single, searing slant of those dark eyes.

Her silk sheath dress was the colour of cappuccino, and she teamed it with a pair of towering nude-coloured shoes. She'd twisted her hair into an elaborate knot, and her only jewellery was a pair of dangling pearl and diamond earrings which sparkled and gleamed against her neck.

'Who bought you those?' he questioned suddenly.

She finished applying lip gloss and turned

round as something in the tone of his voice brought a sudden tension into the room. 'Do a woman's jewels always have to be bought for her by somebody else?'

'They usually are when they're as expensive as those ones clearly are.'

There was a pause. 'I bought them myself, if you must know.'

'Of course you did.' He gave a short laugh and his voice took on a hard note, as if he was remembering something. 'The ever-independent Justina Perry.'

'That's me,' she said lightly, but his words hurt—as she suspected they were meant to. Maybe this was a timely reminder that nothing between them had really changed. Before she started allowing herself to believe that it was safe to start loving him again she needed a reality check. Yes, they had the most amazing sex, but underneath he was still the same judgemental man.

'And the jewels which I bought you? What happened to those?'

'I tried to give them back to you.'

'And I told you to keep them. Apart from the ring, of course—which, as you know, was a family heirloom.' There was a pause. 'So where are they now?'

Justina wriggled her shoulders uncomfortably. Why couldn't he just let it go? 'I sold them.'

He frowned. 'All of them?'

'There's no need to look at me like that, Dante. I gave the money to charity.'

'I told you to keep them,' he repeated. He remembered a bracelet he'd had specially commissioned—a circlet of yellow diamonds, chosen because they reminded him of her eyes. He remembered the way she had smiled as he'd slipped it onto her wrist, and the dreamy way she'd said that one day their daughter would wear it. So much for her vow that she would treasure it for ever! 'They were bought for you and only you. I don't want some other woman wearing them.'

'Oh, come *on*, Dante.' Should she tell him that the sight of all those baubles had made her heart ache every time she'd looked at them? Jewels which most women would long to own had seemed to represent nothing but failure. They'd reminded her of the man she'd loved and lost— and who could live with that? 'Since when did any woman ever wear stuff given to her by her ex-fiancé?'

The bell rang for dinner, putting an end to their discussion—but Dante found himself remembering one sentence in particular which his lawyer had drummed into him. "Independent women make the worst adversaries in any custody battle, Dante. A needy woman is always much more amenable."

If that was the case then no female on the planet could be more fiercely independent than the one who stood in front of him. 'Come on,' he said abruptly. 'Let's go.'

Justina was aware that his mood was cool as they walked along the stone-flagged corridor, and tentatively she linked her arm through his, wanting him to lose that hard and grim expression. 'So who else will be at dinner?' she questioned softly. 'Apart from your mother.'

'My brother, obviously. You remember Luigi?'

'How could I forget?'

'And my sister has travelled from Rome to be here. My cousins are eager to meet you again, but I felt that it might be a bit much to subject you to mass scrutiny on your first evening. So we'll save that for another day.'

She let go of his arm just before they walked into the main salon, where Dante's brother was throwing a large log onto the fire.

'Hello, Luigi,' Justina said quietly, and he looked up. He was as tall and as powerfully built as his brother, but his skin had the darker glow of someone who spent their life working outside. Dante had told her that Luigi had run the vast estate since the death of their father, and was now one of the world's leading wine experts. She thought that his eyes were cool and watchful as he greeted her.

'Justina,' he said. 'This is an unexpected pleasure.'

She smiled up at him. 'It's good to see you again.'

'Indeed. And I believe I must congratulate you on giving birth to my brother's child?'

'Thank you,' she said, thinking that was a characteristically *possessive* D'Arezzo way of phrasing it.

'Now, what can I get you to drink?'

She was longing for one of the glasses of prosecco which stood on a tray, but she was mindful of the fact that she was breastfeeding—so her nerves would have to remain ruffled. 'Some fizzy water would be perfect.'

At that moment a beautiful girl ran into the room, her arms outstretched in greeting. Giulia D'Arezzo was the only female in the family, and rather more demonstrative than both her brothers, and Justina found herself laughing as she was enveloped in an enthusiastic hug.

'Oh, Jus! I'm so happy to see you again—I can't tell you! I've only just arrived—the traffic from Rome was atrocious. Am I too late to see Nico? Have you put him to bed already?'

'I'm afraid I have—or rather Dante has. Babies of Nico's age seem to spend most of their time sleeping—but we can creep down later and peep at him if you like,' said Justina. 'Giulia, you look wonderful.'

'*Grazie*. And so do you—though your dress is much longer than the ones you used to wear! Why are you blushing when what I say is true? Now, tell me, are you still making sweet music?' Giulia demanded. 'And why did you stop sending me your albums?'

The warmth of Giulia's welcome made Justina relax, as did the flames from the flickering fire. She sipped at her drink, listening to the younger woman's chatter and managing to skirt around the subject of why she'd felt it was best not to let her friendship with Dante's sister continue. Because that would have been impossible, wouldn't it? She'd needed to cut all ties with the D'Arezzo family once he'd called off their engagement.

By the time they sat down to dinner she had begun to feel genuinely hungry——though she was seated next to Luigi, who seemed to have some sort of not-very-hidden agenda going on. He asked her how her songwriting was going, and when she tried to play it down told her that he'd read recently that one of her songs had been at number one in Australia. But he said it as if she'd committed a crime instead of doing something to be proud of.

The pasta course was cleared away and Luigi poured himself a glass of red wine, nodding his head approvingly when she refused the same. 'You are intending to go back to work, I suppose?' he enquired, leaning back in his chair to look at her.

'Well, I need to support myself,' answered Justina equably.

'But surely you have accumulated enough money during your career never to have to work again?'

It was a question she got asked all the time—but people always underestimated how much money you needed to live on for the rest of your life. Justina had seen people lose their fortunes and be left scraping around and had vowed it would never happen to her. She'd seen for herself what could happen to women who didn't work. She'd seen her own mother clinging to rich men who discarded her when someone younger and prettier came along.

'I have a very strong work ethic,' she said carefully. 'And besides, the work I do is very flexible.'

'I'm sure it is.' Luigi ran a fingertip around the tip of his wine glass. 'But what will happen to Nico while you are occupied with this songwriting of yours? Will you be able to concentrate? Will you hear him above the music if he cries out for his *mamma*?'

'Luigi,' said Dante warningly.

Justina put her glass of water down with a hand which wasn't quite steady. 'Probably not. So I'll just leave him to fend for himself,' she said. 'I can probably arrange the baby equivalent of a cat-flap. You know—a saucer of milk, maybe a rusk or two. He can just crawl in and out and help himself.'

Luigi pushed his glass away and said something to his brother in a low stream of Italian—a statement clearly designed to exclude her. But Justina was listening carefully enough to register some of the words. She saw the look which hardened Dante's face before he made a furious response which was too rapid for her to understand.

Forcing herself to pick at food she didn't want, she was glad when the meal ended and she could fulfil her promise to Giulia by taking her to see the baby. But her heart was aching as they walked into Nico's bedroom to where he lay sleeping.

He was swaddled inside the cot and Giulia stared down at him for a long moment. Her voice was a breathless whisper when eventually she spoke. 'Oh, but he is beautiful, Justina. Absolutely beautiful.'

'I know he is.' Justina felt the stupid lump which rose in her throat as they stood there, and her fierce sense of maternal pride was blotted out by the terrible sense that nothing was really as it should be. That everything was so damned *complicated.*

But she managed a smile as she and Giulia moved away. 'Tomorrow you shall hold him as much as you like. I might even let you change his nappy if you behave yourself!'

Giulia was still laughing when they returned

to the dining room, where coffee was being served, and Justina took the opportunity to excuse herself before slipping back to their suite.

She fed and changed Nico and put him back in his cot, and was standing in her silk robe, staring out at the starry night sky, when she heard Dante enter the room behind her.

She didn't turn round immediately. Just said in a flat and emotionless voice, 'What was Luigi saying to you over dinner?'

There was a pause. 'We spoke of many things, Justina. You were there, remember?'

At this, she turned round—her body automatically responding to the way he was removing his tie and unbuttoning his silk shirt to reveal a triangle of dark, honed chest beneath. *Keep it real,* she reminded herself. *Don't let yourself be swayed by how much you want him.*

'I listened to him insulting me by implying that I was a neglectful mother. I know that.'

'And I put him right. I told him that you are a brilliant mother.'

'Did you?'

'Certainly I did. I said that no mother could be more devoted nor more loving than you are.'

That took the wind right out of her sails. She didn't want Dante praising her because that was distracting. She wanted to get to the bottom of what Luigi had been saying. 'I'm thinking more specifically about when he spoke to you in Italian.'

'I don't remember.'

'You don't? That's quite unusual for a man with your sharp sense of recall, Dante. Perhaps I'd better jog your memory for you. He said *matrimonio*—which means marriage, and which I imagine is understandable in most languages. But he also said *avoccato*.' She frowned. 'Which means lawyer, if my memory of my Italian classes serves me well.'

There was a moment of silence before Dante spoke. '*Brava, tesoro*,' he said softly. 'I had no idea you were so advanced in my language.'

'Please don't patronise me, Dante. Just tell me what you were talking about.'

For a moment he didn't answer, and there was no sound other than the faint clatter of metal on wood as he put his cufflinks down on the dresser. He had intended to say this to her, yes—but not in this way. Not as something produced as a defence against a heated accusation made at the end of a long day. He had planned to wait until she had softened. Until he had made love to her and she was lying in his arms in one of those rare moments when he sensed she might be close to letting her carefully built defences fall away.

He met the amber fire in her eyes. 'I had planned to ask you to marry me.'

CHAPTER TEN

JUSTINA FLINCHED, THINKING how *wrong* Dante's words sounded. It was the coldest marriage proposal she could have imagined—and how it mocked her. The first time he'd asked her to be his wife he had been brimming over with love—but now his voice was completely different. It was like playing a familiar piece of music and discovering that the disc was covered with dust, so that the sound came out all distorted.

'Right,' she said, somehow managing to keep her voice steady. 'That's why your brother mentioned matrimony. But that wasn't all you were talking about, was it? I'm interested to know why you mentioned lawyers. It's not usually a top topic for dinner conversation—particularly as you both switched to speaking in Italian.'

Dante's eyes narrowed, because surely she knew him well enough to realise that he would have covered this particular base. And if she was missing the point then wasn't it time he enlightened her?

'I've spoken to my lawyer,' he said. 'Obviously.'

'Oh, *obviously*,' she echoed sardonically. 'And what did your lawyer say?'

'She advised me that in our particular situation marriage would be the best solution.'

She? Justina nodded. Of course Dante would have a female lawyer—*of course he would!* 'But a solution implies some sort of problem.'

'*Si!*' he agreed hotly. 'There *is* a problem! A big problem. Surely you can see that for yourself? We have different lives but a shared child. And for as long as we remain unmarried I have no legal say in what happens to that child.'

He felt his lips harden with determination. What had his lawyer said? *"Marriage just makes things easier, Dante—because even if the marriage doesn't endure the law is on your side. Without it you must rely on the woman's benevolence in order to see your child—and this woman might not be feeling particularly benevolent towards you."*

He looked at Justina now, her black hair sil-vered by the moonlight which streamed in through the unshuttered windows. He thought how majestic she looked, with the flow of her satin robe clinging like oil to the soft curves of her body. He thought of her talent and the lov-ing way she was with his son.

'Marry me, Justina,' he said.

There was a long silence as Justina looked into his eyes and tried to steel herself against their dark beauty. She told herself that this was not the time to listen to her heart—that the soft dip in his voice was simply Dante at his most charmingly manipulative. For her son's sake she had to be governed by reason and nothing else.

'And if I do. What's in it for me?' she ques-tioned.

'Security, of course.' He smiled. 'And family.'

Justina smiled back, because he was clever. Oh, he was *very* clever. He had picked on the two things which had always eluded her. The two things she'd always yearned for. A sense of home and being rooted and a sense of being safe. But how could she be safe when what they had was only the mirage of a family... And once that mirage had disappeared, what would be left behind? A man who didn't love and a woman who did.

She shook her head, fighting against the temptation to leap at it, telling herself that she had too much to lose by buying into a dream. 'It isn't enough.'

'Why not?'

'Because…' And then the words came tumbling out. Words she'd buried in some deep place inside herself now spooled out in a dark stream. 'Because I can't be married to a man I don't trust. A man who can just walk away from a woman he was supposed to marry and a few short days later take somebody else to his bed!'

He winced. 'What's the point of bringing that up again?' he questioned wearily. 'I thought we'd done all this. It's in the past, Justina. It's done.'

'But the legacy of that day continues, Dante. It threatens any future we might have—can't you see that?'

'No, I damned well can't. Our relationship was *over*,' he bit out. 'You know that. I wasn't expecting you to walk in on me. That was the last thing in the world I wanted.'

'But that's not the point, is it? The point is that you were….you were with *her*.' Briefly she covered her mouth, as if she was afraid she might be sick, before letting her fingers slide down to rest against her neck. 'I thought what we had was so special—but how could it have been? How the hell could you replace me so quickly?'

'She was not *replacing* you! She could never have replaced you. Nobody could. I know it was wrong. God help me, I know that now. But I was hurting. And I missed you,' he said simply. 'I missed you so much.'

'You had a funny way of showing it.'

'And I was angry,' he admitted. 'More angry than I'd ever been. That played its part—of course it did. I was angry that you kept going away on tour—that you were prepared to put your career before our relationship. I guess I blamed you for the split, and I did what countless other men have done in the same situation. I went to a bar and drank a little too much, and she—'

'*I don't want to hear this!*'

'Well, maybe you should!' His black eyes burned into her. 'Maybe it should all come out so that we can be rid of it once and for all. She came on to me like women are always coming on to me—only I'd never looked at another woman from the moment I'd met you. It was never even a consideration. Only this time it was different.

We were over. Finished. This time I wanted… comfort.'

'Stop it!' she hissed. 'You wanted sex and you damned well got it! You were just unlucky that I came in and caught you.'

'I was *wrong*,' he repeated harshly. 'I just grabbed at the first thing which came along and it was too soon—much too soon. And if its purpose was to try to forget you, then I can assure you that it didn't work.'

'It's easy to say that now.'

'*Easy*? You think this is easy?' he demanded, his face so tense that it looked as if it might shatter at any moment. 'If I could go back in time I would. If I could change it then I would. But I can't. Nobody can do that.' His eyes were the colour of molten jet as he held both hands up in a gesture of appeal. 'I'm asking you to forgive me, Jus. I'm asking you to take me back and to marry me—to let me spend the rest of my life making you happy.'

Justina's heart contracted with a pain which was complicated by a temptation so strong that she didn't know if she'd be able to resist it. Because she *wanted* to reach out and tell him that, yes, she would take him back. She *wanted* to have him hold her and kiss her and keep her close. She *wanted* to buy in to the dream that they could be the perfect couple and the perfect family. But it *was* just a dream—how could it be anything other than that when the trust between them had been severed?

He said that he wanted only her—but he'd said that once before, hadn't he? Who was to say that Dante wouldn't stray next time they ran into some kind of difficulty, as inevitably they would? There were a million women out there, just waiting to "come on" to him. She knew that. There was always a woman waiting in the wings for a married man to have a weak enough moment to stray. Hadn't her own mother proved that, time and time again?

And through all his extraordinary declaration—through all his heartfelt words—there remained one startling omission. He hadn't even mentioned the word *love*. Maybe she should be grateful that he wasn't coating his proposal with sweet declarations which meant nothing, but what hope would a marriage have *without* love? Even if she was honest enough to admit to herself that she was falling in love with him all over again that wouldn't be enough to go round, would it? Not nearly enough to protect her from the influence of gorgeous blondes with hunger in their eyes.

She forced herself to say it, even though her heart was sending out a silent scream of protest.

'I can't do it,' she said. 'I just...*can't*. I saw it and I felt so utterly *betrayed*—and I don't think I can get past that. Trust is almost impossible to repair once it's been broken.'

'Justina—'

'No. Please, Dante. I promise I will give you reasonable access to your son, but no more than that. I won't marry you—but that doesn't mean we can't be good parents.' At this she stopped and drew in a deep breath which seemed to scorch her lungs, before managing a smile. 'And I don't see any reason why we can't continue to have a perfectly amicable relationship.'

There was a long pause—so long that for a moment she wondered if he'd heard her. But one look at the expression on his face told her that he had. His features seemed to have been carved from stone; they were hard and unmoving. The silence in the room was tense as Justina waited to see how he would respond—and she was surprised when he walked over to her and caught hold of her, pulling her into his body in a single fluid movement. Through her silk robe she could feel the jut of her breasts pushing against his chest, and instantly she felt an inevitable rush of desire which was quickly followed by a hot wave of relief. He didn't mind! He understood her reservations!

For a moment he stared down at her, and his hand moved down over the fall of her hair before coming to alight on one silk-covered breast. She sucked in a breath of anticipation.

'And this "amicable" relationship of which you speak,' he murmured. 'You don't think that's going to be problematic?'

She spoke with more conviction than she felt. 'It doesn't have to be.'

'Do you have any ideas about how we're going to go about it?'

'We could…we could make it up as we go along.'

'Could we?' His smile was cold. 'So how about we start with something like this?'

He slipped his hand inside her robe to cover the breast which had been straining for his touch. She felt his thumb flick over the nipple and she swallowed.

'Yes,' she breathed, scarcely able to get the word out. *'Yes.'*

'So while we are being good parents, and

being *reasonable* about access, we will continue to enjoy sex—is that what you are suggesting?'

His tone was a honeyed murmur, even if his words sounded a little on the bald side. 'Yes,' she repeated. 'Definitely.'

His thumb caressed one straining bud. 'You want to do it now, I think?'

Justina swayed. 'You know I do,' she moaned.

The hand was removed with almost clinical efficiency, and Justina didn't even realise that she'd had her eyes closed until she fluttered them open to see the look of naked fury on his face.

'You really think that I would tolerate an arrangement like that? To be treated like some common *stud*? In your dreams, Justina,' he said savagely, and walked out of their bedroom with a soft slamming of the door.

For a moment she stood staring blankly after him, until she realised she was shivering, so she climbed into bed and waited for him to return. It took several sleepless hours before it dawned on her that that he wasn't planning on returning. At least not until after a pale dawn had streaked the Tuscan sky and she'd finished tending to Nico.

Dante walked into the room wearing the same formal trousers he'd had on at dinner, and he had clearly just pulled his dress shirt on over his bare chest, though he hadn't bothered to do it up. His feet were bare, too—and his dark hair was ruffled and untidy.

'Where have you been?' she questioned tiredly.

He gave her a look composed in equal measures of ice and fury. 'Where do you think? We're in the middle of the Tuscan countryside— there aren't really a lot of options open! I slept somewhere else, Justina—there are plenty of available rooms.'

She swallowed, telling herself to stay calm. That nothing could be gained from another angry exchange. 'Why did you storm out like that?'

'Why?' he repeated, a look of incredulity darkening his face. 'You really need to ask me that? I asked you to marry me and you said no— but your refusal came with an interesting suggestion.' He gave a bitter laugh before he shot the words out as if he was firing them from a pistol. 'Don't you think it insults me that I'm good enough to *service* you any time you want, good enough to be your stud, just not good enough to be your husband?'

For a moment Justina's resolve wavered. She wanted to blurt out the truth. To tell him that marriage without love wasn't enough, and she was terrified her heart would get broken all over again. But that might sound like a clumsy attempt at emotional bargaining. He might feel cornered into telling her he loved her in order to appease her—and then what? Wouldn't something like that backfire on them in the end?

She pushed her hair behind her ears and surveyed him, her calm expression belying the painful thunder of her heart. 'So what are we going to do?'

'Do?' He pulled off his shirt and hung it over the back of the chair. 'We're going to do exactly what we came here to do. We are going to introduce Nico to the rest of his D'Arezzo family and show him a little Tuscan hospitality and then we will return to England.'

And that, it seemed, was that. End of subject.

Justina was forced to watch as Dante took off his trousers and his underpants. She wanted to avert her eyes as more and more honed olive flesh was revealed, but pride wouldn't let her. Only when he was completely and magnificently naked did he glance up and meet her gaze, his dark eyes mocking her.

'Frustrating, isn't it, *tesoro*? You can look, but you can't touch.'

'I don't want to touch you.'

'*Liar.*'

The soft word sliced through her.

'But let me tell you this, so that there can be absolutely no misunderstanding. That there will be no more *performing* for your pleasure. You don't want me as a husband then you don't get me at all. None of me.'

It was a depressing way to begin the day, but Justina did her best not to let it show because she knew that streams of D'Arezzo cousins were coming over later. And she wanted to salvage something from this trip. Her relationship with Dante might have taken a nosedive, but she wanted his family to approve of her as a mother, even if it was too much to hope for that they might actually *like* her.

She was aware that some of the cousins were a little wary around her when they arrived just before lunchtime—but she was also aware they'd been at an impressionable age the last time she'd visited. She'd probably seemed distant to them and, if she was being truthful, she had *felt* a little distant. She remembered that while she'd been here her management had rung almost nonstop and it had driven Dante to despair. A photographer had even managed to penetrate the grounds of the family estate and a furious Luigi had threatened to punch him, before sending him on his way.

She didn't miss that side of fame one bit, she realised. The irony was that in many ways she felt much more grounded—and Nico was partly responsible for that. She knew that she would make a better wife now than she would have done at the height of her fame. But she also knew that she couldn't opt for an empty marriage.

Instead, she did her best to fit in with the family—and to her surprise it proved easier than she had anticipated. But then, it was easy to join in with the general clucking over Nico and agree with the sentiment that he was the most beautiful baby in the world! Quickly she realised the significance of this lusty little boy—the first of a new generation of D'Arezzos.

She'd made the biggest effort of all with Beatrix D'Arezzo—wanting her to know that she would do everything and anything for her beloved grandson. So when it came to leaving Dante's mother hugged her tightly, with an affection which did not seem feigned and Justina felt unexpectedly choked, having to swallow down an unexpected lump in her throat as their car arrived to take them to the airport.

She felt deflated on the flight back to England, and not just because the D'Arezzo family's warmth contrasted so bitterly with Dante's new coolness towards her. Now that nobody else was around he seemed to have dropped his politely solicitous attitude towards her. And that didn't bode very well for the future, did it? They were both going to have to override their feelings and think of Nico's welfare.

She stared at him. The plane was lavishly equipped, and he was opposite her, working on a large pile of papers. A lock of black hair had fallen onto his forehead and her fingers itched to brush it away.

'I think the visit went well,' she ventured.

He looked up, his eyes focussing on her almost as if he'd forgotten she was there, and Justina found herself reflecting that a look like that could be more hurtful than all the rage in the world.

'On many levels, yes. I think so, too,' he agreed.

'You'll...you'll be going back to New York, I suppose?'

At this he pushed away the smooth tablet of his computer and studied her with an odd kind of smile. 'That's what you'd like, is it, Justina?'

Justina shrugged. What she'd *like* would be

for him to stop sulking. She wanted things to go back to the way they'd been before he'd spoilt it all by asking her to marry him.

'I don't think what I'd like is really relevant,' she said. 'I just assumed you'd be going home.'

'Haven't you learned by now that it's never wise to make assumptions when you're dealing with a D'Arezzo man?' His voice had deepened to a note of dark silk. 'As it happens, I won't be going to New York—no.'

'You won't?' she questioned lightly. 'Why not?'

'Because I'm moving to London.'

She blinked. 'But you work in New York!'

'These days I can work anywhere. That's the beauty of modern communication.'

'But you don't have anywhere to live! Unless you're planning on staying at the Vinoly long-term?'

'A hotel suite is not ideal for a young baby,' he said. 'Which is why I intend on buying a house.'

'You're *what*?'

'With a garden,' he continued. 'Somewhere Nico can sit outside in the fresh air during his access visits.'

'Access visits?' she whispered.

'Of course. Or did you think that they were

going to be on your territory and on your terms? Oh, you *did*?' He gave a disdainful smile as he unclipped his seat belt and stretched out his long legs. 'You know, for someone who has always accused *me* of being the ultimate control freak, you're doing a pretty good impersonation of one yourself, Justina.'

Justina felt spooked. When she'd spoken of access visits back in Tuscany they had been hypothetical. They'd sounded as unthreatening as a dentist's appointment when you knew it was a whole year away. But this...

Dante was moving to London and he was getting a house!

The child in her wanted to scream. She wanted to tell him that she was scared. Scared he would create a *proper* home simply because he knew how to and she didn't. That Nico would grow up preferring to go round to Papa's, while she...

'Miss Perry?'

She'd been so lost in her thoughts that Justina hadn't realised Dante was no longer there. One of the glamorous D'Arezzo stewardesses was standing over her, her perfectly plucked eyebrows raised in question and Justina turned her head just in time to see Dante disappearing into the cockpit. 'Yes?'

'Signor D'Arezzo has decided to land the plane himself, so he's gone in to join the pilot. Would you care to fasten your seat belt?'

Justina felt even more wrong-footed as the stewardess checked that Nico was properly clipped in. What the hell was Dante doing, landing the damned plane? She hadn't even known he could fly!

She glared as he exited the cockpit after a butter-smooth landing. 'I suppose you've learned to walk on water, too?' she questioned acidly.

'Now, now, Justina,' he chided. 'Shouldn't your role be to congratulate me and to tell Nico what a talented daddy he has?'

She didn't trust herself to answer—just felt an increasing swirl of frustration as they prepared to leave the plane. This wasn't how it was supposed to be—although when she stopped to think about it what had she imagined would happen? That Dante would just disappear into the ether, only appearing at Christmas and birthdays, with a smile on his face and a gift in his hand?

Even so, they were halfway back to London before she had plucked up enough courage to ask, 'When do you anticipate moving to London?'

'Straight away,' he replied, shrugging his

shoulders with the lazy gesture of someone who could afford to do exactly what he wanted. 'Why wait? I've had my people look into availability, and I'm taking a house in Spitalfields which isn't too far from you. A rather beautiful Georgian house in a glorious green square, as it happens.' He tapped his finger on his laptop. 'Would you like to see some photos?'

Justina felt queasy. 'I'll pass, thank you.'

Her apartment felt soulless and bare after the faded splendour of the Tuscan *palazzo*. She stood in the centre of the oatmeal sitting room while Dante put down her suitcase and thought how *gorgeous* he looked in his dark suit. And about as accessible as a remote and icy mountain peak.

She fiddled with the button of her jacket. 'Dante?'

He bent to drop one final kiss on top of his sleeping son's head, unprepared for the savage twist of pain he felt at the thought of having to say goodbye. Straightening up, he looked into her wide amber eyes and felt the twist of something else, too. Did she know how far she had pushed him and how close he was to snapping?

'Justina?' he said, striving for a neutrality which was only hanging by a thin thread.

'Can't we…?' *Say it,* she urged herself. *Just say it.* 'Can't we still be friends, at least?'

At that moment he could have gone over there and shaken her. Why was she so damned stubborn? Why couldn't she see what was staring her in the face?

With an effort he fought against the slow burn of rage. 'I'm not sure whether we can ever be *friends,*' he said. 'Not in the circumstances. But I'm hopeful that we can achieve the amicable relationship you said you wanted.'

Justina only just managed not to wince. Had she really been stupid enough to demand something like that?

Because why on earth would she want something which now filled her with such dark foreboding?

CHAPTER ELEVEN

THINGS BEGAN TO go wrong the moment Justina got back to England. It started when the lift in her apartment block broke down and for the next two days, until it was mended, she had to lug everything up and down seven flights of stairs. It might have been simpler if she'd swallowed her pride and asked Dante for help, but she was so determined not to rely on him in any way that she said nothing—just kept reflecting on the fact that he had been right all along and this apartment really was no place to bring up a baby.

It got worse when her breast milk dried up— and she was eaten up with guilt as a result. The midwife told her it sometimes happened as a result of stress, and that she wasn't to beat herself up about it, but that was easier said than done.

Justina's emotions seemed to be veering all over the place. She felt a failure as a woman and now a failure as a mother.

And wasn't she missing Dante like crazy? Didn't the memory of his closeness taunt her to the point of pain when she lay in bed at night, wondering why she felt so empty inside? Hadn't she been left thinking that the "right" decision now seemed all wrong?

She had only managed not to cry during a midwife's visit by the simple expedient of rubbing her balled fists against her eyes, and it wasn't until Dante arrived soon after and started frowning at her face that Justina glanced in the mirror and saw that her mascara-smudged eyes had left her looking like a panda.

'What's happened?' he demanded. 'Is it Nico?'

'No. Yes. Well, in…in a way.' She swallowed. 'I'm not…I'm not producing any breast milk, and the midwife says that I'm to give him a bottle from now on.'

For a moment his eyes softened, and so did his voice. 'That's a real pity, Justina.'

'Yes.' She nodded. For a moment she thought that he was going to reach out and pull her into his arms, and how she wished he would. All she wanted was to lay her head on his shoulder and howl her heart out so that some of this horrible emptiness might go away. She wanted to lose herself in his powerful embrace and have him tell her that everything was going to be all right, and this time around she might be prepared to believe him.

But he did nothing like that. He just gave her arm the kind of gentle pat he might have administered to an aging family pet. 'Babies survive brilliantly on formula milk,' he reassured her.

Hopefully, she looked at him. She'd forgotten that he'd read just about every book which had ever been written on the subject. 'Do they?'

'Of course they do. And in a way this might make things easier.'

'Easier?' Justina blinked at him. 'How's that?'

'Well, up until now the fact that Nico relies solely on you has governed our timetable, hasn't it? But now he'll be able to come over and spend the night with me. It'll free you up to do some work. Especially now that my new house is looking so good.' He smiled. 'I've had a nursery installed.'

It was appalling that in the middle of such disruption and change and worry about her baby Justina should feel completely redundant and *jealous*. But she did. 'You're sure you don't want any input from me?' she questioned. 'About the nursery, I mean?'

'No, thanks,' he answered coolly. 'I have plenty of ideas of my own.'

She forced a stoic smile. 'Right.'

It got worse.

The first time Nico was due to spend the night with Dante, Justina got him ready with everything he needed for his first overnight trip away. She was trying to push off the heavy blanket of sadness which had fallen over her and to quell her own rising sense of nervousness—not least because they'd arranged she should take him over there herself. She had planned to dress up for her first visit to Dante's new home. Maybe wear that cashmere dress he'd never seen, with her hair hanging loose and a pair of decent shoes. She was going to make sure that she looked *amazing*. She hadn't dared ask herself why such action seemed important, because she was afraid of setting herself up for something which might ultimately fail.

But now the doorbell was ringing, and instead of a cashmere dress and sexy shoes she was wearing jeans and a T-shirt liberally smeared with mashed banana. She opened the door to see Dante standing there, his dark hair wind-swept and his tie loosened a little at the neck. He looked formal, yet rumpled, and quite ridiculously sexy, and she had never felt more unattractive in her life.

'I'm supposed to be dropping him round to *you*,' she protested, wiping away the little beads of sweat which were inconveniently forming at her forehead.

'I know that—but I had a meeting nearby and so I thought I'd save you the journey.'

'But...but I wanted to see the new nursery.'

There was a pause. 'You can see it another time.'

She recognised the blocking tactic and her smile froze. *He didn't want her there.* Had her refusal to marry him backfired in the most spectacular way possible? Had she pushed him so far away that there was to be no coming back?

She thought she saw him glance at his watch. 'You seem in a hurry to get away!' she said brightly. 'Can't I persuade you to stay and have a coffee before you go?'

Levelly, he met her gaze. 'I don't think that's such a good idea, do you?'

She looked into the flat expression in his eyes and flinched. 'No,' she said hollowly. 'I suppose it isn't.'

'So why don't I just take Nico and leave you to have a well-earned rest?' He lifted his eyebrows. 'Planning on doing something special on your first night of freedom, are you?'

From some dark and lonely place deep inside her she produced a grimace of a smile. 'I haven't decided,' she lied, as if she had a million different options open to her.

'Well, have a good one, whatever it is. And I'll see you tomorrow.'

The apartment felt so quiet after they'd gone, and so *empty*. She prowled around the big modern rooms as if she was looking for something— she just wasn't sure what that something was. The giant mirror in the bedroom gave her a glimpse of her hair, which was sticking to her clammy brow, and she thought it was no wonder that Dante hadn't been able to wait to get away. But she knew that it was about much more than her looking as if she'd been dragged through a hedge twice over. She had thrown his offer of marriage back in his face and in doing that had wounded his pride—perhaps for ever.

She showered and put on a robe, but still she couldn't settle to anything. She supposed she should eat something, but there was very little in the fridge apart from two fat-free yogurts and half a bar of chocolate. She hadn't been eating sensibly and she was going to have to start.

This is what it's going to be like from now on, she told herself grimly. *This is your future and it's only going to get worse.* She had let fear stop her from taking what she really wanted. Too scared to embrace the start of a brand-new life, she was going to have to sit back and watch while Dante forged a future with someone else. Because sooner or later he would meet a woman. Someone who would love him as a man like him would always be loved. Who would learn to love Nico, too. Why, her beloved son might one day call another woman Mamma.

'No!' Justina shouted forcefully, as if there was someone else in the room to hear her. And then, because it felt so liberating, she shouted it again. *'No!'*

Her hands were trembling as she ran into her bedroom and pulled on some clothes. Then she dashed outside to find a cab, giving Dante's address in Spitalfields in a voice which was shaking.

The air was unseasonably warm and the rush-hour traffic had died away. She stared out of the cab window as they grew closer to his home. Much of the area had been rejuvenated, and everything seemed to be bursting with life. She could see mothers with buggies and the colourful sign for a local nursery school, festooned with bumble-bees and butterflies. Despite its inner-city location it seemed a homely area, and much more suitable for a baby than her sleek apartment block, where she didn't even know a single neighbour.

Nerves threatened to assail her as the cab drew up outside an imposing black front door. She could see lights blazing from a first-floor room. She could hear birds singing in the nearby garden square as she paid her fare, and her thumb was trembling as she jammed it onto the doorbell.

The sound of footsteps warned her that Dante was about to open the door, and when he did she saw a fleeting look of surprise on his face and—yes—annoyance, too. And something else—some dark emotion underpinning all that unwelcoming sternness. Suddenly she wondered what she was doing here—and whether she should chase after that cab and get back inside.

'What is it?' he demanded.

'Am I...' she forced herself to say it '...disturbing you?'

He wanted to say yes, that she had been disturbing him from the first moment he'd met her, when she'd turned those incredible amber eyes on him and he had been lost. But he was through with chasing after Justina and rainbows which didn't exist.

Instead, he fixed her with a questioning look. 'What do you want?'

She sucked in a deep breath. 'Can I come in?'

Wordlessly, he held open the door. She walked past him, and although he was close enough for her to reach out and touch, his body language was so forbidding that he might as well have been on a different planet.

'I'm upstairs,' he said.

For a moment she thought he meant that he was in bed, but as she followed him upstairs she realised it was one of those tall town houses where the sitting room was situated on the first floor.

The scene which greeted her was curiously cosy. A half-drunk glass of red wine stood next to an open newspaper and the sound of Puccini was filling the room. He had hung several huge oil-paintings on the walls and bought furniture so stylish that it must be Italian. It looked like *home*, she thought wistfully. The kind of home she'd always known he would be able to create.

She wanted to go and sink into that squashy-looking sofa and have Dante join her there, pour her some wine—but the dark expression on his face told her that wasn't going to happen.

'What are you doing here?' he questioned.

She could have blurted out a hundred conventional responses to that bald query. She could have told him she wanted to check that Nico was okay. That she wanted to see his house and the way he lived. All of those things were true, but none of them was the real reason why she was here, and somehow she knew she had to find the courage to tell him what that was.

'I'm here because I miss you.'

'You mean you miss the sex,' he said cruelly.

'No. I miss you. *You.*'

'I find that very difficult to believe.'

'But it's *true*! It's true, Dante,' she finished quietly.

'I'm sorry.' He shook his head. 'Flattering as it is that you should feel that way, I'm afraid that I can't do the kind of relationship you want, Justina. I told you that. I'm not interested in being your "friend with benefits". I asked you to marry me and you threw it back in my face.'

'Because I was being naïve—I was wishing for the stars!' she burst out. 'You never told me that you loved me, and I thought that marriage without love wouldn't stand a chance.' She drew in a deep breath. 'But I'm prepared to concede that I was wrong. Because we're doing this for Nico. I realise that. And if it boils down to marrying you or losing you then I'll marry you tomorrow.'

There was a long pause while his eyes captured hers, as if they were searching for a fundamental truth, and suddenly he knew that there was no turning back. No playing safe or covering his back any more. If he wanted her—*really* wanted her—then he had to have the courage to tell her what he hadn't dared admit until now. Not even to himself. That some things never changed and the most important things never should.

'Not just for Nico,' he said slowly. 'I thought it was, but it's not. My lawyer told me that marriage was the only thing to guarantee my role in his life. But when I stopped to think about it afterwards, I knew there was no way that I would tie my destiny to a woman if I didn't love her. No way I could tolerate a whole lifetime with a woman I didn't care about. I have only ever loved one woman, Justina—and that woman is you. I thought that love had died, but it hadn't. It came springing back to life when you had my baby.'

She realised that the music had stopped and that her rapid breathing was the only sound she could hear. She stared at him, wanting desperately to believe him but still not quite daring to. 'Then why…why didn't you tell me that when you asked me to marry you?'

'Would you have believed me?' His eyes narrowed. 'Didn't you believe we'd spoken of love so often in the past that we had devalued the words by our actions? I wanted the chance to show you that I loved you rather than tell you. But even that won't work if you aren't prepared to forgive me. And I'm not sure you can.'

She felt the ice-cold clench of fear as she heard an awful finality creep into his voice. 'Please don't say any more.'

'I'm going to say it, because you need to hear it.'

'Dante—'

'I know your mother made bad choices. I know you grew up believing that men could never be relied on. And I know I made a mistake—a big mistake.' He lifted his shoulders. 'But if you can't learn to forgive—not just me, but your mother—then the rest of your life is going to be shadowed by the past. Can't you see that? Can't you just let it all go, Jus, and allow yourself to be free?'

And that was when the tears started. Tears she seemed to have been keeping at bay for most of her life. Tears she'd never been allowed to cry as a little girl in case Mummy's boyfriends would think she was troublesome. She'd learnt early that she needed to be strong. To present a cool façade to the outside world and make like she didn't care. She remembered that long night in a hotel suite when she'd been eight—the first time her mother hadn't returned home. She'd lain trembling with terror in bed. And by the morning something had changed. She had survived—she *could* survive—and she could do it on her own. What other choice had there been but to take that forward into her adult life? To forge the independence which had been her one and only anchor and to cling to it?

'I'm sorry,' she sobbed. 'But I was scared, Dante. So scared. And it was a long time since I'd felt that way. My career was the only solid thing I'd ever had and I was afraid that if I let it go—if I learnt to lean on you and rely on you—it would make me vulnerable. That it would all come crashing down around me.' She shuddered in a breath and wiped her wet cheek with her fist. 'The stupid thing was that it all came crashing down in any case.'

'I should never have tried to hold you back,' he said slowly. 'I see that now. I should have re-alised that your talent and your career were all part of the woman I loved, and that trying to stop you from exploring your potential was like putting a bird into a cage. I should have realised you needed to spread your wings.'

'I have done,' she said huskily. 'I went on the flight of my life. Only now I'm tired of flying and I've discovered that I need somewhere to come home, to roost.'

He stared at her for a minute which seemed like an hour before letting go of a sigh which seemed to come from deep, dark place inside him. Then he opened his arms.

'You've found it,' he said simply. 'I'm right here.'

Her heart missed a beat as she stared at him, knowing that this was crunch time. That if she took those few small steps then she really would have to leave the past behind for ever. 'Dante…' she whispered.

'There is just one more thing, and it's probably the most important thing of all.' His lips softened as every fibre in his being ached to touch her. But he knew that she had to come to him. He could not take from her what she needed to give to him freely. 'I love you. You do realise that?'

She read the truth in the molten depths of his black eyes and her heart turned over with longing. 'Oh, Dante,' she whispered back. 'Darling, darling Dante. I love *you*. I tried so hard not to— but I couldn't seem to stop myself.'

He started laughing. 'Then what the hell are you doing over there?'

She moved almost without realising it, until he was holding her, and she was kissing his lips and his nose and his eyelids, and tears were welling up in her eyes and dripping down her cheeks.

'I'm safe now,' she whispered.

He closed his eyes against her silken hair and let her cry as he knew she needed to. He let her cry until there were no tears left, and then he gently pushed her in the direction of the bathroom and told her to go and wash her face. When she returned, she found him on the sofa, with two glasses of red wine on the table before him, and it was as if he'd read her mind—for wasn't this scene what she'd longed for when she'd first walked in?

She walked over and sat on his lap, facing him, before lowering her head to kiss him. She kissed him tenderly. Deeply and slowly. She kissed him with all the love she'd been holding back until she felt him smile against her lips, and when she pulled away he gave a mock-groan.

'Just one more thing,' she said.

'Hurry up,' he grumbled. 'I want you in my bed within the next ten minutes.'

'It's about all those men I told you I slept with.'

His face darkened. 'I am doing my best to be a tolerant and modern man,' he warned. 'But there is a limit, *tesoro.*'

Ignoring his scowl, Justina wriggled her shoulders. 'Well, they don't exist. I made them up.'

'What do you mean, you made them up?'

'Just that.' She shrugged as she met the dawning comprehension in his eyes. 'I pretended that I'd had other lovers because I wanted you to believe I was over you. But I was never over you—I could never seem to stop wanting you or loving you. I invented a whole raft of fictitious lovers so that you would think I had moved on. Only I hadn't. You see, there's only ever been you, Dante. Only you.'

She watched as the implications behind her words registered and he gave a distinctly macho smile of satisfaction.

'Oh, I *see*,' he drawled.

'Now you can kiss me,' she said.

He smoothed back the hair which was clinging to her damp cheeks and smiled. 'I've missed you, Justina.'

'You were doing a good impression of a man who was fine without me. When we came back from Tuscany it was as if you'd stopped caring completely.'

'Because I knew that I had to force your hand. I had to show you what life would be like if we split. I had to push you away in order to get you back. It was a gamble, but it was one I was prepared to take. You had to come to me because you wanted me—because you know your life would be bleak without me. Just as mine would without you.'

She lifted her hand to his face and stared into the brilliance of his eyes.

'I love you so much, Dante D'Arezzo,' she

said. 'And I'm going to spend the rest of my life showing you just how much. But now, if you wouldn't mind, would you please just *kiss* me?'

EPILOGUE

JUSTINA WAS OUT in the garden when the doorbell rang. She'd been writing a song in the autumn sunshine and she glanced at Nico, sleeping
peacefully in his pram, before going into the
house to see who was there. Maybe Dante had
forgotten his key. She hoped so. He wasn't due
home for another couple of hours, but perhaps
he'd managed to cut his meeting short. He was
getting much better at doing that, she thought.
They could take the baby for a walk to the
nearby park—maybe stop off at that new coffee shop on the way home and sit at one of the
tables outside.

But the figure standing on the doorstep of the
Spitalfields house was completely unexpected,
and Justina stood stock-still as all kinds of con-

flicting emotions flooded over her. She felt resignation and slight irritation—but, interestingly,
the thing she felt most of all was *love* as she
looked at her mother.

As usual, Elaine Perry was dressed in a style
which was slightly too young for her years.
Her admittedly very good figure was squeezed
into a pair of jeans, and she was wearing a
soft leather jacket which matched her caramel-
coloured boots. From her narrow wrists clanged
a symphony of narrow silver bands, and the enormous handbag she carried was one which was
regularly toted by supermodels and celebrities.

'Hello, Jus,' she said.

Justina screwed up her nose. 'Well, this *is* a
surprise,' she said drily. 'Where's Jacques?'

'It's Jean, actually, and he's...' The older
woman gave a helpless kind of shrug. 'He's history.'

'Right.' Justina digested this. 'So, are you
coming in? Or are you just passing?'

There was a moment of hesitation while
Elaine Perry delved around in her bag before
holding up a package. It was wrapped in shiny
paper and covered with images of dancing blue
teddy bears. 'I'd like to come in, if I may. I've
brought a present for the baby.' She looked al-

most sheepish as she met Justina's eyes. 'For…
Nico.'

Justina swallowed. There was so much she
could have said in response to that. The old Justina might have commented that she'd thought
her mother was too *young* to be a grandmother,
but she had learned to think before she spoke.
She had learned so much. People changed, Dante
had said—and he was right. People did. She remembered what he'd said about forgiveness, too.
That people couldn't be free to move on into the
future if they stayed shackled to the resentments
of the past. She recognised that this wasn't so
much a toy that her mother was holding out towards her as an olive branch.

'You'd better come in,' she said. 'Because I
know he'd just love to meet you.'

'*Would* he?'

And for the first time in her life Justina saw
her mother through adult eyes. She saw the
vulnerability in her face and the thick make-up
which failed to cover up the deepening wrinkles.
And her heart turned over.

'Of course he would, Mum,' she said softly.
'It's true he's not quite nine months old, but on
some subliminal level he's bound to recognise
you because you're *family*.'

Her mother was still there when Dante came home a couple of hours later, to be greeted by the rather amazing sight of two women sitting close together in the garden, the older one cradling his son.

He wondered what was going on, and then Justina looked up at him. 'Oh, you're home,' she said simply.

He smiled into her eyes and all his questions were forgotten. How could he possibly think straight when she was looking at him like that? '*Si, tesoro.* I'm home.'

Elaine Perry stayed for dinner. She told them—falteringly at first—that she was tired. Tired of being the mistress of some rich man who didn't value her. She told them how hard it was to keep up the perpetual fight to look younger than her years. It was only when she got on to the subject of leg-waxing that Justina quietly changed the subject and gave her mother another hug—though she couldn't help but worry about what the future held for someone who had only ever been reliant on the largesse of men.

It was several weeks later, when Justina and

Dante were lying in bed, that she turned to him, running her fingers through his thick dark hair the way she loved to do.

'Dante?' she murmured.

'Mmm?

'You know my flat in Clerkenwell?'

'I certainly do.' He drifted a finger over her belly and felt her wriggle. 'Are you going to tell me that you're planning to sign it over to your mother?'

'You're a mind-reader!'

He smiled. 'It makes sense. She needs somewhere to live which doesn't come with the price-tag of a man—and we'll never live there as a family, will we?'

She shook her head, but his words thrilled her indescribably. *As a family.* 'No,' she said, then hesitated. 'And while we're on the subject of property...'

'You don't like this house?'

'I do. It's just...'

'Mmm?'

'It's not really where I would have chosen to live. And we didn't choose it together, did we? In fact, it was chosen when we were going through that horrible phase which I'd rather forget. I mean, if you—'

'We'll sell it,' he said instantly. 'Or rent it out. I chose this house because I wanted to be close to you, but now that we're together it doesn't matter where we live. As long as you're happy, I'm happy.'

'Oh, Dante,' she whispered. 'I love you so much.'

'I know you do. And the best thing of all is that I feel exactly the same way about you.' His smile was tender as he pulled her closer. 'So tell me—are you looking forward to our wedding?'

Was she? She couldn't wait! They were flying out to Tuscany to be married at the *palazzo*, and Dante had taken off a whole month for their honeymoon.

She suspected that he wanted to move out to Italy permanently, and she was going to tell him that she was perfectly amenable to the idea. She'd even restarted her Italian lessons in preparation, and this time around she was taking them much more seriously. And the great thing about her job was that you could do it just about anywhere.

In fact she was in the middle of writing a song which she hadn't yet shown him, but she thought it might be the best thing she'd ever done. It was called *Forever*—and it was a powerful tribute to the man she would always love.

Forever.

* * * * *

MARRIAGE SCANDAL, SHOWBIZ BABY!

For Mark. Thank you for believing.

CHAPTER ONE

A THOUSAND FLASHGUNS LIT the sky and the Mediterranean night was turned into garish day as the crowd surged forward.

'Jennifer!' they screamed. *'Jennifer!'*

Jennifer paused and smiled, the way the studio had taught her—"Don't show your teeth, honey—they're so English!"—but the irony of the situation didn't escape her. You could be adored from afar by so many—yet inside be as lonely as hell.

She placed one sparkle-shoed foot on the step of the red carpet—the famous red carpet which slithered down the steps of the Festival Theatre like a scarlet snake. Oh, yes. A snake. Lots of those around at the Cannes Film Festival.

At the back of the building lay the fabled

promenade of La Croisette, where lines of palm trees waved gently in the soft breeze. Beyond foamed the sapphire-edged waters of the Mediterranean, into which the evening sun had just set in a firework display of pink and gold. But, despite the warmth of the May evening which caressed her bare shoulders, Jennifer couldn't stop the tiptoeing of regret which shivered over her skin.

Memories stayed stubbornly alive in your head, and you couldn't stop them flooding back—no matter how hard you tried. She'd been in Cannes with Matteo during that first, blissful summer of their ill-fated romance, and she associated the whole dazzling coastline with him. Matteo had introduced her to the South of France and the heady world of films—just as he had introduced her to white wine and orgasm. Everything in life she thought worth knowing he had taught her.

'You okay, Jen?' came the gruff voice of her publicist, Hal, who—along with an assistant, had been shadowing her like a bodyguard all day, as if afraid that she wouldn't actually turn up for the screening of her film tonight. And, yes, she'd been tempted to hide away in the luxury of her hotel room—but you couldn't hide from the world for ever. Sooner or later you had to come out—and it was better to come out fighting!

Weighted by her elaborate blonde hairstyle, Jennifer dipped her head so that her low words could be neither lip-read nor heard by the crowds who were pushing towards her from behind the barrier ropes.

'What do you think?' she questioned softly. 'I'm being forced to parade in front of the world's media and pretend I don't care that my husband has been flaunting his new lover.'

'Hey, Jennifer,' said Hal softly. 'That sounds awfully like jealousy—and you were the one who walked out of the marriage, remember?'

And for good reasons. But she knew it was pointless trying to explain them. People like Hal thought she was mad. They had told her in not so many words that she couldn't *expect* a man like Matteo to be faithful. As if she should just be grateful that he had cared enough to put a shiny gold band on her finger. Well, maybe her expectations were higher than those of other people in the acting world, but she wasn't about to start lowering them now.

'It's just harder than I thought it would be,' she murmured.

They'd only split six months ago, and yet already the press had started describing her as 'lonely' and 'unlucky in love'—because, unlike Matteo, she had not fallen straight into the arms of a new lover. Maybe it was different for women. Didn't they say that men recovered more quickly from a break-up?

Her pride had been wounded and she wasn't sure she was ever going to be able to replace the man who had been her husband—though that was what the world seemed to want. She just wanted to get through this first public appearance at the world's most famous film festival— then surely anything else would be easy-peasy. Please God, it would.

'Jennifer!' screamed the crowd again.

'Don't even *attempt* to sign autographs,' warned Hal. 'Or there'll be a riot!'

'You mean there isn't already?' she joked.

'That's better,' Hal murmured approvingly. 'Just keep smiling.'

But as Jennifer began to slowly mount the staircase she heard different voices, which somehow managed to penetrate the clamour of her fans. The clipped, intrusive tones of professional broadcasters. Here we go, she thought.

'Hey, Jennifer—have you met your husband's new lover yet?'

'Jennifer! GMRV news! Any plans for a divorce?'

'Jen—are the rumours that Sophia is pregnant true?'

Pregnant? Surely that must be some kind of cruel joke? Jennifer gripped onto her sapphire silk clutch-bag so hard that her knuckles showed up white, but then she automatically relaxed them just in case a camera should pick up the tell-tale tension.

'Jennifer—how do you feel about seeing your husband here tonight?'

At first Jennifer thought that she must have misheard the last statement—her ears playing tricks with her and plucking a wrong note from out of the sea of sound. Matteo wasn't here tonight—he was miles away, in Italy, and she had agreed to attend the Festival because she had known that. They hadn't seen each other in months, and Jennifer was still emotionally wobbly. She wasn't naïve enough to think that their paths would never cross, but had just hoped that it would be without an audience. Especially so soon.

Like a child swimming in choppy waters and searching for a life-raft, she looked round at Hal—but the sudden frozen set of his shoulders made her tense with a terrible growing suspicion.

She tried to catch his eye, but he was steadfastly refusing to meet her gaze. And then the press pack were closing in again, and Jennifer's gaze was drawn upwards, as if compelled to do so by some irresistible force.

Until she saw him—and her ears began to roar as the world closed in on her.

It couldn't be. Please, God—it just couldn't be.

But it was. Oh, it was—for there was no mistaking the dynamic presence that was Matteo d'Arezzo.

Jennifer felt sick and faint—but somehow she sucked in a slow breath of oxygen and managed to keep the meaningless smile on her face as she gazed in disbelief at the man who was standing at the top of the red carpet, surrounded by a small bunch of sychophants—as if he were king of all he surveyed.

His Italian looks were dark and brooding, and his body was lean and honed and shown off to perfection in the coal-black dinner suit. Legs slightly parted, his hands deep in the pockets of his elegant trousers, his casual stance stretched the material over his thighs—emphasising their hard, muscular shafts...leaving nothing about his virile physique to the imagination. Long-lashed jet eyes glittered in the olive-gold of his face, and they flicked over her now in a way which was achingly familiar yet heartbreakingly alien.

Jennifer's heart contracted in her chest. It had been so long since she'd seen him. Too long, and yet not long enough.

And women were screaming his name.

Screaming it as once she had screamed it, in his arms and in his bed.

Matteo.

She felt like a mannequin in a shop window—with the look of a real person about her, but a complete inability to move.

But she *had* to move. She had to.

The cameras would be trained on both faces. Looking for a reaction—any reaction, but preferably one which would provide the meat for a juicy story.

She willed some warmth into her frozen smile and began to walk up towards him, thanking her impossibly tight silk dress for the slowness of her steps.

It was a walk which seemed to go on for ever. The roar of the crowd retreated and the blur of their faces merged, and as she grew closer she could see the dark shadowing of his jaw and the cruel curve of his lips. Men like Matteo did not grow on trees, and his outrageous beauty and sex-appeal often made the casual observer completely awestruck. Well, he would not intimidate her as he had spent his life intimidating the studio. He was her cheating ex-husband—nothing more and nothing less—and she needed to take control of the situation.

She lifted her head as she reached him. 'Hello, Matteo,' she said coolly.

To see her was like being struck by lightning, and Matteo could feel the hot rods of desire as he saw the creamy thrust of her breasts edged by silk as deeply blue as the ocean. He tensed, his mind racing with questions as he stared down at his estranged wife.

Che cosa il hell stava accendo?

But his face stayed unmoving, even though his groin had begun to tighten, and he cursed his erection and despised the unfathomable desire which made him so unbearably hard. For there were women more beautiful than Jennifer Warren—but none who had ever made him feel quite so…so…

He swallowed down thoughts of what he would like to do, and how much he despised himself for wanting to do it. Weak was not a word he would ever use to describe himself— but something about the physical spell his wife had always cast over him was as debilitating as when Delilah had shorn off Samson's hair...

What the *hell* was she doing here? And why the *hell* had he not been told?

He knew that the cameras were trained on him—and on her—waiting for their reactions. A flicker of emotion here. A tell-tale sign there. Something—anything—to indicate what either was thinking. And if they couldn't find out, then they'd make something up!

Training took over from instinct and he kept the tightening of his mouth at bay. Only the sudden steeliness of his eyes hinted at his inner disquiet, and that was far too subtle to be seen. He would give them nothing!

The glance he gave Jennifer was cursory, almost dismissive—but visually it was encyclopaedic to a man who had grown up appreciating women, who could assess them in the blinking of an eye. He felt the quickening of his pulse and the silken throb of his blood, for the bright blue silk of her dress clung indecently to every curve of her magnificent body.

For a moment he ran his eyes proprietorially

over the soft swell of her breasts and the narrow indentation of her waist, and he did so without guilt. Why the hell should he feel guilt? She was still his wife—*maledicala*—even though her greedy lawyers were picking over the carcass of their marriage.

Two of the Festival staff moved towards him to usher him inside, but he waved them away with a dismissive gesture.

Should he turn his back on her? That was what he *wished* he could do. But he decided against it—for would that not just excite more comment from the babbling idiots who would fill their gossip columns with it tomorrow?

Instead, he gave a bland and meaningless smile as she reached him, and looked down into her sapphire eyes, which were huge in a china-white face and blinking at him now in that way which always made him...

Don't do vulnerable, Jenny, he thought. Don't turn those big blue eyes on me like that or I may just forget all the anger and the rifts and do something unforgivable, like taking you in my arms in full view of the world and kissing you in a way that no man will ever come close to for the rest of your life.

'What the hell are you doing here?' she said weakly.

'Wondering if you're wearing any knickers,' he murmured.

'I'm surprised you haven't worked that out for yourself—women's underwear *is* your specialist subject, isn't it?'

How crisp and English she sounded! Just like when they'd met—and then he'd been blown away by it. That cool wit and ice-hot sexuality. But—like a rare, hot-house flower—she had not survived the move to the tougher climes of Hollywood. Her career had flourished, but their relationship had withered.

'Oh, *cara*, don't you know that when you're angry you're irresistible?'

She wanted to tell him that she didn't care. But it wasn't true. Because if she didn't keep a tight rein on her feelings then she might just let it all blurt out and tell him things that he must never know.

That the pain of seeing him was almost too much to bear, and that in the wee, small hours of the morning she still reached for the warmth of her husband in the cold, empty space beside her.

Then remember, she told herself fiercely. Remember just *why* you've haven't seen him in so long.

'I had no idea you were going to be here,' she said, gritting her teeth behind her smile.

'Snap!'

'You didn't know either?'

His black brows knitted together. 'You think I would have come here if I *had*?' he demanded softly. '*Cara,* you flatter yourself!'

Oddly enough, this hurt more than it had any right to and almost as an antidote to meaningless pain, Jennifer forced herself to ask the question which twisted her gut in two. 'Is your girlfriend with you?'

His mouth hardened. 'No.'

Jennifer expelled a low breath of relief. At least she had been spared *that*. Fine actress she might be, and pragmatic enough to accept that her marriage to Matteo was over, but she didn't think that even she could have borne to see the smug and smiling face of her husband's new lover. 'I'm going inside,' she said, in a low voice.

He gave a cold smile as he walked up the red carpet beside her and into the glittering foyer. 'Looks like we've got each other for company,' he drawled. 'Pity we're both on the guest-list, isn't it, Jenny? I guess that's one of the drawbacks of a couple making a film together and then separating soon afterwards!'

'Matteo!' It was Hal's voice. He had obviously judged it safe to talk to them.

Jennifer and Matteo both turned and—for all their differences—their expressions were united in a cold-eyed assessment of their publicist as he panted his way up the stairs and gave them both an uneasy smile.

Matteo spoke while barely moving his mouth. 'You're history—you know that, Hal,' he said easily. 'You tricked me to get me here, and you bring me face to face with my ex-wife in the most awkward of circumstances. I am appalled—*furious*—at my stupidity for not having realised that you would stoop to this level in order to publicise your damned film. But, believe me, I shall make you pay.'

'Now, let's not be hasty,' blustered Hal.

'Oh, let's,' vowed Jennifer, her bright smile defusing the bitter undertone in her voice. 'This is the most sneaky and underhand thing you've ever done.'

An official appeared by their side, a brief look of perplexity crossing his brow as he sensed the uncomfortable atmosphere. He made a slight bow. 'May I show you to your seats, *monsieur, madame*?'

Matteo raised his elegant dark brows. 'What do you want to do, Jenny? Go home?'

She wanted to tell him not to call her that, for only he had ever called her that. The soft-accented and caressing nickname no longer thrilled her or made her feel softly dizzy with desire. Now it mocked her—reminding her that everything between them had been an utter sham. And did he think she was going to hang her head and hide? Or run away? Was his ego so collossal that he thought she couldn't face sitting through a performance of a film she had poured everything into?

'Why should I want to do that?' she questioned with a half-smile. 'We might as well gain something from this meeting. And at least the publicity will benefit the box office.'

Matteo's mouth twisted. 'Ah, your career! Your precious career!'

Censure hardened his voice, and Jennifer thought how unfair it was that ambition should be applauded in a man but despised in a woman. When she'd met him he had been the famous one—so well-known that she had felt in danger

of losing herself in the razzle-dazzle which surrounded him.

It had been pride which had made her want a
piece of the action herself—to show the world
that she was more than just Matteo's wife—but
in the end it had backfired on her. For her own
rise to superstardom had taken her away from
him and spelt the beginning of the end of their
marriage.

She didn't let her smile slip, but her blue eyes
glinted with anger. 'We're separated, Matteo,'
she murmured. 'Which no longer gives you the
right to pass judgement on me. So let's skip the
character assassination and just get this evening
over with, shall we?'

'It will be my pleasure, *cara*,' he said softly.
'But you will forgive me if I don't offer you my
arm?'

'I wouldn't take it even if you did.'

'Precisely.'

Jennifer had been dreading the première, but
it was doubly excruciating to have to walk into
the crowded cinema with her estranged husband
by her side. All eyes turned towards them with
a mixture of expectancy and curiosity as they
took their seats in a box. For a few seconds conversation hushed, and then broke out again in an

excited babble, and Jennifer wished herself anywhere other than there.

But there was no comfort even when the lights were dimmed, because for a start she was sitting right next to him—next to the still-distracting and sexy body. And the giant image which now flashed up onto the screen made it worse. For it was Matteo. And Jennifer. Playing roles which they must have been crazy to even consider when their marriage had been showing the first signs of strain.

They'd been cast as a couple whose marriage was being dissected in an erotically charged screenplay. There were other characters who impacted on the relationship—but the main one was the other woman. The irresistible other woman, who threatened and ultimately helped destroy the happiness of the couple who'd thought they had everything.

Art imitating life—or was it life imitating art?

It wasn't real, Jennifer told herself fiercely. If she and Matteo had been strong together, then no woman—no matter how beautiful—could have come between them.

But it was still painful to watch. And even if she closed her eyes she couldn't escape, for she could still hear the sounds of their whispered lines, or—worse—the sounds of their faked cries of pleasure. Hers and Matteo's. His and the other woman's. How easy it was to imagine the other woman in his arms as Sophia, and how bitterly it hurt.

Jennifer watched as her own screen eyes fluttered to a close, her lips parting to utter a long, low moan as her back arched in a frozen moment of pure ecstasy.

'I'm *coming*!' she breathed.

All around her Jennifer could hear the massed intake of breath as the people watched her orgasm—watched her real-life husband follow her, his dark head sinking at last to shudder against her bare shoulder.

She closed her eyes to block out the sight and the sounds—but nothing could release her from the torment of wondering what the audience were thinking and feeling. Perhaps some of them were even turned on by the blatant sexuality of the act.

It was a ground-breaking film, but now Jennifer suppressed a shudder. It no longer looked clever and avant-garde, but slightly suspect. What kind of job had she been sucked in to doing—to have stooped so low as to replicate orgasm with her real-life husband while the cameras rolled?

And then—at last—the final line. The amplified sound of herself saying the words 'Now she's gone. And now we can begin all over again.' The screen went black, the credits began to roll and there was a moment of stunned silence as the cinema audience erupted into applause.

The lights went up and Jennifer stared down at her hands to see that they were trembling violently.

'Ah! Did the emotion of the film get to you?' mocked the silken tones of Matteo, and she looked up to see that his eyes were on her fingers. 'You've taken your wedding band off, I see?'

She nodded. 'Yes. I threw it away, actually.'

His black eyes narrowed. 'You're kidding?'

'Of course I'm not.' Jennifer wouldn't have been human if she hadn't experienced a thrill of triumph at the look of shock on his handsome face. But any triumph was swiftly followed by anger. Did he think it a comparable shock to seeing those snatched long-range photos of him kissing Sophia in a New York park?

She turned her blue eyes on him. 'What on

earth *does* a woman do with a redundant wedding ring?' she questioned in a low voice. 'I don't have a daughter to leave it to, and I'm too rich to need to pawn it. So what would you suggest, Matteo? That I melt it down and have it made into earrings—or else keep it in a box to remind me of what a sham your vows were?'

He bent his head towards her ear, presumably so that the movement of his lips could not be seen, but Jennifer felt dizzy as his particular scent washed over her senses.

'How poisonous you can be, Jenny,' he commented softly.

'I learnt it at the hands of a grand master!' she returned, as he straightened up and she met his cold smile with one of her own. 'Oh, God,' she breathed, their slanging match momentarily forgotten. 'Here they come.'

Matteo shook himself back to reality, irritated to realise that he had been caught up with watching the movement of her lips and the way that the great sweep of her eyelashes cast feathery shadows over the pure porcelain of her skin. Insanely, he felt himself grow hard.

But he wouldn't beat himself up about it. You didn't have to be in love with a woman to want to…to…

Dignitaries were bearing down on them. He could see a cluster of executives and all the other acolytes that the film world spawned. His eyes narrowed and he turned to Jennifer.

'You're not going to the after-show party, I presume?' he demanded.

'Why not?'

'Perhaps it bothers you that I will be there?'

'Don't be silly, Matteo,' she chided. 'You aren't part of my life any more—why on earth should it bother me?'

His eyes hardened. 'Then we might as well go there together. *Si?*'

That hadn't been what she'd meant at all. Jennifer opened her mouth to protest, and then shut it again. Maybe this way was better. She would have Matteo by her side as they walked down the endless red carpet and into the waiting car. And while he might not have been faithful at least he had always protected her, and she missed that. Badly.

'People will talk.'

'Oh, Jenny.' His laugh was tinged with bitterness. 'People will talk anyway. Whatever we do.'

She met his eyes in a moment of shared understanding which was more painful than anything else he had said to her, for it hinted at a former intimacy so powerful that it had blown her away.

And suddenly Jennifer wanted to break down and weep for what they had lost. Or maybe for what they had never had.

'Come on,' said Matteo impatiently. 'Let's just go and get it over with.'

CHAPTER TWO

SOMEHOW THE LONG SCARLET flight of steps seemed safer this time around—and so did the legion of press waiting at the foot of them. As if Matteo had managed to throw the mantle of his steely strength over Jennifer's shoulders and was protecting her and propelling her along by the sheer force of his formidable will.

Even the questions which were hurled at them about their relationship had somehow lost their impact to wound her. As if Matteo was deflecting them and bouncing them back with one hard, glittering look and a contemptuous curl of his lip which made women go ga-ga and photographers quake.

The party was in one of the glitziest hotels along the Croisette itself, but Jennifer found herself wishing that it was being held in one of the restaurants which lined the narrow, winding backstreets where Matteo had once taken her. The *real* Cannes—where such luminaries as Elizabeth Taylor and Richard Burton had eaten. But it didn't really matter where the party was— she was going to stay only for as long as necessary and then she was leaving. That way she would save her face and save her pride.

They were in a room which was decorated entirely in gold—to echo the colour of the Festival's most prestigious award, the Palme d'Or. The walls were lined with heavy golden silk, like the inside of a Bedouin tent, and there were vases of gold-sprayed twigs laced with thousands of tiny glimmering lights. Beautiful young women dressed in belly-dancer outfits swayed around the room, carrying trayfuls of champagne.

But once she had accepted a drink Jennifer deliberately walked away from Matteo. She didn't need him, and she was here to show him *and* the rest of the world just that. She was an independent woman—why would she need anyone? That was what her mother had always told her, and it seemed that her words had been scarily prophetic.

The party might have had a budget to rival

that of a small republic, but it was a crush—and less hospitable than some of the student get-to-gethers Jennifer had gone to in her youth.

An aging but legendary agent was holding court. A nubile starlet was not only falling out of her dress but also falling over from too much wine, by the look of her. A raddled-looking rock star was looking around the room with a stupid grin on his well-known face and suspiciously bright eyes. And from out of the corner of her eye she saw Matteo being surrounded by a gaggle of glamorous women.

Welcome to the world of showbiz, thought Jennifer wryly. But inside she was hurting more than she could have imagined it was possible to hurt.

She dodged passes, questions, and having her glass refilled—managing instead to find a very famous and very gay British actor who was standing in the corner surveying the goings-on with the bemused expression of a spectator at the zoo. Jennifer had played Regan to his King Lear, and she walked up to him with a sigh of relief.

'Thank heavens,' she breathed. 'A friendly face with no agenda!'

'Hiding from the vultures?' he questioned wryly.

'Sort of. Congratulations on your knighthood, by the way. What are you doing *here*?'

'Same as you, I imagine. I may be an old queen—and a knight now, to boot—but I have to please my publicist like a good boy.'

'Don't we all?'

He surveyed her thoughtfully. 'I see you arrived with that adorable man you married—does that mean you're back together?'

In spite of the room's heat, Jennifer trembled—but she was a good enough actress to inject just the right amount of lightness into her voice. 'No. We're just playing games with the press. The marriage is over.'

'Sorry to hear that,' he said carelessly. 'Occupational hazard, I'm afraid. You'll get over it, duckie—you're young and you're beautiful.' He sighed, his eyes drifting to Matteo once more. 'Mind you—so is he!'

Jennifer grimaced a smile. 'Yes.'

'Go home and forget him,' he said gently. 'And stay away from actors—they're feckless and unfaithful and I should know! Marry a businessman next time.'

'I'm not even divorced yet,' she said solidly. 'And even if I were, this thing has scarred me for life—I'm through with marriage. Anyway— better run. Lovely to see you, Charles.'

They exchanged two butterfly air-kisses and then Jennifer resolutely made her way towards the door and slipped away—not noticing that she was being followed by a Hollywood icon who had just gone through divorce number four.

Not until she was in a quiet corridor and he moved right up close behind her.

Jennifer jumped and turned round. 'Oh, it's *you*, Jack!' she exclaimed nervously. 'You startled me!'

He flashed his trademark smile. 'Well, well, well,' he drawled softly. 'Maybe my luck has changed for the better. You look damned gorgeous.' He crinkled his blue eyes and directed his gaze at her chest. 'So, how's life, Jennifer?'

Jennifer knew that his fame meant he got away with stuff that other men would be prosecuted for, and she should have been used to the predatory way that such men feasted their eyes on her breasts, but the truth was that she didn't think she'd *ever* get used to it. 'I'm fine, thanks,' she said blandly.

'Well, since we're in the same boat, maritally speaking…' His voice dipped suggestively and his swimming pool eyes gleamed. 'It can get a little lonely in bed at night—what say we keep each other company?' And then his eyes narrowed as a shadow fell over him and he looked up into a pair of black, glittering eyes. 'Well, well, well,' he blustered. 'If it isn't the Italian Stallion!'

Matteo wasn't bothered by the star's slurred insult, but he felt a shimmering of intense irritation as he saw the fraught expression on his wife's face. That and the blunt hit of jealousy.

'Are you okay, Jenny?' he demanded.

She wanted to tell him that it was none of his business, but instead she looked straight into his eyes. And, in one of those silent looks between two people who have lived together which speak volumes, her eyes told him that, no, she wasn't okay. 'I was just leaving.'

'What a coincidence,' Matteo murmured. 'So was I.'

The sex symbol frowned in confusion, looking from Matteo to Jennifer like a spectator at a tennis match. 'But I thought—'

'Well, don't,' Matteo interjected silkily. 'You're not paid to think—you're paid to act... pretty badly, as it happens, which is why your career is on the way down.'

And he took Jennifer's hand in a proprietary

way which made her momentarily long for the past and loathe herself for doing so as he led her down a corridor.

'What do you think you're doing?' she demanded, shaking him off once they were out of sight.

'You wanted to get away from that *strisciamento*?'

'Well, yes. But not with *you*!'

'Are you certain?' His eyes glittered. 'I've discovered a service lift which bypasses all the press—if you're interested?' He arched his dark eyebrows as they came to a discreet-looking steel door at the end of the corridor which was light-years away from the luxury of the guest lift they'd ridden up in.

'Aren't you the clever one?' she questioned sarcastically.

'But of course I am—we both know that. Coming?'

Jennifer hesitated.

'Unless you're secretly hot for the *bastardo*?' he suggested silkily. 'And want to stick around?'

Jennifer glanced back along the corridor and then stepped into the lift beside Matteo, pointedly moving as far away from him as possible as the doors slid shut on them.

'You're going to have to watch your step, Jenny,' Matteo said softly as the lift began to whirr into action. 'Men like that eat women for breakfast.'

Jennifer stared at him in disbelief. 'How dare you?' she questioned. 'In view of what's happened how *dare* you take a holier-than-thou opinion on another man's behaviour? Have you tried looking at your own lately?' She clenched her hands into two tight fists, her breath coming hot and fast as the words came spilling out of her mouth. 'How's your *girlfriend*, Matteo?'

Matteo's eyes narrowed. 'Jenny, don't—'

'Don't you *dare* tell me "Jenny, don't"! Remind me of her name again.' Jennifer faked a frown. 'Oh, yes—Sophia! Not exactly a household name at the moment, but I guess that'll soon change with the magic of the d'Arezzo influence.'

'You didn't knock it when you used it yourself,' he challenged softly.

'You *bastard*! At least I was known for being a good actress *before* I met you—and not for pouting and lounging around half-naked in some over-hyped perfume advertisement! So, was she worth it?'

Matteo's black eyes flared. Had he meant so

little to her that she could enquire after another woman as if she were asking the time? For, while he accepted that their marriage was over, Matteo knew that if he bumped into any lover of *hers* he would want to tear him limb from limb.

'I don't think that's any of your business, do you?' he drawled. 'You wanted a divorce—and you're damned well getting one! Technically, that makes me a free man, Jenny—and at liberty to date whom I please.'

'But you weren't *technically* free in New York, when you started your affair with her, were you, Matteo? When the cameras caught you kissing her?' The words were out before she could stop them and he stared at her, an odd expression in his eyes which Jennifer had never seen before.

'I hadn't slept with her then,' he said slowly.

The use of the word *then* cut through her like a knife. 'But now you have?' She swallowed. 'Slept with her?'

It was both a statement and a question, and there was a long and uneasy pause. For, no matter what the circumstances leading up to the act had been, Matteo knew he had broken his marital vows. 'Yes.'

Jennifer clamped her clenched fist against her mouth as the cold rip of jealous rage tore through her heart. But what had she expected? For him to carry on denying a physical relationship? To pretend that his undeniable attraction towards the stunning Italian starlet had remained unconsummated?

Matteo was a devastatingly attractive and *virile* man. He needed sex like most men needed water. Well, she had asked the question, and she had only herself to blame if he had given her the answer she had dreaded.

She had thought that the pain of their breakup couldn't possibly get any worse, but in that she had been completely wrong. He had said it now. He had slept with Sophia. His body had lain naked against hers, warm skin against warm skin. He had entered another woman, had pushed inside her and moved and then thrown his head back and groaned out his pleasure in the way she knew so well—the way he had done with her.

And spilled his seed inside her? Made this other woman pregnant, like the pressmen had suggested earlier?

Biting against her fingers, Jennifer fought hard to prevent herself from retching. The mind could be a wonderfully protective organ—allowing you to block things out because they were too painful to contemplate—but it could be capricious and cruel, too, and Matteo's words triggered an inner torment as images of his infidelity came rushing in, like some unwanted and explicit porn film.

Jennifer leaned against the steel wall of the lift, beads of sweat gathering above her upper lip as she pictured her husband naked with another woman.

Matteo frowned and made an instinctive move towards her. '*Cara*, you are faint?'

'Don't you *dare* call me that!' she spat, and shrank even farther against the metal, which felt cold against her bare back. She wiped the back of her hand over her clammy face. 'And don't you dare come *near* me!'

A wave of sadness washed over him and he wondered how something which had seemed so perfect could have deteriorated into a situation where Jennifer was staring at him as if he was her most dangerous and bitter enemy.

Maybe he was. Maybe that was what inevitably happened when a marriage broke down. Maybe the myth of an 'amicable' divorce was exactly that—a myth.

He stared at her as she moved a little restlessly, as if aware of how tiny the enclosed space was. Her proximity was distracting. Matteo's

senses felt raw—as if someone had been nick-
ing at them with a razor. Yet when he looked at
her he felt nostalgic for times past, and that was
always painful—for it had never been real. Because memory played tricks with your emotions.
It tampered with the past and rewrote it—so that
everyone saw it differently. He knew that Jennifer's version of it would be different from his
own, and there was nothing he could do about
that.

But maybe that was only part of it. For the
eyes didn't lie, did they? He studied her and
thought how much time had changed her. Tonight she was all sleek Hollywood film star—
her heavy blonde hair caught up in an elaborate
topknot with a few artistic tendrils tumbling
down around her face. Her gym-tight body was
encased in clinging sapphire silk, and she was
bedecked in priceless diamond and sapphire jewellery.

How little she resembled the rosy-cheeked
girl with tousled hair and bohemian clothes he'd
fallen in love with. Was it the same for her? Did
she look at him and see a stranger in his face
today?

And a floodgate was opened as the reflection
triggered a reaction. Forbidden thoughts rushed

into his head with disturbing clarity, and Matteo remembered the pure magic of meeting her. Of feeling something which had been completely alien to him.

CHAPTER THREE

MATTEO HAD BEEN FILMING in England. The 'Italian Heart-Throb'—as the newspapers had insisted on calling him—had agreed to play Shakespeare. It had been a gamble, but one Matteo had been prepared to take. He had been bored with the stereotypical roles which had brought him fame and riches, and eager to show his mettle. To prove to the world—and himself—that an Italian-American could play Hamlet. And why not? All kinds of actors were switching accents in a bid to show versatility in the competitive international film market. Some had even won awards for doing just that.

Jennifer had been playing Ophelia—but not in his film. She'd been what they called a 'serious' actress—stage-trained, relatively poor, and rather aloof. He had gone along one evening to watch her perform and had been unable to tear his eyes away from her.

They'd been introduced backstage, and he'd been both intrigued and infuriated when she'd given a slightly smug smile which seemed to say *I know your type.*

'I loved your performance,' he said, with genuine warmth, before realising that it made him sound like some kind of stage-door Johnny—*him*!

'Thank you. You're playing Hamlet yourself, I believe?' she questioned, in the tone of someone going through the motions of necessary conversation. Almost as if she was *bored*!

'You do not approve?' he challenged. 'Of someone like me playing one of your greatest roles?'

Jennifer blinked. 'What an extraordinary assumption to jump to! I hadn't given it a thought.'

And he knew that she spoke the truth. For a man who held the very real expectation that every actress in Stratford would be anticipating his visit as if it were the King of Denmark himself, Jennifer's uninterest inflamed him.

She was studying him, her head tilted slightly. 'But your reviews have been spectacular,' she conceded, in the interests of fairness. 'So well done.'

He knew that. Every theatre in the world wanted him, and Broadway was putting irresistible offers on his agent's table. But somehow Jenny's quiet compliment meant more to him than all those things. 'Have dinner with me tonight,' he said suddenly.

Jennifer put her head to one side, her tousled hair falling over her shoulders. 'Why should I do that?'

A stream of clever retorts could yield entirely the wrong result, Matteo realised. For the first time in his life he anticipated that she might do the unthinkable and *turn him down*!

'Because my life will be incomplete if you do not,' he said simply.

'You can't say things like that!' she protested, biting her lip with a mischevious kind of fascination.

'I just did,' he drawled unapologetically.

She stared at him for a long, considering moment. 'Okay,' she said, and smiled.

And there it had been—like all the old songs said—something about her smile.

Matteo had never really believed in love—considering it something which existed for the rest of the world, but which excluded him. He had seen glimpses of it, but never before had he felt the great rush of passion and protectiveness he experienced with Jennifer that day, which had been the beginning of their tempestuous and ultimately doomed union.

And now?

Now he believed that what had happened had been a cocktail of hormones which had combusted at a time in his life when he'd craved some kind of excitement. He had been right all along. Love was not real. It was a story they fed you which sold movies and books. That was all.

Jennifer rubbed distractedly at her forehead. 'This lift is taking for ever.'

He had been so lost in his thoughts that he hadn't noticed.

'Is it?' he questioned, as there was a sudden lurching kind of movement, followed by complete and deafening silence. Matteo looked from the disbelieving accusation in Jenny's eyes to the stationary arrow on the illuminated panel. 'Maybe you're right,' he mused. 'Seems like we've run into a little trouble.'

'Please tell me you're joking.'

'You think I'd joke about something like that? You think perhaps I've set this up?' he demanded. 'Lured you into this lift so that I can be alone with you?'

Jennifer turned glacial blue eyes on him. 'And have you?'

He gave a short laugh. 'Have I? Believe me when I tell you, *cara*, that I can think of a lot more agreeable companions to be stuck with than a woman who does not seem to know the reason of the word "trust"!'

'And I'd rather be with the devil himself than some arrogant and egotistical sex maniac who can't resist chasing anything in a skirt!'

His black eyes narrowed as he felt the bubble of rage begin to simmer up. 'You dishonour me with such a description!' he declared furiously.

'It's the truth!'

'Ah, but it is *not* the truth, and deep down you know that, Jenny! You saw the amount of women who threw themselves at me! It was never the other way round.'

Yes. Those women who would pass him their telephone numbers openly in restaurants, right in front of her face, as if she were just part of the furniture. Or those others, who would use more devious methods to get the attention of the devastatingly handsome actor.

The shop assistants and the flight attendants

who would slyly slide him their details. The doctors and lawyers who would invent the need for a meeting with him. It seemed that none of them had any shame—any woman with a pulse wanted her husband.

'Did you ever stop to think what it was like for me, as your wife?' she demanded.

'Of course I did! You made it damned impossible for me to do otherwise!'

'Did you? I think you used to treat it as an amusing little game—batting those gorgeous eyes as if to say, *I'm not even doing anything, and still they bother me!*'

'Oh, Jenny—that was *your* insecurity talking, not mine. I'd gone beyond the stage where I needed fans to bolster my ego.' His eyes darkened. 'But, beyond refusing to leave the house, the only way to stop women coming on to me was to increase our security—and that brought its own claustrophobia.' There was a pause. 'And anyway, you know damned well that I pushed those women away.'

'But you stopped pushing eventually, didn't you, Matteo?' she questioned, and she felt that familiar pain stabbing at her heart. And although part of her wondered why she was putting herself through yet more pain, she couldn't seem to stop herself. 'When you looked at Sophia. And you wanted her. Are you denying that?'

There was another kind of silence now—fraught and terrible in the already silent lift. Yes, he had been guilty of the sin of desiring another woman, but it should have remained just one of those unacted-upon desires which made up a human life. People were not immune to desiring other people even if they *were* married. Only the truly naïve believed otherwise. And it was the naïve who fell victim to mistaking that forbidden desire for love. Matteo had seen it, and known it for exactly what it was. Unfortunately, Jenny had not.

He had been filming with Sophia, and their on-screen chemistry had been so hot it had sparked off the set. Everyone in the industry had been talking about it. And eventually Jennifer had got to hear about it.

But even if she hadn't developed such an obsession with it their marriage had already been at crisis point. Their work schedules had kept them apart so much that all she'd been getting were reports from the newspapers and photos of him with Sophia. She had picked away at the rumours—like a teenager worrying at a blemish on her face—until eventually her jealousy and suspicions had blown up. Trust between them had already been destroyed by the time he had kissed Sophia.

'You can't deny it, can you, Matteo?' she persisted. 'That you wanted Sophia?'

'What do you want me to say?' he demanded. 'Because by then what I did or didn't do was irrelevant! We were no longer a real couple. We were so far apart from each other that we might as well have been existing on different planets.' He looked at her across the confined space and his dark eyes were sombre. 'You know we were.'

Jennifer bit her lip so that he wouldn't see it trembling, because now there was pain in *his* eyes, too, and somehow that made it worse. It was far easier to think that Matteo was immune to the hurt of their break-up. Because if he shared even a fraction of her heartbreak, then somehow that only emphasised the precious thing they had shared and now lost.

'Oh, what's the point in discussing it? There's nothing left to be said.'

Matteo stilled. 'Well, for the first time in a long time we are of one accord, *cara*,' he said softly.

Another barb. Yet more pain. But Jennifer silently thanked her ability to act as she kept her face from reacting and flicked him an impatient look instead. 'Look, just concentrate on getting us out of this mess, will you, Matt—since you're the one who got us into it.'

'Are you implying that I've trapped you?' he laughed softly.

'No implication,' she answered. 'You have.'

He narrowed his eyes and listened. 'Can you hear anything?'

'Unfortunately, no.'

'Got a phone?'

'No.'

'Me neither. The truly successful never carry phones to events like this, do they?' he mused. 'That would make us far too accessible to the big wide world—and there's always someone to take our messages for us.'

For a moment Jennifer was surprised by the unfamiliar note of cynicism which had crept into his voice. 'Surely Matteo d'Arezzo hasn't become disenchanted with the jet-set world which brought him riches and fame?'

'Isn't that inevitable?' he questioned drily. 'Doesn't it happen to everyone?'

'Not to you.' She shrugged. 'I thought that success was your very lifeblood.'

'Success on its own isn't enough,' he said

tightly. 'I don't want to stay on this merry-go-round of a life until it chews me up and spits me out.'

Jennifer blinked. 'I can't believe you just said that.'

He looked at her and his eyes were like chips of jet. 'Was I really so ruthless, Jenny?'

She thought about the way they'd pored over their working schedules like two prospectors who'd just struck gold and now she recognised her own ruthlessness, too. Oh, how stupidly short-sighted you could be when fame came tapping at your door. She shrugged her shoulders. 'Maybe we both were.'

She felt the hot pricking of sweat on her forehead and ran her tongue over parched lips, noticing that his black gaze was trying not to be drawn to them. She hoped to God that he didn't think she was giving him the come-on. Fractionally, she moved away from him. 'What are we going to do?'

'We don't have a lot of choice. We wait.'

'For how long?'

'How the hell should I know?' Did she think this was easy for *him*? Her standing so close and off-limits—her luscious body barely covered in some flimsy gown which made her look like…

'Do you want to sit down?' he suggested carefully. Because surely that way he wouldn't have to be confronted by the tantalising thrust of her breasts?

Jennifer didn't know if she dared move. She was aware that her panties were growing damp and that if she wasn't careful Matteo would guess. He had always been so perfectly attuned to her body and its needs that his senses would be instantly alerted to the physical manifestations of desire. Briefly, she shut her eyes, summoning thoughts which would kill that desire stone-dead. But it wasn't easy.

'You're okay?' he asked softly.

She opened them. *Think of his betrayal. Of his doing with another woman what he had stood up in church and declared was for her and her alone.* 'Oh, yes—I'm absolutely fine! Just wonderful! I'm trapped in a service lift in a foreign country with my cheating ex-husband. *Exactly* the way I would choose to spend my Saturday night!' She rubbed her fingertips against the necklace which was digging into her throat.

'Why don't you take that off?' he suggested, as he saw the red mark she'd left there. Her skin was moist and a damp tendril of hair was clinging to her neck.

She met his eyes. 'I beg your pardon?'

He gave a snort of savage laughter. '*Madre de Dio*—don't look at me like that!'

'I wasn't looking like anything!'

'Oh, yes, you were,' he contradicted softly. 'With shock and horror written all over your face. As if I were suggesting some kind of strip-tease when all I meant was that your necklace doesn't look very *comfortable*.' He ran a disparaging glance over the heavy, wide choker which gleamed around her slender neck. 'Studio told you to wear it, did they?'

'Yes.' But he was right. She was aware of the costly gems digging into her flesh, making her feel as if she was wearing some upmarket dog-collar. Blindly, her hand reached up behind her, tried to reach the clasp, but failed—and there was no mirror...

'You want me to do it for you?' he questioned.

Jennifer hesitated, because it seemed almost too intimate a thing to do. The putting on and the taking off of a necklace was the kind of thing a husband did for his wife in the seclusion of their bedroom when they were properly married—not about to enter one of the biggest divorce battles of the year. Yet what choice did she have?

'I guess so. Never has the word "choker" seemed so appropriate,' she added sardonically.

He gave a wry smile. 'Turn around, then.'

But, confronted with the sight of her bare back, Matteo found his mind slipping into forbidden places. He silently cursed as he felt his erection grow even harder, thankful that she couldn't see his face—for he was certain that it had contorted into a pained expression of exquisite sexual frustration.

'You see…ex-husbands do have *some* uses,' he observed evenly, and lifted his fingers to unclasp the necklace, letting it slide into the palm of his hand like a heavy and glittering snake. 'There. Better?'

'Much…thank you.' Jennifer composed her face and turned—noting the dull flush of colour which was accentuating his high cheekbones. She knew what it meant when he looked like that—or at least she thought she did. Was he just getting overheated, or…?

Did he still want her? Was he imagining what they would have been doing in here if they were still married? Him rucking up her dress and pushing at her panties, unzipping himself and thrusting deep inside her, with her back pushed against the steel wall?

Oh, Lord—what was the matter with her? How could the thought of sex with him be so unbearably exciting despite everything that had happened between them? Everything they'd said and thought and done and accused each other of.

'Do you want me to put it in my pocket?' he asked.

'What?' asked Jennifer blankly.

He held the gems up. 'This.'

'Sure.' She nodded her head and turned away, unwilling to watch him slide them into his trousers, some sixth sense telling her what her eyes did not want to see—that he was hard and aroused.

So why did that thought give her some kind of primitive satisfaction instead of shocking her to the core?

As the minutes ticked by she could feel beads of sweat trickling down her back and a faint dampness gathering beneath the heaviness of her breasts. Shifting her position in her high-heeled shoes, she could see the faint sheen on Matteo's olive skin, and she swallowed as their eyes met in an uncomfortable moment of awareness.

'It's hot,' he said huskily.

'Yes.' She looked into his face because there was nowhere else to look. Nowhere to run. The bare steel walls seemed to be shrinking in on them, and suddenly Jennifer was terrified of this false intimacy—frightened of the sensations which were beginning to creep over her skin and the thoughts which were flooding into her head.

She turned away from him and lifted up her fist, pounding it hard on the metal surface of the wall and wincing as she struck.

'Help! Let us *out*!' she called. But the silence was deafening. She raised her voice. 'Let us *out*!'

'Why do you shout when no one will hear us, Jenny?'

'Somebody's *got* to hear us! Because being in here with you is driving me mad!'

'I thought you liked that aspect of our relationship.'

'I wasn't talking sexual!'

His eyes drifted over the hard points of her nipples. 'Weren't you?'

'Oh, can't you keep your mind on something other than your bloody libido?'

Matteo almost smiled. She *was* angry. And she was aroused, too. He knew that with a certainty which only increased his own desire to an almost unbearable pitch. Would he ever again know a woman as intimately as he did this one?

She wished he would stop looking at her. She

wished he was anywhere other than here. Because just his presence was making her have the kind of thoughts which were forbidden. Longing thoughts. Wishful thoughts.

'Help!' she screamed again, and this time she began to drum both fists against the wall. 'Please, somebody—*help* us!'

'Jenny, don't—'

But his words inflamed her even more—or maybe she was just in the mood to be inflamed. And seeing his insufferably enigmatic face as he calmly watched her losing it was like pouring paraffin on an already blazing fire. 'I'll do as I damn well please!' she retorted furiously. 'And you can't stop me!'

He wanted to marvel, because this raging woman was utterly magnificent, but he could see from the rapid movement of her breathing that she was in danger of hyperventilating. 'That's enough! Now, stop it,' he said flatly.

'No!' she yelled, and hot, angry tears began to spill from beneath her eyelids. 'No, I won't stop it!'

Swiftly he moved towards her, wrenching her away from the wall, and she whirled round, imprisoned in his arms, and began to beat against his chest instead.

'*Si,*' he urged her softly. 'Hit me. Hit me if it makes you feel better, *cara*!'

'Bastard!' She slapped him. 'You bloody, bloody cheating bastard!'

'*Si.* That, too.'

'*That's* for that bitch you slept with!'

He took her furious punch without flinching.

'And so is that!'

She made a little roar of rage as she drummed against his chest until her hands ached. And then suddenly her rage became frustration, and all the fight went out of her, to be replaced by a different kind of emotion. She shook her head, trying to deny it, her hands falling as she looked up and saw something change in his eyes, too.

The look of understanding, of empathy, and the fleeting look of sorrow had been replaced by something else. Something she knew all too well and had never thought to see again—even though she had longed for it in the sleepless nights which had followed his departure. And it was wrong. *Wrong.* Oh, so wrong. He had been to bed with another woman!

'Was she better than me?' she demanded.

'Jenny, stop it.'

'No, seriously—I want to know. Did you do

it to her lots of times? Like you did to me when we first met?'

He winced as if she'd hit him, and then the need to destroy her foolish fantasy simply overwhelmed him. 'You want to know the truth?' he exploded. 'I did it to her *once*—just once—and it was the biggest non-event of my life. Do you know why that was? Because all I could see was *your* face, Jenny. All I could feel was *your* body.'

'Don't,' she croaked.

'But it's the truth,' he said bitterly. 'It's flawed, and it's not pretty—but it's the way it was.' His black eyes glittered at her bleakly. 'There— doesn't that make you feel better now?'

'Are you kidding?' she demanded. 'It still makes me wretched to think of you with another woman, no matter how much you hated it!'

But that was not the whole truth, for the stark admission had made her tremble with an unwelcome new emotion and her heart began to ache with sadness and regret. How the hell had it all come to this? How could love be so quickly transformed into all these other hateful negative emotions?

His eyes blazed black fire as they roved over her trembling lips. 'You want me,' he declared unsteadily.

'No.' Could he see the terrible need in her? 'No, I don't!'

'Yes. Yes, you do.' He reached out for her and pulled her into his arms in a movement which felt as natural as breathing.

'Stop it, Matteo,' she whispered.

'You want me to do this.' He began to massage the little hollow at the base of her spine, the way he'd always done when he wanted her to relax, and as if she was acting on auto-pilot she shut her eyes.

'Even if I do—we mustn't. We mustn't do this,' she whispered, half to herself. But, oh, the touch of his body made her feel as though great warm waves had washed over her.

'Why not?' he whispered.

'You know why.'

'No, I don't.'

'You do. We're separated.'

'What's that got to do with anything?'

Her eyes fluttered open. 'That...that...woman.'

'I just told you. It is over. Believe me, Jenny—it never even began.'

And Jennifer was so lost in the thrall of the soft black look in his eyes that his betrayal of the other woman thrilled her. Later she would be appalled at how easily she could be seduced. But not now.

Now her lips were parting with a greedy anticipation she could not seem to deny herself as he slowly lowered his head towards hers.

CHAPTER FOUR

IT FELT LIKE A LIFETIME since Matteo had last kissed her, and Jennifer's arms reached up to clutch onto his broad shoulders as if she was afraid that her knees might give way. But only her lips did that—parting in a soft sigh as he began to kiss her.

Because to her horror—but not to her surprise—Matt's touch was like lighting a touchpaper. Jennifer's skin was on fire, and her heart was skittering away with excitement and almost a touch of desperation—like a drowning woman who had kicked up to the surface of the water for one last gulp of sweet air.

I just want one last kiss, she told herself. One last kiss from the man I loved enough to marry. The man I thought I would have children with and grow old with. One kiss—is that so very wrong?

But adults didn't just 'kiss' and nothing more—particularly those who had been married and who were still in the throes of a powerful sexual attraction.

Jennifer tore her mouth away from his as he began to rove the flat of his hand over one swollen breast, circling it over and over again until the nipple felt so exquisitely hardened that she sobbed aloud with frustrated pleasure. 'Matteo!' she gasped.

'*Si.*' He ground the word out in between hot and shallow breaths, scarcely able to believe that this was happening. That he was doing this to her and that she was letting him—and, oh, it was good. Too good. *Madre de Dio*—it had been so long. And it was never as good with anyone as it was with Jenny. He teased her lips with his in a soft and provocative kiss.

With a disbelieving sob she moved her mouth fractionally from his, knowing that this was wrong—worse than wrong—it was a kind of *madness*!

'Matteo, we…we…*mustn't*. You know we mustn't!'

God forgive him, but he used his hands as ruthlessly then as he had ever done in his life.

He had never wanted a woman more than he wanted Jenny at that moment. Not even on that first night when he had taken her to his bed. Nor the time when he had been a teenage virgin and the older woman who had seduced him had made him wait. *Because a woman likes a man to wait,* she had purred. Well, there was to be no waiting now—he didn't want it and, to judge by the frantic grinding of her hips, neither did Jenny.

For the first and only time in his life he wanted her so badly that he thought he was about to come in his trousers. But he reined his desire in with a rigid self-control not betrayed in his sensual movements. He drifted his fingers beneath the thin bodice of her dress and took her bare breast in his hand, cupping it experimentally and feeling her knees buckle as she relaxed against him.

'Oh!' she squealed.

All she knew was sensation. She felt the rush of pleasure overwhelm her—and somehow all thoughts of this being wrong just melted away. A hunger both sharp and irresistible bubbled inside her like darkest, sweetest honey, and carried her along in its heavy flow as he touched her nipple.

'Matteo!' she gasped again, only this time

the word was spoken in wonder and not in half-hearted protest.

Desire was jack-knifing through him in a way that was barely tolerable. He felt the hot pumping of his blood, the frantic pounding of his heart. Could see the gleam of her eyes and the soft moistness of her lips. It was like entering another world—of love and intrigue and lust and betrayal. One where his powers were weakened. And she weakened him. Just as she always had done. Like no one else did.

Stop me, Jennifer, he begged silently as he touched his fingertips to the silken tumble of her hair.

Il Dio lo perdona! He lowered his head, brushing his lips against hers—a fleeting, butterfly graze—giving her time to realise. Time to stop.

But she did no such thing. Her hands moved from his shoulders to his neck, pressing his face closer, so that the kiss deepened almost before he had realised, and she was lacing her tongue with his.

He moved his hand to the fork between her legs and pressed there, hard. She almost jumped out of her skin.

Her words were slurred yet shaky with disbelief. 'Matteo…

'*Si, cara mia?*'

'You…you shouldn't be doing that.'

He felt her wetness through the silk of her evening gown and closed his eyes. 'Oh, but I should. You know I should. You were born for just this, Jenny. Oh, God!'

She would stop him in a minute. Just a little more of this sweet pleasure and then she would push him away. Her head fell back against the metal wall of the lift as he began to ruck up her dress, and it was so close to her illicit fantasy of earlier that Jennifer almost fainted with pleasure.

His hand was on her bare thigh now.

Stop him.

And now it was moving up to her damp panties. Maybe she would let him bring her to orgasm first, and then she would call a halt to it.

Matteo felt her thighs parting and he could scarcely believe what was happening. *She wasn't going to stop him!*

He said something soft and very explicit in Italian, and Jennifer knew exactly what it meant for she had heard it many times before. It should have made her put the brakes on, halt this madness once and for all. And every ounce of reason in her body was screaming out at her to do just that. But she was so hot and hungry for him—hotter than she had ever been in her life—that she would have died right there and then sooner than not have him do this to her.

She whimpered as he slid her panties across and she heard the rasp of his zip. He rubbed his thumb across her swollen clitoris and Jennifer gave a tiny scream.

And then, to her utter horror—and his—the lift gave a slight lurch and they heard a distant mechanical thrumming.

They stilled as they listened—every nerve-ending straining for the sound that neither wanted to hear. The lift stayed unmoving.

Oh, thank God, thought Jennifer.

'You want me?' he demanded starkly.

Against his neck she nodded her heavy head mutely.

Matteo acted decisively. Ripping apart her delicate panties so that they fluttered redundantly to the floor, he plunged deep inside her and then effortlessly lifted her up so that she could wrap her legs around his back.

He began to move, slowly at first, wanting to prolong it—to make this heaven last until the end of time and then a little longer still. He made a broken little cry as he thrust in and out of her, knowing that he had never been this hard before, feeling her tremble uncontrollably in his arms. He felt the thrust of her hips towards him in unspoken plea, a gesture he knew of old. And Matteo cupped her buttocks and plunged deeper still, hearing her throaty moan of satisfaction.

And then the lights began to flicker, catching fragments of their movements like an old black and white movie. He moved faster still as the lift began to whirr into life.

Jennifer felt herself beginning to come. 'Matteo, no!' she gasped, but she knew in her heart that it was too late. Sensation caught her up and carried her away and she heard his oh-so-familiar groan as he went with her, felt the helpless shuddering of this big man in her arms.

Mixed in with intense relief and pleasure was confusion and anger as Matteo orgasmed inside her—aware that he had just put both their reputations on the line in a way which was scarcely believable. The flickering lights righted themselves just as he withdrew from her, and all he could see was her horrified face. 'Jenny—'

'What have we *done*?' she whispered.

His mouth twisted. Surely it was a little late in the day for regrets? 'You want a biology lesson?'

Her eyes were huge sapphire saucers. 'You seduced me!' she accused hoarsely.

He almost laughed out loud at her temerity. 'I *seduced* you?' he repeated incredulously. 'You may have always had a problem differentiating between truth and fiction, but that really is taking it a little far, Jenny!'

She wanted to hit him again. And she wanted him to make love to her again. Oh, what was she *thinking*? That hadn't even gone close to 'making love'. What had just happened had been a quick wham-bam-thank-you-ma'am.

All it had been about was swift gratification and intense pleasure. On a physical level it had been wonderful—on an emotional one completely empty. She turned her head away, not wanting him to see the shame and self-contempt in her eyes.

'Now what do we do?' she questioned shakily.

So she couldn't bear to look at him now? Was that it? She hadn't been so damned picky when she was grinding her hips against him! 'There's no time for an in-depth analysis,' he grated, as he heard an echoing shout in French from the bottom of the lift shaft and bent to pick up her discarded panties. 'I think we're about to be rescued.'

The blood was pounding at her temples and in her groin, and she closed her eyes in despair. Rescued? Dear God, no.

Despite his anger and misgivings, Matteo knew that he had to take charge—because otherwise this would develop from a regrettable one-off into a drama which could have lasting repercussions. Quickly he adjusted his clothing and raked his gaze over her, a nerve beginning to work at his temple as he saw that the front of her silk dress was dark with the stain of love-juice.

'Damn!' he exploded softly, as he stuffed her tattered panties into his jacket pocket.

She followed the direction of his gaze and blushed a deep scarlet. Oh, how *could* they have? But she saw the detached look on his face and took her lead from it. She would take it in her stride—as he was so obviously doing. Maybe he does this kind of thing all the time these days? she thought bitterly. 'So, now what do I do?'

'Here. Put my jacket on,' he instructed tersely. He helped her wriggle into it and buttoned it up for her as if she were a child.

Frantically she smoothed down what she could of her hair and wiped a finger under each eye, wondering if her mascara had smudged.

For a moment their eyes met, and Jennifer

swallowed, wondering whether she would meet contempt or triumph in his. For what man could not be forgiven for feeling either or both those emotions when a wife who was supposed to hate him had just let him have frantic sex with her?

But there was nothing.

Not a clue, not a glimmer of what might be going on inside his head. He was as enigmatic as she had ever seen him—no, more so—and it was like looking into the eyes of a complete stranger.

Her own senses were clouded and confused, and she was having real problems telling fantasy apart from reality. Sex did funny things to you—it transported you back to another place and another time. It must have done. For why else would she have to stop herself from running her fingertips lovingly over the shadowed rasp of his jaw and following the movement with a series of tender little butterfly kisses? The way she'd used to.

Was that because women were made weak and vulnerable by the act of love in a way men never were? Women's bodies and minds were conditioned to mate with one partner—while men were programmed to spill their seed all over the place.

And at that thought Jennifer blanched. Had she remembered...?

Matteo's eyes narrowed. 'You aren't going to faint on me?'

'Faint?' She spoke with a brightness she was far from feeling. 'Don't be silly.'

He shook his dark head with dissatisfaction, because even though his jacket covered her to mid-thigh her cheeks were flushed and her eyes were wild. Her appearance gave away *exactly* what they had been doing. And this *was* a service lift, true, but that didn't guarantee that some sharp-eyed employee looking to make a quick buck wasn't waiting at the bottom armed with a camera or a mobile phone which could transmit an offending picture around the world in minutes. Was he prepared to take the risk? Did either of them dare?

No.

Without warning he bent and scooped her up into his arms, cradling her automatically against his chest so that she could feel the muffled thunder of his heart.

'What the hell do you think you're doing?' she demanded.

He thought that was maybe a question she should have asked *before* they'd had that highly charged and erotic encounter, but he chose not to say it. Even thinking about it was making him grow hard again. He shifted position slightly, not wanting her to sense that he had another erection—because having sex with your soon-to-be ex-wife once could be classified as a mistake. But twice? No. That would defy description.

What was done, was done—they just had to deal with the immediate fall-out before they parted again for the last time.

'What do you think is going to happen now?' he demanded. 'That you are just going to stroll out of here with your messed-up hair and your smudged make-up and your rumpled dress? You don't think that will excite some sort of comment?'

She shrugged. 'Well, obviously—but—'

'But what, Jenny? You don't think that anyone with more than one brain cell will put two and two together and come up with exactly the right answer?'

'So what's your solution?'

'That you act! Just act, Jenny,' he urged, as he saw her perplexed frown. 'Act like you've passed out and you're leaning on me—act as if your life depended on it.'

And maybe it did, in a way—when she stopped

to think what he'd just said. Certainly her reputation and her dignity demanded that she emerge from that lift not looking as though she had been ravaged by her unfaithful ex-husband.

The lift juddered to a halt, and it was worse than Matteo had anticipated. Outside was an excited crowd of four waiters, a couple of chefs, what looked like a maître d' and a cleaner.

But no one from the studio. Thank God. He knew that their giant protective machinery would have whirred into action to minimise the outcome, but then it would be out of his control. And he would not let that happen. Not in this case.

He saw one of the waiters surreptitiously slide a mobile phone from his jeans and spoke in furious and rapid French to him. The chastened man shrugged and replaced the phone.

Jennifer's ear lay against the strong pounding of his heart and she closed her eyes—Matteo's words seemed to come at her from a great distance. His French was as fluent as his English, and she didn't even attempt to understand what he was saying, only knew that there was an excited and jabbering response from the staff.

He bent his head and whispered in her ear.

'Don't worry,' he said softly in English. 'You're going to be okay.'

She wished he wouldn't talk in that masterful and protective way to her, even though he was being both those things. But it was going to make it harder, she just knew it was—so much harder to say their inevitable goodbyes.

She opened her eyes to find that they were following someone down a long and draughty corridor and then outside, through an ill-lit yard which was lined with bins and a large skip containing hundreds of empty bottles.

We must be at the back of the hotel, Jennifer thought, and pressed her head against him as an overwhelming fatigue began to wash over her. But then sex with Matteo always made her sleepy. What was that she had read once? That some hormone was released when you orgasmed, which made you want to curl up and snooze.

'You okay?' he asked.

'You bring me to the nicest places,' she mumbled, and gave a low laugh.

The sound was so delightfully inappropriate that Matteo couldn't prevent the memory which stole over his skin as he remembered the precious gift of laughter which they had brought to each other in the early days. Ruthlessly, he blocked it.

'It won't be much longer,' he said tightly. 'They're getting hold of a car for us.'

She had to stop herself from snuggling up to him, as if they were real lovers instead of estranged spouses who just happened to know the way to turn each other on.

'I ought to get back to the Hedoniste,' she said unenthusiastically.

'That's where you're staying?'

'Isn't everyone?'

Matteo's mouth twisted with scorn. The marble-built palace of a hotel was situated on the choicest part of the Croisette, and would be full to the brim with other actors, producers, directors, models and wannabes. 'No,' he said shortly. 'It's too much of a goldfish bowl—you can't risk going back there in that state. I'm taking you to where I'm staying.'

He wasn't asking her whether she'd like him to. He was *telling* her, in that autocratic manner which came naturally after a lifetime of having people run around after him. But Jennifer was too tired and too confused to argue—and, if the truth were known, she was glad that he had taken over.

Somehow he had managed to commandeer the use of a luxury car, and he settled her in the soft leather seat beside him, adjusting his jacket so that it modestly covered her and then barking out a terse instruction in French as the vehicle began to move away.

Dreamily, Jennifer turned her head to watch out of the window as the glittering crescent of coastline sped by in a blur of lights. They passed the cool marble splendour of the Hedoniste—and suddenly Jennifer was relieved that they weren't going near it, with its hordes of paparazzi and heaven only knew who else.

'Where's your hotel?' she questioned.

Matteo stared out of the opposite window—anything to avert his eyes from her, and from the knowledge that she was all rumpled, her dress all stained…by *him*… His fingertips were still sticky and warm from having been inside her, and if he drifted them close to his face her particular feminine scent pervaded his nostrils with a potency which made him hard all over again.

'It's not really a hotel.' He swallowed as the car swept through wrought-iron gates, past the dark shapes of lemon trees and cypress.

In the bright moonlight she could see that the hedges were fantastically shaped, and there was an odd-looking sculpture which was emphasised by soft lights pinned into a nearby tree. It looked old and very beautiful, and Jennifer blinked at it in astonished surprise.

'What is this place?' she asked quietly.

'It was once a villa belonging to one of Cannes's most famous residents—an English aristocrat who discovered the perfect climate here, and the stunning beaches. Now it is owned by an eccentric Frenchman—who will let rooms out, but only if the mood takes him.'

He turned his head and saw her looking down at her crumpled state of undress. 'He is very particular and very discreet,' he added. 'There will be no need to be seen by him, or by anyone else for that matter. One is able to bring guests to a place like this without the whole world knowing. For people in the public eye it is a godsend.'

She couldn't stop torturing herself with images of him bringing other women here in the future. Perhaps similarly unclad, and also recipients of his remarkable brand of lovemaking.

But Jennifer knew that she couldn't bring the subject up—certainly not now, when she was already feeling so vulnerable. The sex had been a mistake—but there was no need to compound that mistake by starting to quiz him about his future plans. That would only make her self-esteem tumble and put her in an even more vulnerable position.

Matteo had every right to do whatever he wished. Sex gave you no rights—not even if it was with the man to whom you were still legally married.

But then she remembered what he'd said about Sophia—and for the first time she was able to think about the actress without feeling sick. Had it been true what Matteo had said, about it only being the once and thinking about *her* all the while? Should the fine detail actually matter?

Of course it *mattered*. A one-off mistake—if that was really what it was—was completely different from a long-term affair which had been shrouded in secrecy and deceit.

But in a way that was worse—because it gave her a faint flicker of foolish hope that maybe the relationship wasn't doomed after all. But it was. Too much had been said and done to ever go back. A bout of wonderful sex wasn't a cure-all. Their marriage was in its death-throes, and that had just been one final, bewitching puff of life breathed into it.

She had to take responsibility for what had

just happened between them back there, and then let it go.

But as he led her up a carved wooden staircase which was scented with sandalwood, Jennifer felt a very real shiver of fear ice her skin. *What if she wasn't able to just let it go?*

Well, you don't have the luxury of choice, she told herself. You'll have to.

At least the room was exquisite enough to distract her from her uncomfortable thoughts—with tall, shuttered windows which led out onto a moon-washed balcony. In the distance she could see the coloured glimmer of the town—like a muted version of the fireworks which would later explode in the night sky as part of the Festival celebrations.

'Oh, it's beautiful,' she said automatically, and turned round to find that he was watching her. She gave a nervous kind of laugh. 'What the hell am I doing talking about the view? Isn't this the kind of situation where you wish you could just wave a magic wand and suddenly it's different?'

'Don't you think I spend most of my life doing that?' he questioned bitterly.

'Matt—'

He shook his head. 'Let's not waste any time with recriminations. There's no point.'

'No. But I have to say this. Thanks for...rescuing me and bringing me back here.'

'A while back you were angry with me for having had my wicked way with you.'

She didn't answer straight away, but she knew that she couldn't continue to act like an innocent little virgin who had been coerced into something against her will.

'Maybe I was angry with myself, for having allowed it to happen.'

'*Si,*' said Matteo slowly, in an odd kind of voice. 'I can understand that.' He gave the ghost of a smile. 'So, let's forget it ever happened, shall we?'

'Yes,' she said slowly, hoping her pain didn't show. 'Let's.'

He stared at her, washed pale by the moonlight. 'You can stay here—there's no way you can appear at the Hedoniste tonight—not looking like that.' His black eyes were hard and glittering as he saw her lips part in protest. 'Oh, don't worry, Jenny,' he drawled. 'We won't have to endure the temptation of sharing. I'll see if there are any more rooms available. Jean-Claude is bound to have something.'

'But I don't want to kick you out of your suite!' she protested.

His lips curved in a smile which was almost cruel. 'Then what else would you suggest?' he taunted softly. 'That I sleep on the sofa? Or perhaps we vow to share opposite sides of that huge bed?' He nodded his black head towards its satin-covered expanse. 'Want to try it, Jenny?'

And show him what a walk-over she was?

'Forgive me if I pass up your delightful offer,' she said tightly, and heard his bitter laugh as the door closed behind him.

But after he'd gone, reaction to all that had happened set in and a wave of lassitude washed over her. Her head was spinning and her limbs were aching, but really she ought to go and 'freshen up'. To remove all traces of Matteo from her body. If only you could take a bar of soap and scrub your heart clean at the same time.

Outside, she could hear the sound of circadas as she kicked off her shoes and wriggled out of her dress, letting it fall carelessly to the floor. She didn't care. The designer who had loaned it to her for free publicity would let her keep it. And given the state it was in she was going to *have* to keep it—but she knew she would never wear it again. How could she? She would never be able to look at it again without remembering...

Naked and shivering, she washed her hands and face and then poured herself a glass of wine from the heavy decanter which stood on the antique table by the window.

She meant to take only a sip, but the blood-red liquid filled her with a fleeting peace and contentment and she finished the glass and went over to the bed.

It was a typical Matteo bed, with a novel lying half-open on the pillow. She looked at it with interest until she saw that it was Italian and she didn't understand a word. But when was the last time she had read a book? She'd used to devour them in those days before the merry-go-round of publicity had filled her every spare hour.

On the bedside table was his mobile phone, and for a moment she was sorely tempted to flick through it and look at the messages. But she resisted. Dignity, Jennifer, she told herself sleepily. Try to retain just a little bit of dignity.

She sat down on the bed, moved the novel to one side and lay down, putting her head on the soft pillow. In a minute she would go and wipe off her make-up, but for now the room was spinning. She groaned and shut her eyes. Please make everything all right, she prayed. Let this all be over without any more pain—and please don't let me dream of him. Especially not to-night. Just let me have one night off from the tempting beauty of his dark face.

She hadn't been intending to sleep, nor to dream. But she did, and it seemed that her dreams were impervious to her pleas. One came to her which was frighteningly vivid. Through half-slitted eyes she could make out his lean, dark body bending over her. The raw, feral scent of him drifted upwards towards her nostrils.

She writhed against the mattress, holding her arms up, wanting him to stay with her. 'Matt,' she moaned softly. 'Oh, Matteo.'

When she awoke it was morning—with sunlight coming in bright horizontal shafts through the slats of the shutters. Jennifer sat up, blinking as she looked around the room. But the bed was empty, and so was the chaise-longue which lay underneath the window.

Her eyes strayed to the ornate wardrobe door, from which hung a floral sliver of a dress in layers of silk-chiffon in her favourite pink, and a pair of sandals which matched perfectly. Jennifer frowned. Where the hell had that come from? Had the good fairy flown into the room overnight and waved her wand?

Slowly, she got out of bed and went over to investigate. As well as the dress there was a matching bra and pants set, and Jennifer did not have to look at the size to know that they were exactly her measurements. And that somehow Matt had got hold of them at some god-forsaken hour and left them here for her.

And then she found the note.

Jenny. You looked too peaceful to wake and I found myself another room for the night. Don't worry about Hal—I will deal with him. In fact, try not to worry about anything. You should give yourself a break for a while—you look exhausted. Be kind to yourself and let's try to keep the divorce as amicable as possible. Matt.

It was a pleasant note, a reasonable note—the perfect note on which to end a marriage.

So why did she clutch it with white-knuckled fingers, tears beginning to stream down her face as if they were never going to stop?

CHAPTER FIVE

LONDON WAS RAINY and the flat felt cold and un-welcoming. Jennifer had been living there since the marriage split—she and Matteo had agreed that the luxury apartment would be 'hers', just as the ancient stone house on the island of Pantelleria would become 'his'.

The accountants had suggested that they sell their home in the Hollywood Hills, because apparently prices there had rocketed since they'd first bought it. Jennifer wasn't going to break her heart about *that*. It had never felt like a real home to her anyway. But then, where did?

Their schedules had been so frantic that they'd never seemed to have the time to do the things which other newly-weds revelled in. There had been no careful choosing of furniture or browsing over curtain material. Nor had there been any of the usual concerns about what they could or couldn't afford.

They'd been able to afford almost anything!

Matteo had made an almost obscene amount of money since leaving drama school, and his asking price now ran into millions of dollars.

That was one of the reasons why Jennifer had allowed herself to be tempted away from the stage and gone into films herself. Matteo had made hundreds of opportunities possible, and she had seized them with eager hands—for surely it would have been crazy to turn down such chances?

She'd wanted to be his equal in all ways—and yet when her own asking price had rocketed she had felt none of the expected joy or satisfaction. Just a kind of nagging feeling that somehow she'd sold out. And the price she'd paid for her glittering career had been frequent separations from her husband which had fed all her insecurities and doubts.

Sometimes she had found herself wondering what it would have been like if they had created a proper place together. Spent ages lovingly choosing items together, instead of suffering the incessant march of an army of interior designers who had transformed each one of their homes into dazzling displays which celebrity magazines had fallen over themselves to feature. Matteo had drawn the line at that. 'We have little enough privacy as it is,' he had told them angrily.

Maybe she should have done something to try and claw some of that privacy back—but Jennifer had been a brand-new player in the celebrity game, and she'd been too busy enjoying it to want to pull the plug on it. How easy it was, with the benefit of hindsight, to recognise the mistakes she'd made.

She glanced uninterestedly at the unopened post and the pile of film scripts waiting to be read. Then her mobile rang, and in spite of everything her heart leapt. Because she'd be lying if she denied fantasising about Matteo on her flight back from Cannes. She felt as if he had poured all her emotions into a mixing bowl and stirred them up. Maybe he was ringing her to ask if she'd got back safely? Or maybe just to say hello—because if the divorce truly *was* going to amicable then why *shouldn't* he say hello?

She picked up her phone and made her voice sound as cool as possible.

'Hello?'

'Jennifer?'

Jennifer's heart sank, and she immediately felt guilty that it had. 'Hello, Mum.'

'Where *are* you?'

Jennifer held the telephone away from her ear as the loud voice came booming down the line. Her mother always described herself as an actress too—though she had never progressed beyond the strictly amateur productions at their local village hall. The rest of the time she had spent living out her fantasies through her only child.

Quashing the terrible temptation to say that she was anywhere but England, Jennifer murmured, 'I'm at the London flat.'

'*Why?*'

'Well, why not?' questioned Jennifer. 'I *live* here.'

'No, I mean why aren't you doing the round of parties and interviews in Cannes? There's hardly been a *thing* about you in any of the papers!'

'That's because…because—'

'Because that bastard of an ex of yours was there, I suppose?' interrupted her mother viciously.

Jennifer bit her lip. 'Mum, I won't have you talking about Matteo that way.'

'Then you're an idiot, darling. He's made a complete and utter fool of you!'

'Look, I've just flown in—was there anything in particular you wanted?'

'Well, actually, yes! I was hoping to run an idea of mine past your agent! Or that rather nice publicist I met...what was his name? Hal? Yes, that was it! Hal! I think he took a slight shine to me!'

'Mum—'

'There are such *rubbishy* screenplays around at the moment that I thought to myself—well, why *shouldn't* I have a go?'

Jennifer counted to ten. And then on to twenty. Now was not the time to tell her mother that she'd sacked Hal. Or why.

Promising to visit very soon to talk about it, she managed to finish the call and went through to the kitchen while she listened to all the messages that had arrived while she'd been in France.

There were four calls from her agent. Two magazines wanted her on their cover, and a very famous photographer wanted to include her in his coffee-table book of the world's most beautiful women.

But Jennifer didn't feel in the least bit beautiful—she felt empty and aching, almost worse than she had when she and Matt had first split. At least then there had been endless, explosive rows, and she had felt that breaking up was the best thing to do. She had been carried along by the powerful storm of her anger and hurt.

But the episode in Cannes had been poignant and bittersweet. It had emphasised her vulnerability around him and reminded her of what they had once shared—but a pale imitation of the real thing. It had taunted her with what she was missing…that feeling of being properly alive. Because Matt was like the blazing sun in a summer sky, and when he wasn't around the world seemed dark and cold.

She spent the next few weeks lying low. She wore nondescript clothes and no make-up and kept her eyes down when she went out. As she had intended—no one recognised her. If you were a good actress, then no one should. It was more than just appearance. You could slope your shoulders and make your body language as low-key as possible.

She knew she ought to start trying to rebuild her life as a single woman, but her high-profile marriage had affected the way people saw her. She was famous now—and that had a knock-on

effect on everything she did. She could no longer
have normal friendships, because people wanted
to know her for all kinds of different reasons.
These days their motives had to be scrutinised,
and Jennifer hated that. Fame separated you—
left you lonely and isolated.

And going back wasn't easy. There were people she had been at drama school with, but she
hadn't seen them for years. She'd just been so
busy, with film after film, and she'd been living
on the other side of the world. Fame and money
changed your life—no matter how much you
swore they weren't going to.

And then, before she could relaunch herself
on the world, she began to feel peculiar. From
being full of energy, she found that she could
hardly drag herself out of bed in the mornings.

And her appetite increased. When she'd first
met Matt she'd had the normal rounded body
of a healthy young woman, but he'd taken her
to Hollywood and she had realised that wasn't
good enough. It was stick-thin or nothing. She
had trained her appetite to be satisfied with spar-
row-like portions, but suddenly they were no
longer enough.

Now she found that she simply *couldn't* control her hunger, and it was scary to find herself

wolfing down a bowl of porridge for breakfast every morning—and covering it with golden syrup!

She blamed the syrup for the nagging tightness of her jeans. But even when she cut out the syrup and dragged herself down to the exclusive gym in the basement of the apartment complex there was no marked improvement. In fact, quite the contrary.

When it hit her, she realized she'd been very stupid. She wasn't comfort-eating at all. But of course she had denied it—as she expected women who'd taken risks had done ever since the beginning of time.

Except she hadn't taken any risks!

Telling herself it was hysteria, she upped her sessions at the gym and began to wear more forgiving trousers.

But there came a day when her warped kind of logic refused to be heard any more. And that was the day she sent her cleaning lady out to buy a pregnancy testing kit.

She didn't really need to sit and wait to see whether a blue line would develop. She had known for weeks and weeks what the result would be.

Jennifer sat down on one of the sofas and bur-

ied her head in her hands. In that moment she
had never felt more lost or more alone. But it
wasn't as though she was going to waste time
worrying about what she was going to do.

There was only one thing she *could* do.

She kept putting it off. And meanwhile time
was ticking away. Her shape was changing and
the appetite which had consumed her had now
deserted her. Maybe that was a blessing in disguise—because she didn't *dare* venture out to
the local stores. Thank God for online shopping.

But she couldn't put off telling Matt for
ever—and one morning, when the bright blue
of the early-autumn sky seemed unbearably poignant, she hunted down her phone and found
Matteo's programmed-in number. It rang for a
while before he picked up, and his voice was
wary in a way she had never heard it sound before. That in itself was a shock—the thought
that Matteo was moving on, changing and growing and leaving her behind, while she remained
stuck firmly in the groove of the past.

'Jennifer?' he said slowly. 'This is very unexpected.'

Was it really? Didn't it occur to him that she
might want to discuss what had happened between them in France? Unless the caution in his

voice was there for a more pragmatic reason—because she was disturbing him in the middle of…

Her words came out as if someone was strangling her. 'Can you…?' She swallowed. 'Is it all right for you to talk?'

He frowned. 'Sure.'

He wasn't giving her any kind of help—but then, why should he? *She* was the one who had instigated this conversation, and soon all his ties with her would be severed completely. She bit her lip. Except that they wouldn't. Not now.

'Matteo, I have to see you.'

His voice hardened. 'No, Jenny.'

The room swayed. *'No?'*

'There isn't any point.'

Jennifer felt the blood drain from her face as she realised that she had put herself in a position to be rejected. And that only increased her pain. 'Matt, you don't understand—'

'Oh, but I do—believe me, I do. I've been thinking about it a lot.' More than he'd wanted to. More than he could bear to. Matteo closed his eyes, wishing that he could blot out the memory of her legs laced tightly around his waist while he thrust deep inside her. Or—even more poignant—the memory of her blonde hair spread all over his pillow in Cannes. But their frantic coupling had been nothing but a mockery of a simple and tender intimacy which was gone for ever. Well, he would tolerate it—but he would *not* be used as some kind of stud to satisfy his ex-wife's sexual needs!

He kept his voice terse. 'What happened between us proved that we're still sexually compatible. That's all. Nothing more. That's not enough basis for a relationship—and it would destroy even the memory of what we once had.'

In her outrage and her shame Jennifer nearly dropped the phone. He thought she was ringing him in order to get him back! He thought she was begging him to come back into her life! Trying to resurrect a relationship that was dead!

She wanted to hurl the phone hard against the wall—to finish this conversation and all future conversations with the arrogant and egotistical *bastard* in the most satisfyingly violent way possible.

But not yet.

'Oh, don't worry,' she said coldly. 'Such an agenda couldn't be further from my mind.'

He felt a nerve flickering in his cheek. 'I'm glad we understand each other.'

'Perfectly.'

'So. Why are you ringing?'

She couldn't say it over the phone. She couldn't. It was the coward's way out and she wanted to see his face. *Needed* to see his face.

'There's some paperwork I need you to look at.'

And what? Look into those big sapphire eyes again and start seeing what he wanted to see instead of what was real? Letting himself confide in her and share his thoughts with her? Start wanting to tear her clothing off, with her letting him? Or would she? Maybe this time she would torment him by saying no, by flaunting her magnificent body and torturing him because it was hands-off.

'Can't you get someone else to deal with it?' he questioned impatiently.

'That's your answer to everything, isn't it, Matt? Why bother doing something when you can pay someone else to do it for you? No wonder you're becoming increasingly remote from reality!'

There was a short, angry pause. 'Do you really think I *want* to see you?' he demanded hotly. 'That I would voluntarily put myself in a position where I lay myself open to being insulted by you?'

'Matt, you *have* to see me.'

'*Have* to?' he repeated dangerously. '*Cara*, nobody, but nobody, tells me that I *have* to do something.'

She realised then that there was no way out of telling him over the phone. And maybe this way was best. At least it would be short—if not sweet. She would provide the information in the starkest way possible and leave him with the options. Maybe the best one was for him to leave her completely alone.

'I just thought you'd better know that I'm pregnant,' she said, and then she hung up.

For a moment Matteo listened blankly to the burr of the dial tone, his eyes staring unseeingly at the wall in front of him. And then her words slammed into the forefront of his mind with the impact of a sledgehammer.

'Jenny!' As if saying that would suddenly put her back on the line! He dialled her number, but predictably she let it go through to voicemail.

He shook his head as a floodgate of feelings swamped him. Disbelief and anger and frustration made his heart-rate soar, but the tiniest flicker of hope and joy dazed him.

A baby?

He didn't even know where she was!

Strega!

His mind worked around all the possibilities. She could be anywhere...but it was most likely that she was in their London flat. *Her* London flat, he reminded himself. He knew she wasn't crazy about staying in hotels—not if she was on her own. And then he remembered the night in Cannes, and his heart contracted.

He frowned as he rang the service number of the exclusive apartment block and spoke to the concierge, using blatant influence, charm, and a hefty bribe to ensure that his enquiry was not passed on to Signora d'Arezzo. But, yes, she was there.

He allowed himself a brief, hard smile of satisfaction and then set about flying to England. Normally he might have cursed at a back-to-back flight from the States, but this wasn't normal. He didn't get told he was going to be a father every day of the week.

Beneath the knitted black brows his ebony eyes glittered with a hundred questions. But the one uppermost in his mind was the most important.

Was she telling him the truth?

CHAPTER SIX

THE KNOCKING ON THE DOOR wouldn't stop, and Jennifer knew that she could not lie there for ever, pretending that the outside world did not exist.

Slowly she made her way to the hallway and began to unslide the great bolts which had made their flat into a fortress. When she finally opened the door she was not surprised to see Matteo standing there, but it was a Matteo she scarcely recognised.

Uncharacteristically, he had not shaved. His dark hair was unruly—and his black eyes wild and angry. He walked straight in and shut the door behind him, and when he turned to face her his breathing was unsteady—as if he had been running in a long, long race.

'Now I see that your words are true,' he breathed, because for the first time in his life he felt out of his depth as he raked his eyes over her body.

She *was* pregnant! Rosily and unashamedly pregnant! Oh, the curve of her belly was not huge, but on a woman of Jennifer's slenderness it *looked* huge. Her breasts were swollen, and she had a look about her which made her appear quite different—but he couldn't pinpoint what it was. An experience which had changed her? The most profound experience a woman could have? Or just a kind of luminous fragility which almost took his breath away?

'You thought I would lie about something like this?' she questioned wearily.

He lifted his dazed eyes to her face to study that, slowly and properly, and there he could see changes, too. For her skin was whiter than milk and there were dark shadows beneath her eyes. He knew that pregnant women were supposed to glow from within, yet her eyes were dull, with none of their customary inner fire.

'*Dio!* What have you been doing to yourself, Jenny?' His eyes narrowed. 'Come through and sit down!' he commanded. 'At once.'

Jennifer laughed. After doing his utmost to

wriggle out of coming to see her—how *dared* he? 'It's *my* home and I won't stand for being bossed around by you!'

He sucked in a low breath. 'I will forgive you your stubbornness because of your hormones. But I am telling you this—if you do not do as I say and go and lie down on the sofa, then I shall pick you up and carry you there myself!'

'Isn't that how we got ourselves into this whole mess to begin with?' she questioned bitterly.

Matteo opened his mouth to ask the question which was uppermost in his mind, but something told him to wait until she was comfortable.

He went through to the kitchen to make coffee while she settled herself, clicking his lips with disapproval as he looked inside the fridge. He carried the tray through and poured her a cup—just the way she liked it—and watched with approval as she slowly sipped it. His own lay cooling. Suddenly he could wait no longer.

'It is mine?'

She put the cup down quickly, before she dropped it. She had been expecting this, and had tried to tell herself that it was not an unreasonable question under the circumstances. But knowing something and feeling something were two entirely different things, and Jennifer felt as if he had driven a knife of accusation through her heart.

'Yes.'

'You are certain? There is no other candidate?'

Her mouth crumpled with hurt and scorn. *'Candidate?'* she echoed. 'You make it sound like a presidential election! No, there isn't another "candidate". I haven't slept with anyone else since the day I first set eyes on you.'

He looked up. 'You haven't?'

She heard the macho pleasure in his voice and felt as if she'd been scalded. 'No. Unlike you.'

His eyes narrowed. 'But…how can this be, Jenny? How can it?'

She looked at him. 'You're thirty-three years old, Matteo—do you really need me to tell you?'

'You took a chance like that when we were separated?' he demanded incredulously. 'You risked getting pregnant?'

Something inside her snapped. The weeks of waiting and wondering and worrying all came to a head. 'How dare you make it sound as if it was something I *planned*?' she exploded. 'It happened in a *lift*, for God's sake! A lift which *you* found! If anyone planned it, it must have been you!'

'Oh, don't be so ridiculous!' he countered, and he saw her eyes darken in response. With a giant effort of will he drew a deep breath, trying to contain his emotions. But it wasn't easy. Yet he knew that he had to make allowances for her condition. He had to. For Jenny held all the cards, and if he was not careful…

'If you were unprotected then you should have told me, Jenny. And, yes, we were hot for each other—but there are other ways we could have pleasured each other without risking this type of consequence.'

Jennifer clapped her hand over her mouth as if she was going to be sick. 'I'm having a baby!' she choked. 'And all you can think about is mutual masturbation!'

'Jenny!' he protested. 'How can you say that? This is not like you!'

'What isn't? I don't know what *is* like me any more! And what do you expect me to say in the face of your monstrous accusation? If you must know—I *was* still on the Pill—'

'And why was that?' he shot back immediately. 'If, as you say, there was nobody else but me and we were divorcing?'

Jennifer's hand fell from her mouth to lie protectively on her belly as his suspicions reinforced how hopeless it all was. 'Because my periods are heavy—*remember*? My doctor thought it advisable. But it must have let me down.' She gave him a crooked kind of smile. 'Don't they say that the only surefire form of contraception is abstinence?'

'But you never got pregnant when we were married—when we were having sex every second of the day!'

'Maybe I wasn't taking it as fastidiously as I used to.' Jennifer shrugged listlessly. 'Blame it on me, if it makes you feel better.'

'I don't want to *blame* anyone!' he grated. 'Recriminations aren't going to help us.'

Matteo was silent for a moment as for the first time in his life he felt authority slip from his fingers. He could not get his way here by coercion or charm. Jennifer was in the process of divorcing him. She no longer loved him. What happened now was *her* decision. She was in the driver's seat, and suddenly he felt out of his depth. 'What do you want to do?' he questioned quietly.

'I'm having the baby,' she said flatly.

'Of course you are!' But a great warm wave

of relief rolled over him and for the first time he smiled—a smile so wide that he felt it might split his face in two. 'And look at you, Jenny— you are so big...it must be...'

She could see him doing mental arithmetic and the expression on his face was almost comical. Jennifer smiled too—realising how long it had been since she'd done *that*. 'Nearly sixteen weeks.'

'That long?' he breathed. 'My God. Jenny... this is a miracle.'

'Yes,' she said simply. And in that moment the divorce and the anger and the bitterness and the tearing apart of a shared life all seemed inconsequential when compared to the beginning of a brand-new life.

But her emotions were volatile, and hot on the heels of her heady exhilaration came the despair of the situation into which their baby would be born.

A shuddering sob was torn from her throat and Matteo sprang to his feet, going over to her side and taking her hand between his. 'You are in pain?' he demanded.

She shook her head. 'No, I'm not in pain,' she sobbed. 'I'm just thinking how hopeless this all is.'

'Shh.' Now he lifted his hand to her wet cheeks and began to smooth the tears away, his heart contracting in genuine remorse as he saw the expression in her blurry eyes. 'It is not hopeless,' he said softly.

'Yes, it is! We're getting a divorce and you don't love me!'

'But, Jenny, I will always—'

'No!' She sat up, her face serious, the tears stopping as if by magic. 'Never say it, Matteo,' she urged. 'Don't say something to try and make it better, because if it isn't true then it will only make it worse. I'm not a little girl who needs to be given a lolly because she's hurt her knee. This isn't about me, or the way I feel, or the mess we've made of our relationship. This is about someone far more important than both of us now...our baby.'

Matteo stared at her, his fingertips lingering for one last moment on her face. 'You sound so strong,' he breathed, in open admiration.

'I have to be,' she said simply. 'I'm going to be a mother—maybe it comes with the job description.'

And he needed to be strong, too.

He needed to take control. But he must not do it in a high-handed way or she would rebel; he knew that. He must allow Jennifer to think that *she* was making all the decisions.

'Have you thought about what you want to do?'

'I've tried.' There had been a fantasy version, about taking a time machine and fast-rewinding so that the episode in the lift had never happened. Or back further still, to a time when they'd still been in love and they could have conceived their baby out of that love, instead of out of lust and anger and passion.

But she was dealing with reality, not fantasy—and that posed all kinds of problems.

'Oh, Matt—I just don't know *what* to do for the best. If I stay around here—or even if I go back to the States—it'll soon become obvious that I'm pregnant.' She glanced down at the swell of her belly. 'Though you can tell that even now, can't you?'

'Yes. Any eagle-eyed observer would spot it—and there are hundreds of those out there.'

'I know. And once word gets out everyone will want to know who the father is—and I won't know what to say.'

'But you *do* know who the father is!'

'And think of the questions if we tell them! Are we getting back together? And if we aren't then *why* am I pregnant by you? Or what about the worst-case scenario? Some sleazy journalist bribing someone at the hospital to get my due-date! Then they could work it back to the Cannes Festival—and I'll bet that at least *one* of the staff at the hotel could be bribed into giving them a story that we came out of the lift in a state of partial undress! Can you imagine the scoop *that* would provide?'

'Jenny—'

She shook her head. 'Or, if we *don't* tell them, then the questions and conjecture will be even worse! Every single man I've so much as said good morning to will come under intense scrutiny! There will be all kinds of tasteless headlines—*Who Is The Father Of Jennifer's Love-Child?*'

'Jenny, Jenny, aren't you getting a little carried away?'

'Am I?' Her blue eyes were clear and defiant. 'Think about it, Matt—is it really such an incredible idea?'

And that was the worst of it—he *could* see it, quite plainly, as if someone was playing a film inside his head. In a way, fame robbed you of simple humanity. They had become *things*—to be dissected and picked over. He shook his head and his eyes were clouded with a bleak kind of sadness. 'And I brought you into this crazy world of showbiz,' he said huskily. 'What kind of a lover would do that?'

A few months ago she might have agreed with him, but so much had changed—and not just the baby. Though maybe *because* of the baby. And it was all to do with responsibility—acknowledging it and accepting it. It took two to do everything in a relationship—to fall in love and then to wreck it. You couldn't place the blame on one person's shoulders.

She shook her head. 'Oh, Matt—that's not what I'm saying! You didn't frogmarch me into the studios with a gun at my head, did you? I wanted fame, too. I saw what you had and I wanted it with a hunger which sometimes frightened me—but not enough to stop me! But none of that's important. Not now—we can't change the past. But I don't want any more pressure—because that will put pressure on the baby.' She looked at him with an appeal in her eyes. 'Just what kind of story *are* we going to give the press?'

He swore in Italian, getting up to pace up and down the polished oak floors of a flat in which he had slept for barely more than a dozen nights in the two years he'd owned it—he, a man who'd grown up in a cramped tenement building in New York? How crazy was that?

'Why should the press be our first consideration?' he exploded.

And, in spite of everything, Jennifer's lips curved into a rueful smile. 'That's like asking why the grass is green!'

He let out a pent-up sigh and went to look out of the window. Below lay Hyde Park in all its glory. Joggers moved along the paths and mothers and nannies strolled with pushchairs beneath trees which were beginning to be touched with autumn gold. Soon winter would arrive. The London streets would be washed with rain or dusted with frost or even—if they were very lucky—heaped with snow.

And Jennifer might trip and fall!

He turned round. 'Have you told your mother?'

'Are you kidding?'

'Don't you think you should?'

'Why? The first thing she'll do is think that being a grandmother is going to make her sound old. And the second will be to give me a hard time over the damage this is going to do to my career.'

'She hates me,' he observed.

'She hates all men, Matt, not just you. Ever since my father walked out her view of the world has been distorted.'

It occurred to him that Mrs Warren had influenced her daughter more than Jennifer had perhaps ever acknowledged. Had she learned at her mother's knee that all men were inherently unfaithful? Was that why she had always been so suspicious of him? Only now could he see—too late—that maybe he should have sat down and talked about it with her instead of becoming increasingly frustrated at her lack of trust and her willingness to believe the rumours instead of listening to *him*.

'You're going to have to tell her some time.'

Jennifer briefly closed her eyes. 'I know I am. Just not yet. If we think outside interest would be intrusive, then just imagine...'

Matt shuddered. 'I would rather not.'

It occurred to him that the two of them had not spoken with such ease for a long time. And that was good, he told himself. Jenny was right—they could not change what had happened, and in the conventional sense their relationship was over. But civility between them must be maintained. He had wanted that before, but in view of the baby it had now became imperative.

'Shall we go to Pantelleria?' he asked softly. 'To the *dammuso*? We could both do with a little rest and recuperation.' His eyes narrowed as they took in her pinched face and pale skin. 'Particularly you,' he added.

Her mouth suddenly dried, but only her attitude of mind could save her from plunging into regret. For surely Matteo's suggestion made sense? A place which she knew offered refuge and peace. Possibly the only such place in the world—at least for them.

Pantelleria—the black pearl of the Mediterranean. The beautiful island where they had spent their honeymoon. Where wild flowers bloomed and rare birds visited.

There, Matteo owned a simple square white house built of volcanic stone, with shallow domes and thick white walls which stayed deliciously cool in summer. She remembered them lying together in bed on the last morning of their honeymoon and vowing to return as often as they could. But of course that had been one of many promises broken by a lack of that most precious commodity…time.

And nothing had changed there.

She stared at him blankly. 'How can we? I've got two films lined up.'

Matteo shrugged. 'Cancel them.'

'I can't do that!'

His black eyes glinted. 'Can't? Or won't?' he challenged softly. 'What's more important to you—your work or your marriage?'

'I notice you're not offering to do the same!'

'Oh, but that's where you're wrong, Jenny.' He gave a brief, hard smile and his eyes were as brittle as jet. 'If I have to cancel a couple of films to take this course of action, then so be it.'

It was like seeing a side of Matteo she'd never seen before—it was certainly the first time she'd ever seen a chink in the tough armour of his ambition, and Jennifer was momentarily taken aback. 'You'd risk your career?' she whispered. She nearly added *for me*, until she reminded herself that it wasn't for *her*—but for their baby. And what was wrong with that?

'My career will always pick up,' he said arrogantly. 'But films can wait. This can't,' he finished, with another shrug of his broad shoulders.

Jennifer knew that despite his almost careless air this was a supreme sacrifice for Matteo. He had made films almost back to back ever since she'd known him—and way before that. As if he was frightened of stepping off the merry-go-round of successful work which bred still more work.

And now that it had become a real possibility—instead of a throwaway remark—Jennifer could see the sense in Matteo's suggestion that they escape together, to a place which she could see might act like a balm on their troubled spirits.

The island lay halfway between Africa and Sicily—where Matteo's ancestors had come from and where secret-keeping was legendary, taught from the cradle. On Pantelleria Matteo wielded the influence of his birthright, not that of the fickle fame brought about by celluloid.

They had been happy there—and part of her wanted to hang on to those precious memories and leave them intact.

He saw her hesitation and suspected he knew its cause—for did he not have misgivings about returning there himself? Would it not unsettle him—reminding him of the dreams they had shared and never realised?

'You know you would be safe there.'

Safe? Alone with Matteo? That was a definition of *safe* she wasn't sure existed. Jennifer felt as if her life were a pack of cards which someone had thrown into the air to see where they would land. 'But how long would we stay there, Matt? I mean—I don't want to have the baby there.'

The brittleness had gone and now his eyes gleamed. 'You think that no child has ever been born on Pantelleria?'

'How long?' she persisted quietly.

'Long enough to bring the colour back to your cheeks and for you to rest and eat good food.' There was a pause. 'And long enough to decide what we are going to tell the world. To decide what our strategy will be.'

From a supposedly hot-headed and passionate Italian it was possibly the coldest and most matter-of-fact declaration Jennifer had ever heard.

CHAPTER SEVEN

MATTEO ORGANISED THEIR TRIP to Pantelleria
with a degree of organisation to rival a military
campaign. Despite the loyalty of his staff—who
these days had to sign a watertight confidenti-
ality agreement—he entrusted relatively few of
them with the knowledge of their whereabouts.

As he said to Jennifer—this was just too big
a story to risk.

And that was all this was, she reminded herself. A damage limitation exercise over a story
which had the potential to explode in their faces.

Jennifer had forgotten how extraordinarily
protected you could feel in the exclusive coterie
of Matt's inner circle—but this time there was
a subtle difference.

'Your staff are being unbelievably nice to me,'

she said, as they waited for their baggage to be loaded onto the private jet which would fly them to the island.

Matteo snapped shut his briefcase and frowned as he looked up at her. 'Aren't they always?'

Jennifer switched her phone off. 'Oh, forget I said anything,' she said airily. She certainly wasn't going to blow the whistle on anyone.

But Matteo laid his hand on her arm, and the unexpected contact caught her by enough surprise to lower her defences. 'Jenny? Tell me. Because if you don't then how the hell will I know?'

And maybe it was her duty to tell him. Nobody dared tell Matteo anything. And even when they did they told him what they thought he wanted to hear. 'They normally put a barrier between you and the rest of the world.'

He narrowed his eyes. 'Well, yes, I suppose they do—but surely you can understand why?'

'From the world, yes—from your family, no.' She hesitated. 'Once, I remember trying to get through to you on the phone, and being completely stonewalled and unable to reach you. They dismissed me as if I was some kind of disgruntled ex-employee! It made me feel so...'

'So what?' he prompted.

Jennifer hesitated—but what did she have to lose by telling him? 'So isolated, I guess.' Jennifer shrugged. 'Mind you, that was after we had separated. Maybe they were acting on your instructions.'

His face darkened. 'I gave no such instructions.'

In fact he remembered feeling pretty isolated himself. The rupture of their relationship had given him a sense of being cut adrift from all that was familiar. Because even when their marriage had been in an appalling state they had still been in contact. She had still been his anchor, the person he turned to to confide in. He'd telephoned her from locations around the world, or she him. But once she had left—that had been it. Nothing. As though he had never even occupied a tiny part of her life. She had cut contact completely—or so he had thought.

Now it seemed that his staff had been instrumental in that sudden severing of all ties, and his eyes narrowed thoughtfully as he stared at her. He employed people to act on his decisions, not to make them for him.

'So, how many of the famous d'Arezzo workforce will be accompanying us to Pantelleria?' asked Jennifer.

'None.' He savoured the moment. *'Nessuno.* Just us.'

Jennifer blinked in surprise. 'No chef?' she echoed. 'But you always take Gerard with you!'

A sense of regret washed over him. Was this what he'd intended when he had started chasing his dreams? To employ so many staff that he seemed to have lost control of his own life? 'I'll do the cooking,' he drawled.

Jennifer's surprise increased. *'You?'*

'Do you really consider me incapable of living my life without any staff to help me, Jenny?' he demanded exasperatedly. 'That I never knew what it was to be cold or go hungry? Or to take jobs that I hated in order to survive before I got my big break?'

'Well, in theory, no—of course I don't. But when I met you you were so successful that it was hard to imagine you being anything else. Like a slim person telling you they once had a weight problem. You can't quite believe it.'

'Well, believe it,' he said quietly, and smiled. 'And come and meet our pilot.'

He had given her a lot to think about on the flight, but the reality of what they were doing hit her when the luxury private jet touched down, and she turned to him with wide eyes. 'Are we completely mad, do you think?'

He gave a lazy smile. 'Very probably.'

And the easy intimacy of that smile spelt danger, reminding Jennifer to be on her guard. To be careful to protect her feelings. Because nothing had changed between them. This trip didn't mean that they were compatible, or that they weren't in the process of getting a divorce. She was having a baby. That was all.

Pantelleria's October air was still deliciously warm, and coastal flora bloomed in a profusion of pinks and reds and yellows. The crystal blue waters which surrounded it were rich in lobsters, and in the fertile valleys of the interior grapes grew as large as plums. It was like paradise.

Matteo felt the weight of expectation lift from his shoulders as he drove along the familiar unchanged roads to the Valle della Ghirlanda and his *dammuso*.

These days, superstars visited the island, but Matteo had fallen in love with Pantelleria as a child—when his parents had saved up enough money to send him to stay with one of his aunts during one long, dry summer. His family had laughed when he said he'd own a house there one day, but sure enough he'd done it—buying the *dammuso* with his very first film cheque. He had set about completely modernising the old building, whilst making sure it retained its natural charm.

It offered two terraces—one by a vast swimming pool which had a backdrop of the distant sea. The high walls hid a secret pleasure garden, with an irrigation system which had been built by the Arabs during their four-hundred-year occupation.

But it was the cool, domed main bedroom which Jennifer longed and yet dreaded to see—with its huge bed and restful simplicity. If only she could close her eyes and take herself back to the person she'd been then...would she have done anything differently? Would he?

'I guess you'd better sleep in here,' said Matteo, as they both stood in silence looking into the room.

'And you?'

He shrugged. 'The guest room is prepared.' He wondered if she would heed the unspoken question in his voice. Was she thinking of inviting him into her bed—to maybe build some kind of way back through the physical intimacy of being close once more?

But Jennifer didn't hear; she was struck dumb by the chain reaction of feelings which had been sparked by being in this room, this house. Delight, sadness, regret, and sorrow—all those emotions and a hundred more besides flowed over her in a bittersweet tide.

She stared at the bed as if it was a ghost—and in a way it was. And imagine if the ghost of her honeymoon self were to look up and see what had become of her and Matteo. Separated—with only an unplanned baby holding them together. How heartbroken that madly-in-love Jennifer would have been.

'Our baby should have been conceived in a bed like this,' she whispered—as much to that ghost of her former self as to the man by her side. 'Not in some seedy lift.'

'So many *should haves*, Jenny,' he said, and his deep voice was etched with pain, too. 'We should have listened more. Trusted more. Talked more. We should not have been too proud to say what was on our minds.'

'We should not have been parted so much,' she ventured—because this was a game it was frighteningly easy to play. There was a whole list of things they had done wrong without meaning to. Had she and Matteo just got unlucky? Or had they simply been too bound up in selfish interests to cherish their marriage properly?

'Do you think those problems happen with all couples—only some work out how to deal with them?' she questioned.

'I think we both struggled so hard to make it in our own careers that we forgot to put any work into the relationship,' he said slowly. 'And I think that once success arrived we felt that our lives were charmed and nothing bad could touch us.'

'But we were wrong,' she breathed.

'Oh, yes.'

'Oh, Matt,' she said brokenly.

He wanted to take her in his arms and hold her tight against him, kiss away her cares, but she looked so tense—as if one touch would shatter her into a thousand pieces. In the dim light of the shuttered room he thought how pale her face looked.

'And now?' he questioned. 'What must I do to ensure that there will be no regrets in the future?'

Be in love with me again, she thought. But you couldn't ask for that. A precious gift like love could only be given, never demanded. 'You think I have a magic formula?'

Now he noticed the shadows which darkened her eyes and he wanted to kiss them away—but he had forfeited the right to tenderness a long time ago. 'I am burdening you with too many questions. So sleep,' he instructed grittily. 'I will leave you in the peace and the silence and you will sleep.'

And, miraculously, she did. For the first time since she had left Cannes—and maybe even before that—Jennifer slept as if someone had drugged her.

SLIDING ON A filmy white kaftan over her swimsuit, she left her hair loose beneath a wide-brimmed hat and went out into the bright sunshine to find Matteo.

He was lying on a lounger by the pool, wearing wraparound shades and reading a film script. He had on nothing but a pair of swim-shorts, and Jennifer's feet faltered as she grew closer, for the sight of his near-bare body was utterly spectacular. And, let's face it, she thought, you haven't seen it for a long time.

His skin gleamed like olive satin, each muscle so carefully defined that he could quite easily have featured as an illustration in a medical student's anatomy book. Dark hair curled crisply over his chest and arrowed down to a V over his hard, flat belly, darkening over the powerful shafts of his legs.

She blamed the heat for the sudden drying of her mouth as Matteo slowly lifted his head. His eyes were unseen behind the shades, but Jennifer knew that he'd been aware of her watching him.

'Enjoying the view?' he questioned softly.

She jerked her head to stare out at the sapphire stripe of distant sea. 'It's…exquisite.'

He smiled. 'Come and sit down over here. I'll fetch you something to drink.'

Her legs felt like cotton-wool, and inwardly she despaired. Wasn't the whole point of being here to get herself fit and rested? If she started living on her nerves and constructing fantasies about her ex then she might as well have stayed in England and faced the press.

He brought her something cool and fizzing which tasted of lemons, and she gulped it down.

'Hungry?'

'Not really.'

'Am I going to have to force-feed you, Jenny?'

'No. Just give me a little time to acclimatise.

Anyway, I ate on the plane—and I'm not stupid.' She sank into a lounger. 'Ooh, that's nice!'

'Isn't it?' He gave her a hard smile as his eyes flickered over her kaftan. 'Aren't you going to get a little sun on your body?'

What could she say? An excuse would sound feeble but the truth would sound far worse. That she felt suddenly and inexplicably shy about disrobing in front of him.

But you're having his baby, for God's sake! And you were married to him!

'Of course,' she said lightly, and turned her back.

Behind his dark glasses, a thoughtful look came into Matteo's eyes. Shyness indicated that she was uncomfortable. Or was it something else? He leaned back against his lounger, affecting rest—but his body was tense as she turned around again and a sigh of something approaching wonder escaped from his lips.

In the bikini, her pregnant shape was like a visual feast—with its brand-new curves and soft shadows. He saw the swell of her belly properly for the first time and was filled with a fierce and primitive pride. For—no matter what the circumstances of the conception—nothing changed the fact that beneath her heart, his child grew.

His own heart pounded, and he swallowed down the sudden lump in his throat. His child.

And Jenny was still his wife. By law they remained married, with all the rights that gave an individual—even in these days when marriages could be dissolved so easily. Was he really going to let that go so easily now, when there was a baby on the way?

True, she might grow strong and well here on Pantelleria, and true, they might fabricate such a wonderful explanation about why she was pregnant with his baby that no one would ever bother them again. But even if this latter and extremely unlikely scenario occurred—where did that leave him?

On the sidelines, that was where. While Jenny would go on to give birth and, sooner or later, another man would fall for her pale blonde beauty and her quirky character and her particular talents—and then what?

He would be relegated to weekends, and then to less and less contact with the child. And why not? He would never have lived properly with its mother—so why should he expect the child to love him?

An unbearable pain caught him unawares. It churned in his guts and twisted in his heart.

At that moment he saw Jenny slide her leg up to bend her knee, and he knew that he still held a powerful weapon. Could he not work on her desire for him and tie her to him with *that*, even if that was as far as it went?

He lifted the sunglasses from his eyes and put them on the ground as the sun glinted off the pale flesh of her thigh.

'You'll burn,' he said thickly.

She heard the note in his voice and knew what it meant. She knew that she had a choice. She could either thank him for his concern and go up to her room and cover herself from head to toe in Factor 20, or...

She shut her eyes. 'Do you want to cream me up?' she murmured.

Her words made him so aroused that for a moment he wondered if he had dreamt them. But the languid pose she was holding told him that she had said them and meant them.

He noticed that she had her eyes closed, and that amused him as he moved slowly towards her. Was she trying to block out the sight of an erection which felt as hard as a rock against his belly?

He kneeled down beside her and squeezed a dollop of cream into the palm of his hand.

'Turn over,' he commanded.

She wriggled onto her stomach and, starting with her back, he loosened her inhibitions, unclipping her top and massaging the cool cream into her baking skin.

'Now lie on your back,' he instructed huskily.

Jennifer tensed as he peeled down her bikini top, and she nearly passed out with pleasure as he began to circle the palm of his hand over one hard globe, marvelling at the new and intricate tracing of blue veins there.

The cream felt deliciously cold, and Jennifer squirmed as her nipple peaked against his hand. 'Oh!'

But Matteo said nothing, for he sensed that words might shatter the highly charged atmosphere of erotic desire. He began to work on the other breast instead, hearing her gasp and seeing her squirm as he let his fingertips slowly glide down over the swell of her belly.

It was like being on familiar territory but discovering a whole new landscape. Like finding that a lush orchard had grown on a piece of previously barren land.

Wonder made him momentarily break his vow of silence. *'Madre de Dio!'* he whispered, and pulled down her bikini bottoms, sliding his finger to her wet, warm heat and hearing her gasp again, only sharper this time.

He began to kiss her until she moaned in an unspoken plea and he kicked off his shorts, carefully lowering himself on top of her so that they were properly naked at last. Her arms encircled his neck and Matteo buried his face in her soft neck and sighed. like a man who had come home.

They stayed like that until he lifted his head at last, tracing her mouth with his fingertip. 'I don't how I'm supposed to do it with a pregnant woman,' he murmured.

'You?' Her voice was slumberous as she smiled. 'Just do what you normally do.'

'But I don't want to hurt you. Or the baby.'

Matt could hurt her in a million different ways, but never like this. 'Just do it,' she urged. 'Let go.'

He reached down to find that she was soaking wet, and with a sigh of exquisite relief he thrust inside her. He began to move, slowly at first, teasing her and teasing her and teasing her. Enjoying the luxury of a long coupling—but it was never going to be long enough. He could barely wait for her to orgasm, but somehow he managed it—and then he let his own happen, in glorious golden waves which just kept on rocking him.

It seemed to take for ever to come back to earth, and when he did he lifted his head to look down at her, inordinately pleased at the dreamy smile of pleasure which curved her mouth.

'Jenny?' he whispered.

Her eyelids fluttered open and she looked up at him. *I love you,* she thought. *Is there any chance that one day you could love me, too?* 'What?' she mumbled drowsily.

'Can I sleep with you tonight?'

The wind made music out of the chimes which hung in the trees, and the world seemed suspended as it waited for her answer.

Jennifer closed her eyes and touched her lips to his neck. It was not what she had wanted to hear, but it would do. 'Yes,' she breathed. 'Yes, you can.'

THE DAYS DRIFTED into one another, like a river running into the sea, and Jennifer grew brown and slow and contented. She slept and ate good food and swam like a fish—sometimes in the pool and sometimes Matteo took her out in his boat to splash in the clear waters—and her hair grew pale and he told her she looked like a mermaid.

And every night he slept with her, and made love to her in a hundred different ways, both in and out of bed.

In fact, it was almost like a second honeymoon—except that honeymoons were held together with the glue of shared love, not the unreliable adhesive of an unplanned pregnancy.

'What is it?' he questioned softly one afternoon, when they had gone upstairs to lie beneath the cool, curved dome of the bedroom ceiling for their customary siesta.

'I didn't say anything.'

'You didn't have to. You were frowning.' His fingers traced an imaginary line just above her nose.

Jennifer closed her eyes, because the subject playing on her mind was one that she would rather keep hidden away. It was so like paradise here that she didn't want to introduce the serpent of reality.

And yet hadn't their inability to communicate been one of the primary causes of their breakup? Geographical distance had been the reason for that—but you didn't need to be thousands of miles apart from someone to fail to interact with them on an adult level. And they couldn't keep pretending that there weren't a million unresolved issues simmering beneath the surface of this extended holiday.

'Well, we haven't discussed how long we're staying here, or what we're going to do when we get back—in fact, we haven't made any real plans at all. We've been burying our heads in the sand, and—whilst it has been lovely—I feel a bit as if I'm in limbo. As if the real world were a million miles away.'

'Well, that *was* the intention in coming here.'

'But it can't continue indefinitely,' observed Jennifer, smoothing her hand over her belly and watching as his black eyes followed the movement with fascination.

She remembered the very first time she had slept with him. In the morning she had woken first and lain there feeling slightly dazed, thinking, *I'm in bed with Matteo d'Arezzo!* 'Can it?'

'No.' The rumpled sheet lay tangled around his naked thighs as he moved over her, the powerful shafts straddling her, and for a moment Jennifer thought that he was going to drive his erection into her aching body. But his face was dark and full of tension. 'Tell me what it is you want, Jenny.'

She shook her head. 'That isn't fair. Are you too frightened to say what it is that *you* want?'

And at that moment he *did* know fear—he who had been fearless for most of his life. But it was time to take a gamble. To lay down the guidelines for the only situation he could see working for the two of them. He just hoped that he had softened his prickly ex-wife enough for her to be agreeable.

'I'm Italian—' he began.

'You were brought up in America,' she pointed out. 'And what's that got to do with it?'

'I *believe* in marriage,' he breathed. 'But especially a marriage which involves a family. I want us to try again, Jenny' he said, and Jennifer heard the unmistakable ring of determination in his voice. 'To be man and wife. To bring our baby up within a secure family unit. Don't you want that, too?'

She nodded, too choked for a moment to speak. Had she thought that he might threaten her with a legal battle if she did not accede to his will? Possibly. The very last thing she had expected was that heartfelt appeal, and it affected her more than was probably necessary. Or wise.

'Of course I do,' she said eventually. 'It's what every mother wants for her baby.'

Not for herself, Matteo noted coldly, but he nodded and kept his face impassive.

She wanted to say, *And if there were no baby, would you still want me, even then?* But she wasn't strong enough for that. Because she might still be in love with Matteo but not so much that she would let it blind her. Because if there was no baby, then there wouldn't be a relationship.

'We need to do it properly this time around.' He tilted her chin up and his black eyes were hard and glittering. 'We will not lead separate lives again, *cara*. I don't know how we'll work it out, but we will.'

'And I won't listen to rumours…won't allow jealousy to flourish.'

'I won't give you cause to feel jealous ever again,' he grated.

'You're going to give up being a film star?' she said, half joking.

He smiled, his mind already working out their schedule. 'Shall we fly to England and tell your mother together? And I'll tell my office to answer any enquires with a short statement announcing that the divorce is off.'

Jennifer recognised the light of triumph which

burned at the back of his eyes as she nodded her head in agreement. This might be as good as it got, but she wasn't going to knock it. She had tried living without him, and that was much, much worse.

CHAPTER EIGHT

'I CAN'T BELIEVE IT!'

'Just say you're happy for us, Mum!' pleaded Jennifer.

She and Matteo had driven straight from the airfield to her mother's elegant cottage near Bath, knowing that as soon as they were back in England word would get out about the pregnancy, and wanting her to hear it from them first. But now, looking at her mother's expression, she began to wonder why they'd bothered.

Mrs Warren's heavily made-up eyes flicked over her daughter and came to rest on Matteo again. She shook her head in disbelief. 'But I'm too young to be a grandmother,' she declared.

Matteo's expression didn't flicker, and he did not risk glancing over at Jennifer. He squeezed her hand instead. 'Of course you are,' he said smoothly. 'Everyone will believe that you are the baby's aunt!'

'Do you really think so?' Mrs Warren looked slightly mollified as she automatically patted her faded blonde hair. 'Does this mean the marriage is back on?'

This time he *did* risk it, and he read the understanding in Jenny's eyes. *'Si,'* he said slowly. 'It is. We have settled our...*differences.'*

Mrs Warren nodded. 'Well, I suppose I'd better look on the bright side—I always got much better service on airlines when I mentioned that Matteo was my son-in-law!'

Matteo's mouth twitched. 'Then that is a good enough reason for the marriage to continue, surely?' he said gravely.

'Mum, Matteo's going up to London on business, and I thought that I might stay here with you for a day or two. We could have lunch, if you like.'

Mrs Warren brightened. 'In a restaurant, you mean?'

Jennifer nodded. Her mother loved eating out with her famous daughter, and all the attendant fuss. 'If you like.'

Matteo's eyes narrowed. 'You're sure?'

She shrugged. 'Why not? No good hiding away—we were spotted and snapped at the airport, after all.'

'I'm sending two minders with you,' he said grimly.

'Ooh, goody!' squealed Mrs Warren.

In a pale restaurant overlooking the beautiful old city of Bath, they ate exotic seafood and salad, and Mrs Warren drank copious amounts of champagne 'to celebrate, darling!' while the minders sat a not-so-discreet distance away. Jennifer even posed for a photo with a little girl who was waiting outside the restaurant with her mother.

Maybe I'll have a little girl too, she thought as she crouched down and smiled. And she'll have dark eyes, just like Matt's, and gorgeous curly hair.

But when they got back to her mother's house there was a crowd of pressmen milling outside, and the minders had to barge their way through.

'What the hell is going on?' asked Jennifer, frowning. 'How ridiculous! Surely one pregnant actress doesn't merit *this* kind of interest?'

The phone was ringing when they got inside, and Mrs Warren took the call, her face growing white as she listened. 'Yes, she's here—I'll see if she'll speak to you.' She held the phone towards Jennifer. 'It's a reporter. Wants to speak to you.'

Jennifer pulled a face and took the phone. 'Hello? Jennifer Warren speaking.'

'Jennifer—were you aware that Sophia Perotta has given an interview to a London evening paper about her affair with your husband?'

'I wasn't,' she said calmly.

'Did you know that he was cheating on you with her throughout your marriage?'

There was a pause. 'I'm not going to comment on that,' she said, still in that strange, small voice of calm. 'And now I'm really going to have to go. Goodbye.'

She put the phone down and ignored all her mother's questions, but inside she felt queasy, and the feeling of nausea just grew and grew inside her. She only just made it to the bathroom before she started vomiting—and the frightening thing was that she couldn't stop.

'I'm calling an ambulance!' her mother exclaimed dramatically. 'I knew you should never have got back with that cheating bastard!'

Feeling as if she was taking part in one of her own films, Jennifer was rushed to hospital with sirens and lights blazing, wishing that her mother would just go away. She rolled around in agony, clutching her abdomen—her stomach was empty but she was unable to stop the dry retching which was making her throat burn. 'Am I going to lose my baby?' she cried.

'Shh! Try to calm down,' soothed the nurse in the emergency room. 'The doctor is on his way down now to see you.'

Which did not answer her question at all. And Jennifer closed her eyes as tears began to creep from behind her tightly shut lids.

All this for nothing. Now she would lose the child she had longed for, and along with that terrible heartache would come her final separation from Matt—for he would not want her without the baby. Why would he?

AROUND A LARGE TABLE, Matteo sat with his lawyers—his face chalk-white beneath the tanned skin. On the front page of London's biggest-selling evening newspaper was a huge photo of a pouting Sophia Perotta—her brown eyes as widely innocent as a baby deer's. And there was the splash:

Cheating Matteo Was A Stallion In The Bedroom!

'Can she say this?' he demanded hotly.

'She already has.'

Matteo's fists clenched and he banged one down hard onto the table, so that the lawyers jumped. 'Let's sue her. Let's take the bitch for every penny she's got!'

'Are you certain you want to, Matteo?'

'It's a pack of lies!'

The lawyer coughed delicately. 'Did you or did you not have sex with her?'

Matteo flinched. 'Once!' he gritted, a feeling of disgust creeping over his skin. 'And only when my wife was divorcing me.'

'That's your story,' said the lawyer stolidly.

Matt turned on him, his black eyes flashing with anger, and suddenly he understood. 'Oh, I see,' he said slowly, and nodded his dark head. 'It's her word against mine.'

'Precisely. She's deliberately vague about dates and times, but explicit enough about your er…skills…in the bedroom department to make it clear that you *did* have sex with her. The dispute is when. She says it was during your marriage. You say it was not. We can try fighting it, if you want, but the publicity…'

He let his voice tail off, and Matteo knew

what he was saying. 'I've only just got back with my wife,' he said urgently.

And she's pregnant.

Oh, Jenny.

Jenny.

It was at precisely that moment that one of his aides came grim-faced into the room, with a message from the hospital.

The journey back to Bath was a like a trip to hell. The worst thing was the not knowing—but no one would tell him anything and he couldn't get hold of Jenny's mother. It was an exercise in powerlessness, and Matteo had never felt so frighteningly out of control.

He made silent pleas to God. He prayed for their baby, and he prayed for much more than that, too. But Jenny would never forgive him for this. How could she?

'I want to see my wife!' he said to the overwhelmed receptionist at the desk.

'Mr d'Arezzo?' she verified breathlessly.

'Let me see her,' he pleaded.

'The doctor wants to see you first, sir.'

'Jenny!' he cried.

'He looked like a broken man,' the receptionist was to tell her colleagues in the canteen later.

Fearing the worst, Matteo paced the room

they'd placed him in, and his eyes were bleak when the doctor walked into the room.

'My wife? How is she?'

'Your wife is fine, sir—'

'And the baby.' Matteo swallowed. 'She has lost the baby?'

The doctor shook his head and smiled. 'No, the baby is fine.'

'It is?'

'Absolutely. The heartbeat is perfect—the scan is normal. We've put a drip up, of course, because your wife was dehydrated, and we'd like to keep her in for—'

'But why has this happened?' breathed Matteo, and dug his nails so hard into his clenched palms that he did not notice he had drawn blood. 'It is shock which has caused this?'

'Shock? Oh, no. Your wife has food-poisoning, Mr. d'Arezzo. You should tell her to keep clear of prawns in future—particularly during pregnancy.'

Hot on the heels of exquisite relief that his wife and his baby were going to be all right came the bleak realisation that Jenny would never want him now. How would he feel if the situation were reversed? Could he bear to think of her in the arms of another man? And then to read about it in graphic detail in a newspaper, even if the facts *had* been twisted?

He walked along the corridor, and when they showed him into her room she was asleep against a great bank of pillows. She looked so small and so fragile that his heart turned over, and seeing the curve of her belly made an indescribable pain hit him.

Feast your eyes on her now, he told himself. For this will be the last time you shall see her so defenceless and vulnerable. Your access to her and to the baby will be barred from now on, and she will look at you in the wary and watchful way in which divorced wives do. From now on your relationship with Jenny will consist of brief meetings and visitation rights—and a whole legal framework.

'Aren't you coming in?' she said softly, without opening her eyes.

He stilled. 'Jenny?' he whispered hoarsely, as if a ghost had spoken to him.

She opened her eyes. 'Hello.'

He started. 'Did you hear me come in?'

'Yes.' And she had felt his presence, too—her senses were so alerted to him.

He rubbed his hands over his face, suddenly weary. 'I'm sorry.'

'So am I.' She managed a smile, wanting to banish some of the bleakness in his black eyes. 'But that's what comes of eating seafood! I shall have to be more careful in future.' She gave him a wobbly smile. 'But the baby is safe, thank God.'

He felt as if she had driven a stake through his heart. 'Jenny, don't!' he said savagely. 'Rail at me and tell me you hate me, send me away, but don't do this to me! For when you are kind it makes it so much harder, and I cannot bear to see it crumble—not what I thought we were on the way to regaining—' He shrugged his big shoulders. 'I just don't think I can bear it,' he repeated brokenly.

Jennifer stared at him. 'Matt—you're not making any sense. Didn't you hear me properly? Don't torment yourself. Please. Your baby is safe. Isn't it wonderful?'

'Yes, it's wonderful,' he said heavily. 'But I deserve all the torment in the world.'

'Would you mind telling me what the hell is going on?'

He blanched, praying for the courage to give his wife the facts which would finally put closure on their marriage. 'You haven't been shown a newspaper?'

Jennifer stilled. 'No. They've been keeping me quiet.'

He nodded. 'Well, you're going to find out sooner or later.'

'Matt, just *tell* me!'

'Sophia Perotta has given an interview claiming that I cheated on you with her throughout our marriage.'

Jennifer stared at him, searching his black eyes, the sombre slash of his mouth. 'You told me that it was just once. Afterwards.'

He nodded.

'So she's lying.'

Matteo stared at her. 'Jenny?'

'You told me you did not stray in our marriage. I believe you.' She had to believe him, or else there was no future for them.

She had done a lot of thinking in that quiet white hospital room, and had come to the conclusion that she couldn't spend the rest of her life reacting like a spoiled teenager. She was a woman with a baby on the way—who needed to look at a bigger picture than pride and hurt feelings.

'I know what happened between you, and I have to learn to live with that—but that doesn't mean I need to torture myself with badly written detail. We've both made mistakes, Matt, and one of those was my lack of trust, I don't intend repeating it. It's the way things were—but I'm more interested in the way things are *now*. And I'm going to work at our marriage—because I want it to survive.'

'Survival?' he asked, and his heart sank. 'That is all you hope for?'

'Isn't that enough? Trust and respect make a pretty good substitute for love. When we were apart I missed you more than words can say, and I want to be married to you. Just as you want to be married to me. B-because we're having a baby.'

'No!' he denied furiously. 'No!'

She started. 'You don't want to be married to me?'

He could have kicked himself. She was ill, and yet managing to be so understanding that she'd taken his breath away—while he was behaving with all the finesse of a bull. 'I don't want to be married to you *just* because of the baby,' he corrected. 'I want to be married to you because I love you.'

'Don't say that,' she said shakily. 'Please.'

And then he saw his own fears and uncertainties reflected in her sapphire eyes. 'Even if it's true?' he whispered. 'And you the great champion of the truth? Do you know something else, Jenny—I will carry on telling you that I love you even if it takes for ever for you to believe me and to learn to love me back again.'

Joy licked over her skin with warm fingers, and tears began to well up in her eyes and spill down her cheeks. 'I'm a quick learner,' she wept. 'I already do. I've never stopped—and if you don't come over here and hold me properly then I shall create a scene as only an actress can!'

He was smiling as he took her in his arms—as if she were a delicate parcel and any pressure might make her snap.

'Hold me tighter,' she protested.

'Later,' he promised, as he eyed the needle in her arm. 'I'm not risking the wrath of the doctors.'

And Jennifer laughed, because she had never seen her husband look intimidated over *anything*. 'Won't you at least kiss me?'

'Mmm.' His mouth curved. *'Posso controllare quello,'* he murmured, and touched his lips to hers. He kissed her until he felt her heart hammering like a little bird, and he rested his palm over it and sighed softly. 'Now you must rest,' he said firmly. 'And listen to what I have to tell you about our future.'

She leaned back against the pillows.

'After my next two films I'm taking a break from acting—because there are a thousand possibilities out there and I don't want to be at the opposite end of the world from you any more. Especially if you're on location with the baby.'

'But I won't be on location with the baby,' she said softly. 'Because I don't want to live that kind of life any more, Matt.' She edged her way a little farther up the bed. 'Acting works well for lots of people, but I want to look after my baby myself, and concentrate on you and me. At least for a while. After that we can reconsider—maybe take it in turns to film. Or maybe I'll just retire and have a big, old-fashioned, Italian-sized family!'

Matteo stared at her, his black eyes full of gratitude and wonder. And excitement. Because for the first time in his life he could understand what it was all about. The houses didn't matter, nor did the awards and the fame and the riches. Jenny and the baby they would have—*they* were what mattered. His family. *Their* family.

They were still blinking at each other like two people who had emerged into the sunlight after a long time in the dark when there was a brisk rap on the door. In walked a nurse, with two minders close behind.

One of them came up to Matteo and spoke rapidly in his ear. When he'd finished, Matteo looked over at Jenny.

'Much as I'm grateful for your mother's spirited defence of my morals—I think I'd better go downstairs, *cara mia*,' he said, a smile playing around the corners of his mouth. 'I'm afraid that your mother has just started to hold a press conference!'

* * * * *